"Go! Bomb! Run!"

The first incendiary bomb went off. Almost, but not quite in the same beat, the others erupted. A white flash and a ball of heat punched Mack Bolan in the small of his back, burning his neck, singeing his hairline. He tried to turn, tried to bring up his arms to protect his head.

Then he was falling. As Bolan floated through the air, as if suspended in space, he turned and saw the finger of thick, black smoke roiling from the instantly flash-burned Chevy, climbing high into the sky in oily ropes.

The pavement rushed up, and darkness claimed him.

Don Pendleton's **Mack**

Bolan®

Radical Edge

A GOLD EAGLE BOOK FROM
WORLDWIDE®

TORONTO • NEW YORK • LONDON
AMSTERDAM • PARIS • SYDNEY • HAMBURG
STOCKHOLM • ATHENS • TOKYO • MILAN
MADRID • WARSAW • BUDAPEST • AUCKLAND

Recycling programs
for this product may
not exist in your area.

First edition June 2012

ISBN-13: 978-0-373-61553-7

Special thanks and acknowledgment to
Phil Elmore for his contribution to this work.

RADICAL EDGE

Printed in U.S.A.

Revenge is sweet, sweeter than life itself—so say fools.
                    —*Juvenal*

There is revenge, and there is justice. One will destroy you.
The other, when you have fought for it, makes it possible for
you to go on living. A man who can't tell the difference is
dead inside.
                    —*Mack Bolan*

CHAPTER ONE

Outside Alamogordo, New Mexico

Mack Bolan, aka the Executioner, put a single 9 mm bullet through the left eye of the tattooed, skinhead terrorist, stepping over the body just as it collapsed onto the dusty ground. Shifting the FN P90 he wore on a sling across his chest, he let the silenced snout of his Beretta lead the way.

Neo-Nazis, Bolan thought with distaste. A dime a dozen. The domestic terrorists were like roaches, forever scuttling about no matter how many you crushed under your boot.

The soldier continued his slow crawl along the fence line surrounding the ramshackle, clapboard safe house. The structure was a mess; it appeared, at first glance, to be a mass of sun-bleached plywood and faded plastic tarps held together with hope and weighed down with cinder blocks.

A second skinhead sentry risked a look around the corner of the building, probably thinking he had heard something. He had, and it was the second-to-last thing he ever *would* hear. The very last thing was the muffled clap of Bolan's Beretta as a 147-grain hollowpoint bullet dug a channel through the sentry's brain.

Bolan moved quickly, crouched low, staying beneath

the sight lines of the open windows. They were covered with heavy plastic over sheets of what was probably Plexiglas. The interior of the safe house buzzed with activity. Heavy-metal music blared from a stereo. Shouts and jeers could be heard. There was a party going on inside. Bolan had to hand it to the terrorists; they were remarkably true to type. When neo-Nazis weren't preying on those they hated, they spent their free time mired in teenage-mentality hedonism. The fact that they had posted sentries at all surprised Bolan, at least mildly.

Hal Brognola, director of the Sensitive Operations Group based at Stony Man Farm, Virginia, had placed the secure satellite call to Bolan in the middle of the night, waking the Executioner.

"They're animals, Striker," Brognola had said, using Bolan's code name. "Latter-day race cultists, worse than every skinhead and white supremacist gang you've taken down in years past. The group calls itself Twelfth Reich."

"That's imaginative," Bolan had commented.

Brognola ignored that. "Their leader is one Shane Hyde. His file and psych profile are long and complicated. 'Delusional nut job' is the short version, but with caveats. He's not so unbalanced that he isn't also extremely dangerous, nor so wide-eyed that he'll tip his hand before he's ready. He has military experience, too. He was discharged from the Army on medical grounds just after Desert Storm. Seems his commanding officer considered him unstable and, after a series of altercations with several black and Hispanic soldiers, Hyde was shuffled around until the Army could be rid of him. He disappeared for a few years after his discharge, only to reappear on the Mexico border at the center of several high-profile immigration disputes."

"I take it he's not a fan of illegal aliens."

"Who is?" Brognola sounded as if he were speaking through clenched teeth. Which meant he was chewing an unlit cigar, something he did under stress. Bolan could hear the edge in his old friend's voice. "Hyde is an avowed racist, but he's not just that. He's got charisma, Striker. He's smart and he knows how to network. He's got a real knack for locating, and absorbing into his plans, people who share his outrage over the plight of the white middle class in America. That's his rallying cry, incidentally. He sees himself as champion of what he calls 'the only group it's socially acceptable to oppress.'"

"He hasn't just talked about it."

"No. We believe he's personally or indirectly responsible for at least a score of racially motivated bombings and murders," Brognola said. "The pace of the crimes tenuously linked to Hyde and Twelfth Reich is increasing, too. They're getting stronger and growing more bold. Until now they've done their best to keep secret, for the most part. The FBI has been on to them, or to parts of several cells, for a while now, trying to build a case that would take the investigation to the top. Hyde's cagey, though. He's managed to stay far enough from his handiwork that most of the 'legitimate' government agencies don't have enough on him."

"That sounds thin, Hal."

"That's because that's not all there is to it," Brognola said. "The Bureau had a special team on this, not long after the intelligence community started getting wind of Twelfth Reich as a cohesive organization. They put an undercover group on it, three trained operatives. But something went wrong. Two of them never came back. The third lived but, like his fellow agents, he lost his family. Hyde's people are believed to be behind the arson deaths of seven civilians, all told. They staged simultaneous raids on the agents' homes, duct-taped whoever they found inside and burned them alive."

Bolan said nothing for a long moment. Finally, he spoke. "The survivor?"

"Beaten, maimed and left for dead," Brognola said. "At last word, he was living in an assisted-care facility in San Diego. We believe one of the three agents was tortured badly enough to give up the other two. The corpse's fingernails and teeth had been removed."

"Yeah," Bolan said. He had seen it done, seen the aftermath of such barbarity, more than once.

"After the disaster," Brognola explained, "the investigation stalled. Any information the agents might have gathered undercover was lost with them. The survivor, Agent Russell Troy, couldn't or wouldn't talk about it. I'm told he was catatonic for a while. Whatever the reasons, nothing solid on Hyde or his fellow race cultists was produced. Various agencies here and abroad have tried since. Interpol would love to get their hands on Hyde, too, because we've traced him to several trips abroad. He is believed to be spearheading a push for renewed racist violence in Europe, and may well be the man behind three different separatist cells. We know he's been linked to the terrorist group Ausländer Toten, half a dozen of whom were caught with the components of a Russian military surplus nuke in Berlin three weeks ago."

"So Hyde has his claws in a lot of pies," Bolan said. "How do we know? If we can't get anything on him officially, where's this intel coming from?"

"Largely through the efforts of Bear and his people," Brognola said, referring to Aaron "the Bear" Kurtzman, head of Stony Man Farm's computer team. "He's tweaked the internet chatter algorithms we use to screen sensitive and secure or encrypted data traffic. In its infancy it was part of the old Carnivore program that most of the public has heard about. In reality, it's worlds more advanced."

"But what it gives you isn't legally actionable," Bolan said.

"No," Brognola admitted. "Not even a little. Which is where you come in, Striker."

"You had my attention at 'animals.'"

"Twelfth Reich hasn't yet publicly claimed responsibility for what is now a series of increasingly deadly terrorist attacks. Most of these have been covered up, described as gang killings or the results of failed drug deals, that sort of thing. The hope was to prevent a national panic should the extent of Twelfth Reich's involvement at the national level—and its body count—come to light. But Bear and his team have intercepted communications from Twelfth Reich cells that tell us something big is coming. We think they're getting ready to announce themselves publicly. There'll be no ignoring them when they do."

"Which means you'll have a domestically produced al Qaeda on your hands," Bolan surmised.

"Exactly," Brognola said. "Imagine the damage it would do to public confidence in the government, and in Homeland Security, if we can't stop this before it reaches that point. Twelfth Reich strikes conducted multiple times per month, even per week, with sympathetic media outlets serving as mouthpieces for the terrorists. We'll lose control of the playing field, Striker. We'll be on the defensive, reacting instead of intercepting. Once we start down that slope we've got nowhere to go but utter failure."

"You really think it will get that bad?"

"I do. Hyde is laying the groundwork with certain talk show figures and journalists he believes are receptive to his message," Brognola said. "Bear brought us the raw feeds, tied to his keyword sweeps across the web, but to their credit, most of the media figures contacted thus far have since reported the solicitations to the authorities. We're sitting on them, for now. We don't want Hyde to know that we know."

"What do you want me to do?" Bolan asked.

"The Farm has compiled, leveraging the Bureau's past intelligence, a priority list of targets for you. Some of them are places we think Hyde may go to ground. Others are potential targets. We've isolated two of the former, a pair of safe houses located very close to each other in New Mexico, as Priority Alpha. One of these is Shane Hyde's most likely base of operations. We want you to hit them both, and we want you to find Hyde."

"Find and eliminate?"

"No," Brognola said. "That's the problem. He has intelligence that could put us ahead of the terrorist networks in Europe. We need to know what's inside his brain. We need you to take him alive."

Bolan considered that for a moment. "That's not going to be easy."

"I know, Striker," Brognola said. "There are few men I would ask even to try. But we need him breathing and able to tell us what he knows. The Man is getting a lot of pressure from agencies here and abroad. Strings were pulled to make sure we're on point in this, which means we're running interference with the National Security Agency, Department of Homeland Security and the FBI to keep them out of the mix."

"They don't like not knowing who's handling it," Bolan offered.

"Yes," Brognola said. "It's our job now, but there are plenty of people who'd like to take it from us. The Man himself was very clear about this. The President needs this problem resolved before it starts to seriously hinder his credibility with the international law-enforcement community."

"The logical thing to do," Bolan said, "would be to send blacksuits to each target. Simultaneously."

"I can't give the order not to fire on Shane Hyde to that many men," Brognola said. "They'll be walking in there with their hands tied behind their backs. They'll either hold off too long and get shot up, or they'll be too quick to fire, and a stray bullet or a miscalculated shot will take Hyde out for good. There's also the fact that we need to do this more or less discreetly because we're doing it extralegally. We don't have enough hard evidence on Hyde and Twelfth Reich, not to justify an operation as decisive as this. We've been ordered to cut out a cancer. I need a surgeon. I need *you,* Striker."

"Understood," Bolan said. "What about support?"

"We may be able to draw a certain amount of backup from DHS or the Bureau," Brognola said. "It will mean admitting that Justice is in charge, which will get my phone ringing. That's nothing I'm not used to doing whenever you're in the field. But again, discretion is called for…if not simply because the Man needs this done quickly and quietly."

"Or he looks as if he's not in control of the situation," Bolan said.

"Exactly."

"And if I don't find Hyde at this Priority Alpha? Follow-up is going to have to be fast, Hal, if I can't count on simultaneous containment. Frontal, hard assault will get Hyde's attention. When word gets out that I'm rattling cages, he and his men will hunt for cover and dig in. I'll have to run them down site to site."

"I know," Brognola said. "I'm transmitting files to your phone now. Jack has orders to report to your location. He'll bring suitable transportation, something fast with decent range."

Bolan nodded, though Brognola could not see him. Jack was Stony Man pilot Jack Grimaldi, a man whose war against society's predators dated back almost as far as Bolan's own. "Have him bring me something that goes bang."

"I'll make sure the armory sends along a care package."

"Then I'd better go," Bolan said, as his phone vibrated under his hand, signaling receipt of Brognola's data files. "I've got a lot of reading to catch up on."

"You do, at that," Brognola had said. "Good hunting, Striker. I realize I'm dropping you into a meat grinder. I wouldn't ask if I had any other option."

"Yeah," Bolan said.

"And…Striker?"

"Yeah?"

"You *could* say no. You always have that option."

"I know that. Do *you?*"

"I do," Brognola had admitted. "You've made it very clear that what you do occurs on your own terms."

"Then you also know why I won't refuse," Bolan said. "Striker, out."

That had been mere hours ago. Now Bolan's boots were on the ground in New Mexico, his familiar Beretta was in his hand and dead terrorists were already assuming ambient temperature in his wake. A double-edged Sting combat knife rode in a custom Kydex scabbard inside his waistband behind his left hip; a massive .44 Magnum Desert Eagle rode in a similar Kydex holster behind his right. Over the shoulder of his formfitting combat blacksuit he wore an olive-drab canvas war bag, which carried the other munitions and tools he might need. He had not yet deployed his subgun, but he would need it only too soon.

The promised care package had turned out to be the FN P-90, Belgium's contribution to the world's most innovative submachine guns. The lightweight bullpup weapon, no longer than the width of Bolan's shoulder blades, fired 900 rounds per minute of 5.7 mm cartridges to an effective range of 200 meters. Equipped with a tritium-illuminated reflex sight, the weapon fired from a closed bolt for maximum accuracy. It was one of the quietest weapons of its type Bolan had ever fired, with superb ergonomics. Its horizontal magazines were loaded with fifty rounds each.

It was time to knock on the door.

Bolan made sure his Beretta was set to 3-round-burst mode. He reached into his war bag, grabbed a flash-bang grenade and popped the pin with his thumb. Counting silently, he pushed the grenade through the corner of one of the windows, where the Plexiglas didn't completely cover the gap. Then he quickly made his way across the front of the building to the opposite side of the front door, opened his mouth wide and shut his eyes.

His quick surveillance of the building prior to making his run had told him there was only one entrance. Unless they threw themselves from the windows, the skinheads would have to flee through the—

The flash-bang detonated. The explosion, even contained within the house, was almost loud enough to hurt. The flash left afterimages in Bolan's vision through his eyelids. The screams and cries from within were immediate and not surprising. The warped wooden door at the entrance was thrown open, and it banged against the front of the building.

The skinhead who stumbled out carried a .45 automatic pistol in one hand. His eyes were clenched shut and streaming tears. He was moaning, producing no words but making a lot of noise. He had probably been near the door when the flash-bang went off. He had obviously taken some of the worst of it. Bolan raised the

Beretta and squeezed off a 3-round burst into the center of the man's chest. He fell, hard, and did not move.

Moving smoothly, with deliberate, gliding strides, the Executioner made for the doorway. He held the Beretta 93R in a firm, two-hand grip as he crossed the threshold. Within the main area of the house, thin plywood walls had been erected to create a warren of tight, mazelike rooms beyond the central party area in which he now stood. Thermal imaging from Stony Man Farm's satellite photos had told Bolan everything he needed to know about the layout.

There were two skinheads, writhing on the floor, a revolver and a sawed-off shotgun nearby. When the pair heard Bolan's footfalls, they clawed along the floor for their lost weapons.

The Executioner walked through a kick to the head of the closer target, which snapped the skinhead's skull to the side. He couldn't reach both men in time; the second had his hand wrapped around the cracked wooden grips of the oldest and rustiest revolver Bolan had seen in a long time. A single burst from the Beretta put a stop to that.

He heard the scream then. Of course. There would be women here. Wherever there was human trash, there were dissolute paramours. Whatever their sins, if the women weren't skinhead terrorists themselves, they were innocents.

But there was no way to tell, quickly, which they would be.

He heard the shuffle of feet on the other side of the plywood wall he faced, almost felt the clack of a shotgun pump being racked. He threw himself to the floor as the blast punched first one, then another, then a third quarter-size hole through the crumbling wood. The shooter was loading deer slugs.

From his sight angle on the floor, Bolan could see movement behind the slug holes. He waited until the gunman—who was tall and wide enough, from what Bolan could see, that he must be male—blocked the light over all three holes. Bolan heard the sound of the shotgun pump being hauled back again. He lined up his target at the center of the three-hole group and squeezed the Beretta's trigger.

The Executioner's 3-round burst provoked a grunt; the body blocking the holes fell away. Bolan could feel the vibration of the gunman as he dropped to the floorboards.

The soldier pushed himself back to his feet, staying low. The doorway leading beyond was really just a ragged opening in the plywood walls. It offered no true cover, only concealment. He would have to stay mobile to clear the rest of the house. A spray from an automatic weapon could rip through the entire structure with ease, ending his life while mowing down anyone else who happened to get in the way. That option wasn't open to Bolan.

He heard the scream again, followed by an angry retort. That was a male's voice.

"Shut up! Stand there! He's coming!"

That was all Bolan needed. He had the man's position fixed and, diving through the doorway, he punched the Beretta up and out from the floor, flicking the selector to single shot as he did so.

The skinhead, crouched behind a three-legged

wooden table, had a naked, bleached-blond, heavily tattooed woman in a headlock. She wriggled and squirmed, trying to escape the line of fire in which her captor had put her. When she screamed again, the would-be domestic terrorist tightened his arm, choking off her cries. The skinhead glared at Bolan. He held a huge Bowie knife in his hand.

"You just back off, man, or I'll—"

Bolan fired.

CHAPTER TWO

Bolan's bullet plowed a furrow through the skinhead's cheek and kept on going at an angle, blowing his brains out the back of his head. The woman screamed again, falling to her knees as the corpse dragged her to the floor. She had been sprayed with the punk's blood.

The soldier reached for her, pushing to one knee. She would need treatment for shock.

The blade came up in a wild arc that nearly laid open his face, the lightning-bolt SS tattoo on her wrist flashing across Bolan's vision. He counter-slashed with the barrel of the Beretta, knocking the Bowie knife aside, feeling the edge dig into the steel of the pistol's slide. He dropped to a crouch and whipped the pistol against the woman's temple. She bleated once, then folded. The knife she had taken from her dead companion clattered on the floor.

Boot steps on the plywood floorboards were all the warning Mack Bolan needed. He rolled onto his back and pumped several bursts into the corridor opening as more terrorists approached.

They boiled through the opening like angry ants, firing without aiming. Two had heavy pistols; a third had a semiauto MAC-11. Bullets tore runnels in the floor, the walls and in the stunned woman on the floor behind Bolan. She yelped once as her fellow terrorists killed her.

Bolan breathed. He didn't think about the enemy fire; he didn't let the urgency of the moment push him to clumsy haste. He simply aimed and fired, aimed and fired. The 20-round magazine shot free as if of its own accord; the spare magazine rose in his off hand in a single, fluid movement. Then he was racking the slide as he rolled through the filth and debris on the floor of the house, coming up to engage the enemy, pulling the Beretta in close to his body.

He fired from retention, blasting away as the skinheads crashed into him, colliding with him in their panicked rush. He heard the grunt of the first man's death as 9 mm hollowpoint rounds from the Beretta tore into the skinhead's gut three at a time. The weight of the collision bore the Executioner back to the floor, under the dying man, his blood soaking them both.

"Get him! Get him!" someone shouted.

"Renny's in the way!"

"Screw Renny! Kill the bastard!"

Bolan rolled the hapless and dying Renny off his chest to the side. From his back, he had only his legs to protect him. It was enough. As the pair continued to push toward him, dumbly rushing on top of him, he snapped a savage piston kick into the closer man's shin. His heavy combat boot struck with enough force to produce an audible crack.

The scream the skinhead made was inhuman. Bolan drew his Beretta through an arc that covered both the screaming man and the confused skinhead behind him.

He pulled the trigger twice for each, taking them out of play.

Covered in blood, sawdust and pieces of trash, Bolan surged to his feet. He was nearly through the doorway to the rear of the house when yet another skinhead terrorist collided with him, this one from behind.

Instinct had Bolan swiveling before the skinhead could complete the attack. He fired the Beretta empty as the terrorist, an enormous bodybuilder type wearing only camouflage pants, smashed him against one of the plywood walls. The skinhead roared and pulled a double-edged dagger from a leather sheath on his belt.

The Executioner was faster.

He opened his hand and let the Beretta fall away. From his waistband he drew the black-coated Sting dagger. Locking his left hand in an iron grip on the skinhead's knife arm, he succeeded in stopping the blade as it slashed toward him. The wounded bodybuilder howled again, his eyes bulging with shock and pain.

Bolan's knife stabbed into a brick wall. The barrier constricted and now the soldier's own wrist was being crushed under his opponent's left hand. The two men were frozen like that for an instant, the terrorist's strength slowly ebbing from his wounded body, his breath coming in rasps and snarls as he tried to bull Bolan over with his superior size.

The soldier had been careful to position his hand on the terrorist's upper arm, where the dagger could not catch him. The skinhead had taken no such precaution. Bolan curled his dagger around the other man's wrist, carving his way through and out of his viselike grip.

The bodybuilder didn't react as Bolan cut to the bone.

The man's tendons gave way, and as they did so, his grip on Bolan's arm released. The Executioner shoved the knife deep into his flank, jamming the short, double-edged blade in and out.

Finally, the skinhead's strength gave out. His resistance dissolved and he crashed to the floor like a felled tree.

Bolan left the knife lodged in his enemy, scooped up the Beretta and dropped to one knee, ready to slam the other into the dying skinhead's chest, should he rally and try for another charge. The rattle that caught and churned in the big man's throat belied any horror-movie last stands. Bolan waited nonetheless, listening carefully for some sign of further resistance.

He counted off a full two minutes in his head. Most men thought themselves patient, but given a full minute of complete silence, they started getting anxious. Bolan was depending on that. If there were more enemies hidden with the house, he would flush them.

He waited through another full minute. Something wasn't quite right. Scanning the room, he stood, holding the bloody Beretta at the ready. Bracing the machine pistol with his off hand, he took up a position in the doorway. From this vantage he could see the last room of the house, from which the enemies now piled on the floor had come. It was a bunkhouse of sorts. Old wooden twin beds, never intended to be stacked, were sitting one atop another, nailed in place with cross-braces of plywood and metal wire. A makeshift table in the center of the room—just a large wooden utility spool—was piled with cards, trash and empty bottles.

"Striker to G-Force," Bolan said quietly. He shifted to his right.

The shots that came were fired from underneath the farthest of the "bunks," ripping through the mattress and tearing holes in the wall a good three feet away. Bolan simply flicked his Beretta's selector to single shot, took his time aiming, and squeezed off a single round. The bullet punched a hole through the concealed skinhead's mattress where his skull would be. The hole bloomed crimson and movement from underneath the bed stopped.

Bolan let out a breath.

"G-Force here," the voice in his ear said.

"G-Force" was Jack Grimaldi's code name. The Stony Man pilot was even now somewhere overhead, far enough off that the whirring of his chopper's rotor blades wouldn't tip off any hostiles. Bolan wore a tiny earbud transceiver, designed in part by Stony Man electronics expert, Hermann "Gadgets" Schwarz, which transmitted the soldier's words to Grimaldi and relayed critical communications back to him. The earbud could be connected to Bolan's secure satellite phone if required, but at the moment, he and his pilot were just connected locally. Grimaldi was Bolan's lifeline in the sky. Should he become enmeshed in a situation he truly could not handle, Grimaldi would descend, guns blazing. More than once, a well-timed air strike with his colleague at the stick had saved Mack Bolan's life.

"Stand by, Jack," Bolan said quietly. He swapped 20-round magazines in the Beretta and ran his hand over its slide. The knife edge had cut a deep gouge into the well-worn bluing on the steel, but hadn't damaged the machine pistol's function. He eased the weapon back into its custom leather shoulder holster.

"You forgot about *me,* cop," said a voice behind him. "Put your hands up or I'll just put one in your back." The shotgun that racked behind him for emphasis had already been chambered. Bolan heard the heavy thump of the loaded 12-gauge shell hitting the debris on the blood-strewed floorboards.

"I'm not a cop," Bolan said, not moving. His hand was still on the Beretta in its holster under his arm. "I was hoping I could take you alive. You may have information I need."

"I don't know jack," said the skinhead whom Bolan had kicked unconscious. "They don't trust me with nothin'. I do what I'm told and I like it that way."

"Figures," Bolan said.

"Ain't no way I'm going quietly. I ain't givin' up *nobody.* You ain't takin' me alive," the skinhead said.

"I've learned to live with disappointment," Bolan said. He pulled the trigger.

The bullet fired through the open rear of the leather shoulder holster, the muzzle-flash burning the back of Bolan's shoulder. Turning, he left the weapon where it was, not knowing if shooting from within the holster had prevented the action from cycling properly. He ripped the Desert Eagle from its Kydex scabbard and extended the weapon, snapping the safety off. The skinhead had taken a round through the heart and was dead.

"You okay down there, Sarge?" Grimaldi said through Bolan's earbud.

"Affirmative. I had a brief complication." He looked down at the dead terrorist. "It's resolved now."

"Roger."

"Stand by," Bolan said. "I'm going to need you to signal the Farm for a cleanup crew."

"Standing orders on that just came through from Barb," Grimaldi said, referring to Barbara Price, Stony Man Farm's mission controller. "She has a blacksuit contingent on hand to liaise with local law enforcement, make sure the dead bodies get written up the right way."

"Another drug deal gone wrong?" Bolan asked.

"Or something like that," Grimaldi said. "Maybe swamp gas, a weather balloon…"

"Or a classified training mission," Bolan supplied. He could hear Grimaldi chuckling in his earbud.

"Yeah," said the Stony Man pilot. "You've got it exactly."

"All right. Give me a minute to finish up here. Then we'll hit the second safe house."

"I assume negative contact?"

"Correct," Bolan said, his voice carrying a hard edge of irritation. "He's not here."

It had been a toss-up determining which of the two safe houses to hit first. This one was farther out than the second, which stood in a residential neighborhood on the outskirts of Alamogordo. Bolan had opted for the more remote location first, hoping that, with Shane Hyde in custody, it wouldn't be necessary to risk a firefight in a more populated area. Now they would have to take that step, and quickly. Vermin had a way of relaying word to one another, even where no apparent means of communication existed. Mack Bolan suspected that all criminals and predators shared, if not a sixth sense, then a heightened cunning that made them wary of situ-

ations and scenarios out of the ordinary. Losing contact
with the crew here at the safe house would tip off Hyde's
Twelfth Reich terrorists nearby. Of that Bolan had no
doubt. He and Grimaldi were already on the clock.

Bolan removed his secure satellite smartphone from
one of the pouches on his blacksuit web gear. The phone
was equipped with a high-resolution camera, which he
used as he moved from corpse to corpse, still cautious,
expecting no resistance but prepared to be surprised. At
each one, he either leaned in and toed the body over or
grabbed a hank of hair and pulled the head back, pho-
tographing each dead man—and the dead woman—for
Stony Man's files.

The images would be relayed automatically through
the smartphone's data link to Stony Man Farm, where
Kurtzman and his cybernetics team would run them
through facial recognition software. These would be
cross-referenced with the Farm's sometimes extralegal
databases linked to multiple law-enforcement systems,
including those of Interpol. The Farm's files on the indi-
vidual terrorists, where appropriate, would be updated
to reflect their new status as "deceased."

Each bit of information was, Bolan knew, a potential
puzzle piece to solve future problems. Even data that
closed doors was useful, for it helped draw boundaries
in the Stony Man sleuths' search for what was missing.

The frame of the safe house began to rattle, causing dust to filter down from cracks and crevices in the
ceiling. The throb of the chopper's rotors was as familiar as a heartbeat to Bolan, who had made his bones on
battlefields far removed, but no less deadly, than this
one. The machine that Grimaldi brought in for a land-

ing was, at first glance, the familiar Army Black Hawk.
The careful observer would know, however, that the helicopter was anything but.

Bolan's ride was, in fact, a highly modified HH-60G
Pave Hawk, itself a heavily upgraded version of the
Black Hawk. The chopper's fuel capacity had been
effectively doubled with the addition of external fuel
tanks. Its integrated inertial navigation, global positioning, Doppler navigation and satellite communications
systems had the latest Stony Man augmentations, including the encryption technology Grimaldi needed to
exchange data and voice with the Farm without fear of
being intercepted.

Grimaldi had explained to Bolan, during their flight
to the safe house, that the Pave Hawk had an automatic
flight control system, including forward-looking infrared enhancement for low-light and night ops. The chopper's ancillary equipment included a six-hundred-pound
hoist with a two-hundred-foot range, full infrared jamming and electronic countermeasures, including chaff
and flares, color weather radar and an automatic anti-
icing system.

More importantly, one of the two crew-served
7.62 mm machine guns had been replaced with an electric M197 Gatling gun. The three-barreled automatic
cannon fired 20 mm rounds at rates of fire up to 650
rounds per minute, all controlled remotely from Grimaldi's seat. While the Pave Hawk wasn't as heavily armed
as the Cobra and Apache gunships Grimaldi had often
flown in support of Bolan and other Stony Man personnel, both men were confident the chopper's offensive capabilities were sufficient to this mission. What

Bolan needed, more than airborne firepower, was the speed and range of the Pave Hawk. Its large extra tanks fueling twin General Electric T700-series motors, each pushing almost 2,000 horsepower, would get him where he needed to be as quickly as was practical.

Bolan boarded the Pave Hawk as the machine started to lift into the air once more; the runners barely had time to kiss the ground. As he piled in, Grimaldi looked back from the cockpit.

"Forgive the observation, Sarge," he said, "but you look absolutely pissed."

"I am," Bolan said. He strapped himself into one of the seats. Shifting the FN P90 on its sling, he looked the weapon over, removing the magazine and checking the action. He had spent a lot of time rolling around on the floor of the safe house, fighting in close contact. He needed to make sure his weapons would function when he called on them. The FN seemed none the worse for wear for riding along with him through the misadventure.

"Are you injured, Sarge?" Grimaldi called back. His earbud transceiver broadcast his words to Bolan despite the noise of the rotors overhead. He looked worried.

"It's not my blood," Bolan said. The front of his blacksuit and portions of his web gear were stained darker than the rest. He picked several splinters from the latter and from the crease of his canvas war bag before removing, from the bag, a compact cleaning kit. Then he turned his attention to his pistols.

John "Cowboy" Kissinger, the Farm's armorer, would give him grief for the gouge in the 93R's slide. He could almost hear the man's commentary now. Each of the weapons Bolan was issued had been combat-tuned, in most cases by Kissinger's own experienced hands. The goal was always to increase accuracy while enhancing reliability, goals that too often might seem mutually exclusive. Having spent years responsible for selecting and maintaining his own hardware, Bolan was no stranger to the demands on the Farm's armorer. He appreciated the support Kissinger provided.

The Beretta had, after all, saved his life.

Grimaldi called out their estimated time to the second target zone. He looked back at Bolan again. "Sarge," he said, "you okay?"

"Yeah," Bolan muttered. "But I'm mad, Jack. We've just left a trail of corpses behind us, and we're not much further along. Hyde may or may not be at the second safe house. If he's not, we keep moving through our priority list."

"That's the plan," Grimaldi said. He looked at Bolan as if unsure where the soldier was going.

"They're wasting lives," he explained. "Hyde and his hate-filled kind. Terrorists, predators of every stripe. They have motivations, Jack, and while they're all equally deserving of being *put down,* as Hal put it, some make more sense than others." He cleaned the Beretta as he spoke. "Hyde and his ilk want power, sure, but they'll never hold it. Power is an abstract to them. They wouldn't know what to do if they were suddenly in charge, suddenly the kings of their own white-as-snow empire. They kill not for power, not for political change, not for money, but because they hate."

"We've faced a few who answered to that description," Grimaldi said.

"Yeah, and every time, they were wasting lives."

They rode in silence. The thrum of the rotor blades vibrated Bolan's chest. He let his hands work as if of their own accord; he could disassemble, clean and re-assemble the familiar Beretta 93-R in the dark, on the back of a camel, in a sandstorm. The image made him chuckle despite his stern mood. The phrasing was Barbara Price's, shared in a moment's intimacy after the pair had spent some meaningful and only too rare downtime together. Their on-again, off-again relationship was the most Bolan could offer her. It was, for now at least, something she could accept. Neither pushed the other; they were professionals who knew only too well how quickly fates could turn.

He checked the fit and draw of his Beretta in the custom shoulder holster. The leather had been singed by muzzle-blast but wasn't otherwise damaged. Replacing the machine pistol's 20-round magazine, Bolan holstered the weapon, topped off the magazine in his Desert Eagle and secured the hand cannon in its Kydex scabbard.

"Jack," he said. "Time."

"Sixty seconds, Sarge."

Good.

It was time to get back to work.

CHAPTER THREE

Bolan moved briskly through the rear lots of the string of well-tended ranch houses, his boots crunching on gravel and through scrub. There were no manicured green lawns to be found here. Such suburban affectations weren't practical in this climate. The houses were nonetheless nicely maintained. Some yards were strewed with toys and dotted with play equipment—a sobering reminder that innocents weren't far removed from the target area.

The hovering helicopter would, of course, have exposed their operation immediately. Grimaldi had been forced to put Bolan down far enough away from the second safe house to prevent the presence of the Pave Hawk from blowing the surprise. While he hadn't yet seen anyone on the street—the neighborhood was, thankfully, a quiet one—he was certain he had been noticed through windows he passed. He was making no effort to conceal himself, no pretense of being a civilian. The sight of a black-clad man armed for combat and carrying an assault weapon was sure to have the residents dialing 911.

The fallout from that would be managed by Barb Price's blacksuit liaisons, trusted field operatives and veteran commandos in their own right, who would be running interference for Bolan as they helped the Farm coordinate the thorny issues of jurisdiction and author-ity. It was just those issues that would have Brognola's phone ringing before too long, as the many agencies with dogs in the fight started arguing with Justice about just who should be able to tell whom what to do.

Bolan answered to himself first.

The ergonomic and futuristic P90 in his hands was fully loaded. He had semiautomatic and fully automatic modes of fire at his disposal. The two-stage trigger, tuned by Kissinger and similar to that of the Steyr AUG, provided him with crisp fire control from which he could milk single shots or withering, sustained auto-matic fire.

"Sarge." Grimaldi's voice was clear in Bolan's ear-bud. "Something strange is going on. I'm getting telem-etry from Barb. She says emergency services are being rerouted to your location."

"*Re*routed?" Bolan asked. "What do you mean?"

"Something about a massive false alarm across town," Grimaldi said. "Multiple mobile phone calls about a fire and hostage situation. Barb says it's sketchy, but they're getting confirmation in now. A block of va-cant commercial properties was set ablaze, but there are no hostages. Alamogordo SWAT is reporting negative contact. You thinking what I'm thinking?"

"Decoy," Bolan said. "It's a decoy play."

"Barb says they're tracking back to multiple 911 calls reporting gunfire in your target zone," Grimaldi said. "Stuff that took a backseat to what they thought was a terrorist incident in the other direction. Sounds aw-fully convenient. Sarge, I think we may have missed the party."

Bolan picked up the pace, jogging now, the FN P90 in his grip as he moved. He didn't like the sound of that, not at all. A decoy might mean some kind of sacrifice-and-breakout maneuver on the part of Hyde's men, perhaps to cover the terrorist leader's withdrawal. There were countless ways the Twelfth Reich cell might have been tipped off to the threat. He couldn't guess at them. He could only hurry.

As he neared the safe house, he saw smoke. A small fire seemed to be burning at the back of the structure. Neighbors were already coming out of their homes, pointing and crouching, afraid to stand in the open but too curious or worried not to look. When they saw Bolan, some shrank back. One woman screamed. Another man shouted that there was some kind of trouble, pegging Bolan as someone in authority. The soldier could only keep running. He was now closing on the safe house.

The house was, like the others around it, a low ranch. This one had started out a muddy tan, then bleached an uneven beige by the merciless New Mexico sun.

There was a dead man on the porch.

The butt of the stubby FN P90 was already positioned against Bolan's body; he snapped the weapon up to acquire the sights. The man on the porch was down, lifeless, his limbs turned at angles no living human being could endure. He wasn't the threat. Whoever had put him there was.

"Hey! What's happening?" a young man, just a teenager, called from the neighboring house.

"Go back inside!" Bolan warned. "Justice Department!" The kid slammed the door as if monsters were barking up his walk.

Bolan hit the porch in a combat crouch. His boots scattered brass shell casings, which were thick on the porch floor. The front of the house had been shot to pieces, peppered with so many bullet holes that it looked like Bonnie and Clyde's last ride. He couldn't tell, from this vantage, exactly what was producing the black smoke curling from the rear of the building.

He struck the door with a powerful front kick, near the knob, not bothering to try it. Molding flew in three directions as the flimsy, hollow-core door slammed against the interior wall. Bolan ignored that; he was already charging inside, ready to flood the room with 5.7 mm rounds.

The living room was a slaughterhouse.

A smoke alarm was squealing. The fire from the rear of the house was gaining momentum; its crackling was growing louder. Smoke drifted in lazy clouds through the L-shaped living area, escaping through bullet holes spidering the bay window at the front of the home. The plaster walls were pocked with similar holes and sprayed with blood. More blood soaked every visible piece of furniture. There was a dead woman on the couch, two dead men on the floor near a card table and a pair of reclining chairs, and another dead man near a very old and very shattered tube television. The man near the television had almost no head. He had taken what was likely a shotgun blast at close range.

Shells were thicker here than they had been on the porch. Bolan crouched and, using a metal pen he carried in his web gear, fished up first one, then another.

He checked half a dozen casings throughout the living room. All were .40 caliber. He pocketed several, careful not to touch them.

Crouched low, he moved from body to body, making sure. There were no signs of life. The house was a tomb. It was worse than that, however.

The dead hadn't merely been neutralized; they had been mutilated, shot again and again in what could only have been postmortem overkill. Bolan filed that fact for analysis even as his mind worked overtime to make sense of what he was seeing.

Had the skinhead safe house been hit by a rival gang? A conflicting security firm? Counterterrorists, perhaps operating without authority on American soil? The first was possible; the second was unlikely, given the Farm's contacts and Brognola's knowledge of domestic security operations. The third was possible but didn't seem to fit. Bolan had only too recently found himself caught between rival security and black-ops personnel from multiple countries, in playing bodyguard and escort to a Very Important Person whom he had to transport to Wonderland. Even at their most vicious, foreign kill teams wouldn't have wasted the time and firepower necessary to do this kind of job on poorly trained skinhead combatants. An ops team from a nominally allied nation, like Israel, certainly wouldn't kill so unprofessionally.

The term caught in Bolan's mind. That was what bothered him. The position of the bodies indicated that the skinheads had barely had time to process the assault on the safe house. They weren't arrayed behind cover or braced in fatal funnels such as the hallway from the living room to the kitchen. They were, instead, dead where they'd probably been sitting when the attack came. Bolan paused just long enough to snap pictures of the dead, wondering if he would fine Shane Hyde among them. But the Twelfth Reich leader wasn't there.

He moved down the corridor to the kitchen, holding the FN P90 before him. Two more dead men waited here, one stripped to the waist, his tattoos proclaiming the supremacy of his race and stretching in blues and blacks across his back. He had been shot as he sat at the kitchen table. He lay in a puddle of his own brains amid the mess of an overturned cereal bowl and an opened can of beer.

The fire licking up from the stove and consuming the ventilator hood was almost out of control. Bolan grabbed the dusty fire extinguisher from its strap on the kitchen wall, pulled the pin and sprayed its contents across the stovetop. The extinguisher was long expired, according to its pull-tag, but it did the job. Whatever had been burning was now a black, frosted mess in the center of a charred frying pan.

Food, still cooking on the stove…and the man lying dead at the table had been shot down in the middle of his skinhead's breakfast of champions. Something about this was very wrong. Bolan took out his phone and photographed the dead men, noting the flashing icon that indicated transmission to the Farm.

"Sarge," Grimaldi said in his earbud. "The first of the emergency responders is inbound to you in less than three minutes. A pair of uniforms. You're about to have company."

"Understood," Bolan said.

There was a groan from nearby.

At the back of the kitchen, a door that appeared to have been punched several times—perhaps during some skinhead's drinking binge, producing several fist-size holes in the cheap pressboard—led to the basement. The sounds of pain and distress became louder. They were coming from behind the door, which stood slightly ajar.

Bolan didn't wait. He simply ripped the door open the rest of the way, angling the short barrel of the P90 against his body so he could target the space without turning his weapon into a lever to be used against him. The gaunt, shaved-headed man lying on the stairs within had full tattoo "sleeves" up his arms. The mesh muscle shirt he wore was ragged and bloody. He was hugging himself, holding his guts in, trying to staunch the massive wound where he had been shot.

"Don't move," Bolan ordered. The man held no weapon that the soldier could see, but that didn't mean he was unarmed. In his time fighting terror and crime, Bolan had seen every sham I'm-wounded ploy in the book. He wasn't easily fooled. "Who did this?" he said. "Who hit you?"

"I think I'm dying," the skinhead said. "Hell...I think I'm dying...."

"Tell me," Bolan snapped. "Before it's too late. Before you're out of time. You can get even. You can hit back at whoever did this. Tell me who it was."

"You gotta..." the man said. He tried to draw breath and apparently couldn't. "You gotta..."

Just what it was Bolan had to do, he would never know. The man stopped gasping. The light left his eyes.

That was that. There would be no intelligence to be had here.

"Sarge," Grimaldi said in Bolan's ear, "I'm transmitting to the locals. I'm warning them that there is a Justice Department agent on the premises. They don't like it. I'm not getting confirmation that they'll hang back."

"Understood," Bolan said again. "Out."

He placed two fingers against the dead man's neck, knowing he would feel no pulse. A quick check of the skinhead's pockets revealed nothing. Up once more, Bolan made his way carefully back through the kitchen, just in time to confront a pair of uniformed Alamogordo Police Department officers with their guns drawn.

"Freeze!" they shouted, almost in unison.

"Matt Cooper," Bolan said, citing the cover identity that appeared on the credentials issued him by Stony Man Farm. "Justice Department."

"Drop the weapon!" one of the cops called.

"You were contacted," Bolan said. "You're interfering in a federal operation."

"Drop your weapon!" the police officer repeated. His partner looked at him dubiously, though he didn't lower his own gun.

"Continue pointing that weapon at me," Bolan said, "and we're going to have a problem."

"Are you threatening to fire on duly appointed law-enforcement officers?" the first cop demanded.

"No," Bolan said. "I don't shoot the 'good guys.' However, if you don't stop pointing those guns at me—" he paused, and his voice became steel "—I will take them away from you and beat you unconscious with them."

"Put it down, Jimmy," the man's partner whispered urgently.

Reluctantly, the first officer lowered his weapon. The second breathed a noticeable sigh of relief as he did the same.

"How many are you?" Bolan asked. It was only a matter of time before the safe house was swamped with law enforcement and emergency response personnel. He would need to move quickly if he was to find anything useful amid the debris before the place was overrun with competing administrative concerns. The crush of jurisdictional red tape would make Bolan's job more difficult no matter how well-meaning the cops themselves were.

The officers exchanged glances, probably trying to decide if it was safe to tell Bolan anything sensitive. Stepping toward them and lowering his own weapon, the Executioner removed the Justice Department identification from his web gear and waved it under their eyes. That seemed to mollify them, though the cynical part of Bolan's mind told him that it shouldn't have. Were the soldier some sort of assassin or other well-equipped hostile operative, forged credentials would pass such a quick inspection.

"Backup is on the way," Jimmy said. "We're it for now. What happened here, Mr.…"

"Cooper," Bolan repeated. "Agent Matt Cooper, Justice Department." He leaned on the last two words heavily. It wouldn't hurt for these men to know he had the authority of Washington, D.C., behind him.

"I'm looking for this man," Bolan said. He held up his satellite phone and called up the most recent mug shot of Hyde. "Shane Hyde. A wanted extremist with ties to several domestic terror organizations." That simplified the issue quite a bit, but it would be enough to get his meaning across.

"You thought he might be here?" the second officer said. "Did you…did you kill all these people?"

"Negative," Bolan said. He pressed his lips together. Even the implication was disturbing. "This location has been assaulted by a force of armed operatives, size unknown, affiliation unknown."

"You don't talk like a Fed," Officer Jimmy said.

"You talk like a military man," his partner stated.

Bolan ignored that. He gestured toward the kitchen. "Everything around you is potential evidence. Don't touch anything. There's a basement. I intend to investigate." He turned to leave them. Over his shoulder, he said, "Stay out of my way."

He didn't enjoy being brusque with police, who were just trying to do their jobs. He simply didn't have time to be diplomatic. Hyde wasn't here and, if he had been, the assault on the safe house opened multiple worrisome possibilities. Had he already been taken out, possibly by one of the terrorist organizations to which he was connected? Had they mounted a daring coup, hoping to silence the security threat Hyde represented to them?

Bolan rejected that idea. Until his strike at the first of the pair of safe houses, Hyde and Twelfth Reich would have no reason to believe they were being targeted. Hyde's allies, then, would likewise have no reason to be any more concerned than they already were about working with him.

Unless there was something else at ploy here. Some

kind of leak, possibly within the web of law-enforcement agencies already homing in on Hyde. The man had, after all, been previously targeted, with disastrous results for the agents involved.

The Executioner dismissed this speculation. There was little value in it. He would simply have to keep moving forward through the priority list until Hyde, or some sign of him, shook loose. Until he could uncover new intelligence, there were no other options.

The temperature dropped to comfortable levels as he descended the open stairway to the basement, flicking on the combat light attached to the FN P90's rail system. He was ready to fire through the stairs, if need be; he had ambushed plenty of men himself from such a position. The basement was largely empty, however. There were a few cardboard cartons of what appeared to be trash, a water heater, what looked to be a nonfunctioning furnace and several empty metal garage shelves.

Satisfied there was nothing here, Bolan started back up the stairs. It was then that he heard the sound of a thump in the living room.

He hurried back in that direction to find the police officers had ripped a heavy-metal band poster from the plaster wall, ignoring his instructions. They had uncovered a cavity into which a small but sturdy-looking safe had been set. Officer Jimmy and his partner had apparently removed the lockbox and dropped it on the floor of the living room. The safe was oblong, painted black, covered in deep gouges where its paint had been scraped away near the lock and handle lever.

"Don't touch that," Bolan ordered. Jimmy looked up, annoyed.

"There was a tear in the poster," Officer Jimmy's partner offered. He appeared embarrassed. "We weren't intentionally—"

"He's a Fed," Jimmy said. "He's not God, Gray. Relax. We've as much jurisdiction as anyone until—"

"And what happens when everyone else gets here?" Gray asked.

"How many times you going to try to call it in?" Jimmy said, irritated. He reached for the safe.

"I said," Bolan interjected, "don't touch that."

Jimmy looked up. "Listen, Agent Cooper—"

He held up a hand. "Do you hear that?"

"Hear what?" Jimmy asked.

"Oh, crap," Gray said. "I hear it. Metal moving. Like a spring uncoiling. A rasping sound."

Bolan pointed. The sound was coming from the safe.

The soldier went to the wall and examined the cavity. There was a piece of simple, light gauge wire jutting from a hook screwed into the hole in the plaster. Removing the safe had torn something free and snapped the wire.

Bolan looked past the two cops and through the damaged bay window. Despite his warning, civilians had begun to gather before the house, milling about and craning their necks for a better look. The squad car belonging to the police sat in the drive, its LED light bar cycling red and blue.

"We've got to move this fast," Bolan said. He suspected a bomb. The safe was booby-trapped. Whoever had hit the house had missed it during their assault. Now the two police officers had triggered some deadly insurance left in place by the skinheads, probably to prevent their secured information from falling into law-enforcement hands.

There was no way to tell how big the explosion might be. Containing even a moderate charge, the safe would become a huge pipe bomb. Pressure would build within it until the safe itself became shrapnel. They had to get it away from the bay window and the civilians beyond.

"Basement," Bolan ordered. The police officer complied and the three of them managed to lift the safe and shuffle through the corpses and debris toward the kitchen.

"It's speeding up," Gray said. "I can feel it vibrating faster."

"Move, move, move," Bolan urged. They reached the kitchen. "Dump it down the stairs, then take the back door! Get out!"

The cops shuffled with him as far as the dead man at the top of the basement stairs. Then Bolan used one hand to shove the door all the way open before he put his shoulder under the safe.

"Go!" he commanded.

The cops backed away, through the rear doorway. Bolan heaved with all his strength, feeling the muscles in his shoulders burn, sensing the tipping point as the bomb started to fall down the stairway.

He was framed in the basement doorway, his arms outstretched, his hands open before him as he released the heavy, booby-trapped metal box—

The world burst into blinding flame.

CHAPTER FOUR

Mack Bolan was on fire.

He could hear nothing but the wall of pressure building in his head, ringing through his brain, driving an iron spike through his skull. Angry, unseen ants crawled up his arms, burning him with their touch, tearing at his flesh with their phantom jaws. He tumbled in free-fall, unmoored from gravity. Blunt pain in his shoulder and hip, so different from the sharp, searing agony of his hands and forearms, told him he had crashed into a wall or the floor. He tried to force his eyes open and saw only a black-red miasma of exploding, interweaving Rorschach inkblots, tumbling and rolling through his vision.

Knife blades thrust through his palms in dozens of places. He fought the pain and found the stock of his FN P90, fought the pain and found the broad, uneven surface of the torn floorboards, fought the pain and made himself put his legs beneath him. His thighs screamed as he stood, swaying and staggering, crashing into another barrier that could only have been the doorway.

From memory, from his flash-picture of the kitchen layout, he found the back door, careened off the frame, found the door again. Pushing, he plunged through, stumbling through the gravel, rolling, crawling, collapsing. The pain in his head worsened, crushing his skull, reaching a crescendo that threatened to burst his sightless eyes from within…and then slowly, tortuously receded, until the jet-engine whine became only the drumbeat of a sledgehammer crashing against his forehead. As the pain diminished, his hearing began to recover, and the blobs of painful light swimming across his vision began to resolve into shapes.

"Cooper. Cooper. Cooper."

Why did he hear that name? Who was Cooper? What did Cooper want? Was Cooper—

"Agent Cooper!" shouted the mass of burning light that was Officer Jimmy. "Can you hear me? Can you hear me?"

The lines defining the cop slowed and then stopped crawling. Bolan still saw blooms of actinic afterimage as he blinked, but now he could see, could really see. Jimmy and Gray might have been shouting at him from the bottom of a swimming pool, but he could hear them, too, well enough. They were holding his arms by the elbows.

"Oh, man, Jimmy, look at his hands," Gray said. Bolan's vision cleared and he focused on the man's nametag: Graham, P. The tag on Jimmy's uniform read Hernandez, J.

"G-Force," Bolan said. "G-Force. Striker to G-Force."

"What's he talking about?" Officer Graham asked.

"The g-forces, Agent Cooper?" Officer Hernandez suggested. "Is that it?"

Bolan reached up and fumbled at his ear. His earbud was gone, lost in the explosion. He patted himself down, searching for his secure satellite phone. He found it, and when he brought it to his face, he saw the ruggedized unit had been cracked almost in two by the force of the explosion. He tucked it back into his web gear without thinking.

Bolan's hearing cleared further as the sound of squealing tires reached him. He rolled over and onto his hands and knees. As he did, automatic gunfire churned the gravel where he had been. Graham and Hernandez rolled in opposite directions.

The battered, primer-spotted Chevy Caprice swerved as if in slow motion. Bullets fired from the Uzi subma-chine gun in the hands of the unseen passenger ripped across the flank of the squad car, flattening both tires on the driver's side. The car continued on, spraying gravel as it crossed the lawn at the far end. It could only have been concealed on that side of the house, between the bullet-riddled safe house and the residence next door.

Bolan didn't speak. He left Graham and Hernandez to shout after him as he took off from his position on his hands and knees, a track-and-field athlete launch-ing at the starter's pistol. His target was the beat-to-hell Toyota Camry parked across the street. The car was so dented it looked as if it had been rolled down a hill. It was, however, pointed in the right way: aimed to pur-sue the Caprice.

The soldier then rolled his battered body over the hood of the car, ignoring the pain, and landed on the other side. He smashed out the driver's window with the butt of the FN P90, popped the lock and wrenched the door open. Distant alarm signals were jangling in the back of his brain, jarring his awareness every time he used his hands. He ignored them.

Bolan didn't believe in coincidences, nor did he believe "Matt Cooper" was such important a figure on the national scene as to warrant seemingly random assassination. The would-be killers in the Caprice were linked to whomever had assaulted the safe house and killed the skinheads. The gunner, or the man behind the wheel, could even be Shane Hyde. Stealing a car was the lesser of the possible evils. Bolan needed to catch that Chevy.

Once behind the wheel of the Camry, he was as brutal as he'd been gaining entry. The FN P90 was once again his hammer as he smashed, ripped and tore, gaining access to the wires he wanted. He twisted one pair together and was rewarded with dash lights. Using his Sting knife, he cut sections of insulation from the next pair, struck them and made the engine turn over. Dropping the knife on the seat next to him, he floored the accelerator. The beat-up Camry responded ably, leaving a six-inch length of rubber behind the front tires as he spurred it onward.

He drove straight, grateful that traffic was light. Pushing the car as fast as he dared, he trusted his instincts, following his nose, avoiding turns until he came to a fork. Traffic was heaviest to the left; he bore right, hoping the traffic pattern hadn't altered in the last two minutes.

The light ahead of him changed. He ignored it, pressing the accelerator to the floor, veering around honking, outraged drivers who brought their vehicles to screeching stops to avoid him.

Bolan clenched the steering wheel, which felt like sandpaper beneath his bloody palms. Each minute turn of the wheel caused a stabbing pain, and when he glanced down he could see the ragged sleeves of his blacksuit and the livid flesh beneath. He was burned badly, maybe seriously.

He flexed his right hand, picturing the butt of the Beretta beneath it, feeling the FN against his body on its sling, the weight of his canvas war bag, the pressure of his web gear over his blacksuit. His body was screaming, racked with pain and vibration, coming alive again as the numbing effects of the explosion wore off.

Curling his hand into a fist hurt. He was ready for it, expected it, and still it hurt badly enough to surprise him. He would need medical attention.

Later.

Far ahead, at the end of the block, he saw the paint-spattered trunk of the Chevy Caprice. He had guessed correctly. His quarry was there and, for the moment, moving slowly enough that he was gaining ground.

The Chevy's leisurely pace didn't last when the occupants noticed the speeding Camry. The vehicle shot through a four-way stop and sideswiped a minivan, tearing off its bumper and speeding away. Bolan guided his stolen car around the damaged minivan, feeling the Camry threaten to pull up onto two wheels as it heeled past the obstacle.

As he got farther from the target zone, with Grimaldi well out of range, he realized his position was worsening. With both his transceiver and his secure phone lost or destroyed, he had no way to call for help except by conventional means—finding an increasingly rare pay phone, or even use a landline, which meant dialing a scrambled trunk line and waiting as the call was routed through a series of encrypted cutouts. He couldn't do that until he dealt with the immediate threat, followed the immediate lead. He couldn't risk losing the men in the Chevrolet.

Once he pinned down the killers in the Chevy, then he could call the Farm. They could route Grimaldi back to his location, wherever Bolan ended up. Hell, he would send smoke signals if he had to. It wouldn't matter once he'd brought the two men down.

Both cars powered through a red light, the Chevy dodging a panel van. Bolan caught an opening created by terrified drivers, all of them pausing to wait out the adrenaline rush caused by witnessing an obvious and flagrant violation of traffic laws before their eyes. The idea almost made Bolan smile, despite the discomfort in his hands and arms. The average civilian would freeze at the sound and sight of gunfire, but run a red light before him and he was apoplectic with outrage.

We all react according to what we know, Bolan thought.

He was drifting. Accustomed to focusing on the combative task at hand, he realized that his injuries were taking their toll. He shook his head, trying to clear it, tromping on the accelerator again and squeezing another few miles per hour out of the abused Toyota. The vehicle wasn't much to look at, but it responded well, its engine revving gamely as he pushed it for more.

Something was happening ahead. Bolan knew it would be nothing good. The Uzi gunner leaned farther out his window, and as the Chevy passed a slow-moving Smart car, the gunner fired a withering, sustained blast that raked the wheels and punched holes from front bumper to the rear. The Smart car lurched to a stop in the middle of the road, blocking Bolan's path.

He took the Camry up over the curb, praying the wheels would hold as he struck it at speed. Nothing popped. He managed to get the vehicle back on the road, drawing a line of gold paint across three parked cars doing so. Well, the Camry's owner probably wouldn't be able to tell the difference....

Bolan shook his head again and deliberately squeezed the steering wheel. The jolt of pain brought his eyes back into focus. The Chevrolet missed by inches a woman crossing the street. She shouted something he couldn't hear as the Camry rocked past her.

He had to stop this. He had to stop it *now*. The danger to innocent pedestrians and drivers and passengers in other cars was too great for a sustained pursuit. Bolan picked his angle. The Caprice was a big, rear-wheel-drive vehicle, much less nimble than the borrowed Camry. It was heavier, but Bolan knew the physics of what he was about to do. He could make it work.

He needed to make the Chevy turn.

Bolan reached to the back of his web belt and found the cylinder of a smoke grenade. The skin of his fingers cracked as he unclipped the lethal orb. Blood smeared the grenade as he wrenched the pin free with his teeth and waited, counting silently in his head. When the canister was almost ready to burst in his fist, he hurled it with all his strength through the broken window of his driver's door.

The grenade burst in the air. The driver of the Chevy broke right, avoiding the smoke. Moving at high speed, he wouldn't process that the smoke was harmless; he would simply avoid the potential danger.

As his quarry veered to the side, Bolan cut the arc, aiming the nose of the Toyota for the rear quarter of the Chevy.

It was unorthodox, but it worked. The Chevrolet spun, scraping its passenger-side door along a telephone pole. The two men inside, opting for confrontation over flight, started to climb from the vehicle.

Bolan threw the gearshift into Reverse and jammed his feet on the brakes. The transmission banged heavily and then threw him forward. Slamming on the gas, he shifted again. The Camry lurched ahead once more.

The driver was wearing a black T-shirt, jeans and a windbreaker, and he had a SIG Sauer pistol in his hand.

His eyes were very wide as Bolan crushed the life out of him, pinning him between the open door of the Chevy and the grille of the Toyota. Blood erupted from the man's mouth. As Bolan backed up again, feeling the Camry's tire fight against its crushed right front fender, the dying man collapsed back into the Caprice.

Bolan grabbed the back of his vehicle's passenger seat. Pain shot up his arm. Looking over his shoulder, he wheeled around the stricken Caprice. He was going to use the same tactic again. Bullets ripped holes in the roof and smashed through the windshield only inches from his face. The gunman with the Uzi was hosing him down.

The rear of the Camry ripped the passenger door from the Chevy. Bolan's stolen ride stuttered under the abuse he was heaping on it, then stopped when he struck the same telephone pole. The gunman ran his magazine dry and, rather than reload and try again, dived back into the Caprice. Suddenly, the Chevy's engine was roaring and the vehicle was mobile once more.

Bolan threw his door open and jumped from the Toyota. He landed on his feet, stumbled, and managed to recover. The FN P90 was barbed wire in his damaged palms as he brought the weapon to his shoulder and tried to acquire his target.

The Caprice struck another telephone pole. The gunman, practically on top of his dead colleague, went for something out of sight on the floor of the car.

Bolan dropped to one knee and took careful aim. The pain in his hands had the sights jumping around in his vision. The beat of his pulse was a metronome of punishment that rocked its way up his arms with every thud of his heart.

Traffic around the danger zone was slowing. Frightened drivers were honking. Others were screaming. Bolan had to stop this now, before someone wandered into the impromptu battlefield.

His shot was clear.

Bolan squeezed the trigger. Even the light recoil of the 5.7 mm cartridge caused a fresh blossom of pain in his palms when the P90 went off. He fired again and again, punching rounds through the side of the Caprice, trying to hit the Uzi gunner before he could pop up and start spraying the neighborhood anew.

Bullets peppered the pavement by Bolan's feet. His enemy was shooting back through the car door, crouching down below the window. The danger of ricochet had to be severe, yet he kept on. He was either insane or very daring.

Bolan shifted, duck-stepping from his kneeling position. The Uzi gunner was firing blind. The danger was greater for innocents than to Bolan himself, but thankfully, the area behind him was free of pedestrians. It was, in fact, a small parking lot, where some of the parked cars were taking bullet holes. A car alarm went off.

In the distance, above the cacophony, the first sirens could be heard.

Bolan sprayed out the 50-round magazine on the FN P90, holding the trigger all the way back, grouping his rounds in the car door, where his enemy had to be hiding. The soldier then changed magazines, moving quickly. Even that act hurt him. When he slapped the new magazine home, he saw bloody, partial fingerprints on the plastic. He retracted the cocking lever and adjusted his aim for the rear of the Chevy, where the Uzi shooter seemed to be creeping. He was using shadows on the pavement to gauge the enemy's movements.

"Hey!" the Uzi gunner shouted. "You out there! Are you law?"

"Justice Department!" Bolan shouted back. "Lay down your weapon! Come out now with your hands where I can see them!"

"No way, pal."

"Identify yourself!" Bolan barked.

The sirens were louder, but still far enough off that much could happen before emergency personnel complicated the situation. While Bolan normally hoped for the combat stretch to resolve things himself, without endangering others, he had to admit that backup might be useful in this situation. His vision kept fuzzing at the edges.

"Identify yourself!" he repeated. "Who are you? Are you with Hyde?"

"Hyde's filth!" the gunner yelled.

"What's your involvement?" Bolan called back.

"Every last one of them is going to die," the man shouted. "They all deserve it. Don't try to tell me they don't!"

"That's not your call!" Bolan said. "This is bigger than whatever play you're making."

There was a pause. Then, from the Chevrolet: "You'd die for *them?* For white supremacist garbage?"

"I don't intend to die for anybody today," Bolan retorted. "Last chance!"

The gunner rolled on the asphalt, his Uzi held before him, stretched along the pavement. Bolan had expected something like that. The blast went wide, as the soldier thought it might; an automatic weapon, especially a subgun, was no easy thing to control on the fly. He took careful aim, braced himself mentally for the slap to his palms, and fired on full automatic, walking his 5.7 mm rounds up the road and into the gunner.

The man saw it coming and tried to roll back. Bolan's fire stitched him across his shoulder and tore holes in his back. He crawled back behind the Chevrolet, trailing blood without a word.

The passenger door opened. Bolan, on his feet, came around the Chevrolet, his head swimming. He was close to passing out, but cleared the rear bumper of the Chevy in time to see the gunman pulling a leather shoulder bag from the car.

The wounded man's hand came up with a grenade.

No, Bolan thought. Not a grenade. An incendiary device. The red canister was clearly marked. There were more of the weapons visible in the leather bag. It was possible the gunner and his driver had been a mop-up crew, whose job may well have been to burn the safe house to the ground—and shoot down any stragglers in hiding within, who would be driven outside by the flames. It was a proved tactic when cleaning out a nest of vermin.

The hostiles, whoever they were, hadn't counted on being interrupted. Bolan's presence had to have thrown them off their game. Then again, the fire raging in the kitchen would have consumed the house eventually. The occupants of the Chevy might have been waiting to see if that happened, saving them from leaving behind more evidence that wouldn't quite fit with a nice, clean theory of gang warfare among skinheads and other criminals.

The theories flitting through Bolan's mind were sound enough but, he realized, disjoined and oddly timed. He was fading on his feet. The muzzle of the FN P90 began to drift....

The wounded man saw his opportunity and took it. He popped the pin on the incendiary and made as if to throw it.

Bolan shot him.

The Executioner tried to snap his weapon back into position, but his knees were turning to rubber beneath him. He managed to hit his enemy in the chest.

The incendiary, pin freed, fell into the bag of similar bombs.

Every hardwired instinct Bolan had told him to go,

and go fast. He turned and found himself stumbling, dragging, rolling. Clawing at the pavement, he nearly fell flat on his face, but then was up and running, pumping his legs, screaming. He let the P90 fall to the end of its sling and bellowed at the bystanders who had not already sought cover from the gunfight.

"Go! Bomb! Run!"

They fled before him, trying to escape the seemingly crazed, bloody man flapping his scorched limbs at them.

The first incendiary went off. Almost, but not quite in the same beat, the others erupted. A white flash and a ball of heat punched Bolan in the small of his back, burning his neck, singeing his hairline. He tried to turn, tried to cover himself, tried to bring his arms up to protect his head.

Then he was falling. As he floated through the air, suspended in space, he turned his head and saw the finger of thick black smoke roiling from the flash-burned Chevy and climbing high into the sky.

The pavement rushed up to meet him.

The soldier didn't feel the impact. He was suddenly prone, staring at the blue sky, watching the smoke climb to heaven. He was losing all sense of time. He heard voices; he saw faces. Were civilians gawking at him? Trying to help him? He had no idea how long he lay there. It might have been seconds; it might have been hours.

As gray snow crawled in from the edges of his vision, finally carrying him to oblivion, he thought he heard the sound of helicopter rotors.

The darkness claimed him.

CHAPTER FIVE

He woke to find himself staring into Jack Grimaldi's face.

"Somehow," Bolan said, "I always knew it would end like this."

"You aren't dead, Sarge," Grimaldi said, grinning widely. "And I'm sure no angel."

"I was thinking just the opposite."

"You must be feeling better if you can make bad jokes. Here. Take a sip of this." Grimaldi handed him a bottle of water and helped the soldier to sit up. Bolan realized they were in the back of the Pave Hawk. He had been lying on an olive-drab Army blanket between the bolted seats.

Bolan took a long sip of water and then looked down at his hands. Grimaldi had sprayed them with translucent, liquid skin. His palms were numb.

"Switch that to your left hand," Grimaldi said, "and give me your right." Bolan extended his right hand, which his friend turned palm-up and began dressing with light gauze.

"How long was I out?" the soldier asked.

"Not long enough," Grimaldi said. "I gave you some painkillers that will be wearing off soon. There's more in the medical kit." He gestured for him to switch hands, then began the process of wrapping his left palm. Bolan sipped more water. It wasn't cold, but was delicious anyway. His throat felt raw.

He looked out past the unmanned door gun of the Pave Hawk. The chopper sat in the center of a broad expanse of scrub and sun-baked dirt on what he took to be the outskirts of Alamogordo.

"You're in rough shape, Sarge," Grimaldi said. "Nothing that won't get better provided you take a couple weeks' vacation."

"I'll get right on that," Bolan told him.

"Right." Grimaldi shook his head. "I shot you up with some of the pain amps in your kit. As much as I dared. It's going to wear off and you're going to hurt again. You'll need to stay on top of that."

"I can manage."

"We've got a blacksuit squad on-site cleaning up the damage," Grimaldi said, "and running interference with the Alamogordo PD, who're hopping mad. All but the two cops whose lives you saved. They've been debriefed."

"Somebody beat us to the safe house. Killed everyone inside."

"Yeah." Grimaldi nodded. "The officers kept asking me if *you* did that. Although I don't think they really believed it."

"The house?"

"A complete loss," Grimaldi said. "The bomb started a fire that burned the place to the ground. You're lucky. It could easily have killed you *and* your two new friends."

"The Chevy," Bolan said. "Getaway car. Two men.

One automatic weapon. They were with whoever hit the safe house."

"Uh…yeah." Grimaldi hesitated. "About that. Both men and the car were burned to a crisp. Any clues we might have found inside…well. You get the idea. We've had the bodies routed to a facility we control, for autopsy, but running their dental records will take time."

"Yeah." Bolan shook his head.

"Here," Grimaldi said. "I made you something." He handed over a pair of leather gloves. Bolan held them up curiously. He realized that the fingers had been removed.

Grimaldi held up a pair of medical shears. "These are yours, too." He put them back in the kit. "Those gloves are sized for my mitts, which are a little smaller than yours. Without fingers, though, it won't matter."

Bolan pulled the leather shells on over his hands. They fit snugly but weren't too tight. The cut-up gloves covered his dressings and protected his scorched palms.

"Thanks, Jack," Bolan said. "You know you've got a pretty decent bedside manner?"

"No, I don't," Grimaldi replied. "I'm about to spoil your mood. You want the bad news or the bad news?"

Bolan said nothing. He raised an eyebrow.

"We've got a big problem," Grimaldi explained. He produced a replacement earbud and his own secure satellite phone. "I can use the transmitter here in the chopper to relay to the Farm," he said. "Use my phone. The earbud is from the spares here."

"The problem?" Bolan prompted.

"Idle hands," Grimaldi said. "You didn't find Shane Hyde at the second target house," he said. "I know, because I've been talking to the Farm while you were out. Shane Hyde and his Twelfth Reich boys have been very busy. If he was here, he was long gone before you got yourself blown up."

"Doing what?"

"I'll let Barb tell you that," Grimaldi said. He pointed to the earbud. "You're hooked in through the chopper."

Bolan put the device in his ear. "Striker here."

"Striker?" Barbara Price sounded worried. "Jack says you've sustained some injuries. If you need to come in—"

"Negative," Bolan said. "I'm all right, Barb."

She paused. "All right. Striker, what I have for you is significant. Bear and his computer team have identified, through a series of account transfers and our internet chatter algorithms, a hijacking perpetrated by Twelfth Reich."

"Perpetrated as in already conducted?" Bolan asked.

"As in happening right now," Price said. "We've checked it at the source and we're confident it's ongoing. So is the domestic intelligence network. Right now Hal is sitting on DHS and the Bureau, who are gearing up to take action. Hal held out for confirmation from you. He's pushing hard to get you in on this."

"What is it?"

"Do you remember O'Connor Petroleum Prospecting?"

"Yeah," Bolan said. "The oil outfit that had some trouble in Honduras when the dictator there nationalized their equipment and took some of their employees hostage."

"O'Connor has finagled a deal with the relatively

new government of Honduras, the powers that are in Guatemala, and the new, moderate regime in Mexico. They're running a pipeline from newly discovered oil fields in Honduras to a refinery in Mexico, from which they'll ship oil across the Texas border and around the country. This energy initiative is very important to the Man and, as you know only too well, is the result of some recently resolved political turbulence in all three nations."

"Yeah," Bolan said. "That sounds vaguely familiar."

"We have identified a series of account transfers, among other things, that helped us identify some suspicious industrial purchases of fertilizer. There were multiple indicators that Bear, on his own time, crosschecked. The pattern emerged slowly—too slowly for us to stop it before it could begin."

"Stop what, Barb?" Bolan asked.

"Twelfth Reich's people have hijacked an OPP tanker train," Price said. "We believe they've packed it with ammonium nitrate fuel oil bombs—ANFOs—in cargo cars attached to the tankers. They're heading for an enormous O'Connor tank field outside of Dallas, one of the largest of its type in North America. The facility is adjacent to a kind of tent city, an encampment that has risen to serve Mexican immigrants working for O'Connor. That's the target. Twelfth Reich wants to kill those people."

Bolan frowned. "Likely casualties?"

"Potentially thousands," Price said.

"Why not evacuate them?"

"These are migrant workers, Striker," Price explained, "many of them in the country illegally. We can't prove it, of course. The Immigration and Naturalization Service has swept the area twice now, and each time, the workers return as soon as they find gaps in the security cordon. It's just too large an area for the INS to patrol. By the time we got enough men in there to link arms and surround it, the train would have arrived. The other problem is that, even if there is no loss of life among the workers, destroying that tank field will deal a serious blow to our economy. The waivers and other incentives needed to get all this moving with OPP were delivered because the nation needs that oil, Striker. Losing that infrastructure will wound us badly.

"The train will cross the border near Piedras Negras," Price went on. "It will then follow a route through San Antonio, Austin and Fort Worth. The terrorists could choose to blow the train themselves at any point, but Hyde and his fanatics don't just want to destroy a train. They want that tank field. This is their ticket to al Qaeda status, as they see it. Their death blow to the hated American regime. They *want* to get where they're going."

"So we have to stop them before they get there."

"That's the problem," Price said. "We can't erect a barrier. There's no time for that, and anything solid enough to halt the train will blow it. Blow the track itself, derail the train, and we risk creating an environmental disaster that will kill whoever's unlucky enough to be nearby. Strike it from the air, it explodes, taking everyone aboard with it—and that's if you can reach it. We have intelligence indicating Hyde may be in possession of antiaircraft weaponry, purchased from the Iranians."

"Not good."

"It's worse. This train is one long bomb, but it's a bomb with hostages aboard."

"How many?"

"There's a very special passenger car attached, near the engine," Price said. "O'Connor, in an effort to protect its employees from the threat of kidnapping, to avoid future occurrences of its Honduras experience, has equipped the train with an armored personnel compartment. There are close to forty employees aboard, all of them O'Connor executives, returning to Dallas from an on-site conference across the border. They attended the opening of the new Mexican refinery, apparently."

"Those people might already be dead, Barb," Bolan said.

"They aren't," she replied. "The train's security passenger car is hardened to external assault and has self-contained communications gear. We've verified that OPP is in contact with its employees. The terrorists can't get in, not without damaging the train so badly they risk derailing it themselves. But those people cannot get out, either. Not with Hyde and his skinheads waiting to take them hostage the moment they do."

"Well," Bolan said. "Isn't that a pretty picture."

"It doesn't get much more complicated," Price admitted.

"Not with an unknown element killing our leads," he muttered. "Jack apprised you of the situation?"

"Fully," Price answered. "He said you recovered some .40-caliber casings on the scene before the evidence burned?"

Bolan patted himself down.

Grimaldi smiled and waved, giving Bolan the A-OK sign. "I've arranged for them to be couriered," the pilot interjected.

"We'll run them, for whatever good that will do," Price said. "I'll let you know."

"So what's the play?" Bolan asked.

"The Bureau and the Department of Homeland Security are running a joint operation outside San Antonio," Price said. "Hal has been leaning on everyone involved, hard, to get you in on it. There's been some resistance, but you know how these tugs-of-war usually play out."

"Hal gets what he wants."

"Most of the time. It doesn't hurt to have the Man backing your play."

"Any chance of getting some backup on this? People I can trust?"

"We're spread thin covering potential ancillary targets," Price said. "We believe Twelfth Reich may attempt, through satellite cells, to conduct parallel attacks while we're occupied dealing with the train hijacking. Able and Phoenix are deployed here and abroad, for some of Hyde's European allies may be involved. We've got blacksuit contingents covering other high-profile target areas. We're just spread too thin, Striker. Except for our allies in Homeland Security and the FBI, you're it." Able Team and Phoenix Force were the Farm's other field operatives.

"Understood," Bolan said. "When do we go?"

"As soon as you signal Jack you're ready to fly."

"Then I'm ready to fly." He looked at Grimaldi, stuck up one finger and rotated his hand in the universal "spinning rotors" sign.

"Striker…" Price said.

"Yeah?"

"You're sure you're up to this." It wasn't a question. The concern in her voice was obvious even through the scrambled, filtered and reprocessed connection.

"I'll manage," Bolan said. More quietly, he added, "Like I always do. I'll see you soon."

There was a pause. Finally, Price said, "Good hunting, Striker. Again. Out."

Bolan, forcing himself to move without grimacing, pulled a pack from the locker bolted to the floor nearby. He unzipped the gear bag inside and began rifling through it. Grimaldi made a mock show of tapping his foot impatiently as Bolan shrugged out of his web gear, changed out the stiff, bloody and scorched shirt of his blacksuit, and donned his equipment. Then Bolan began to check through his weaponry, only to find it had been cleaned and reloaded. He looked at his friend curiously.

"You were asleep for a while," Grimaldi said. "I had to keep busy."

"Idle hands," Bolan repeated. He smiled. "Thanks, Jack." He made a cursory review of both of his pistols and the FN P-90, including removing the slide of the Beretta and checking its custom suppressor. It wasn't that he didn't trust Grimaldi; this was simply long-ingrained habit, the result of years of trusting his life to the weapons he carried. One of the most basic rules of such weaponry was that you never simply trusted a weapon handed to you; you always checked it, for yourself, to make sure.

Grimaldi returned to the cockpit and began the process of firing up the chopper. He restored the in-flight connection, allowing them to speak to each other over the noise of the machine.

Once they were in the air, Bolan closed his eyes, breathed deeply and focused on his limbs. His hands and forearms were still numb, but rapidly warming. The ache that would pervade them could be blunted with painkillers, but these would fog his judgment and reaction time. He would have to err on the side of more pain, more awareness. He accepted as much and shrugged the thought from his mind. There was no point in dwelling on what couldn't be changed.

Starting with his feet and moving up his legs, he tensed and then relaxed his muscles. As his focus moved up his torso, he rolled his shoulders, working the kinks out, feeling the tightness give way. Years of combat had left him a patchwork of scars and potential recurring stress injuries. The human body simply wasn't built for the kind of punishment Bolan put himself through. If he allowed himself to dwell on it, he supposed he would have to chalk it up to effort of will. He was, after all, extremely well motivated. What he did, what he asked the men and women of Stony Man Farm to do with him, and what they did of their own will and motivation, wasn't normal. That of itself was a shame, for a country as great as the United States deserved a citizenry whose every member thought superhuman effort preserving freedom was the norm.

Bolan couldn't, and never had, faulted any man or woman for not following the path he himself had chosen. Lesser men and women might wrongly conclude that this wasn't a choice at all; that circumstance, and tragedy, had forced Bolan to do what he did, to fight as he fought. That, of course, was ridiculous. Most men, confronted with the deaths of those they loved, grieved and absorbed the tragedy, soldiered on as best they could in the most benign sense of the word.

The men and women of Stony Man Farm weren't truly the exception, for deep down, Bolan believed every man and woman had the potential, and the desire, to fight for what he or she valued most. It was simply that the counterterrorists with whom Bolan worked were *exceptional,* and that was the best way to describe them.

He snapped open the replacement satellite phone that Grimaldi had loaned him. A brief update bar appeared and, when it finished scrolling, the phone's screen indicated that its new code assignment was STRYKR2. Grimaldi and Price had wasted no time getting him back up and running.

As Bolan watched, the send-receive icon started to blink. Data files began coming in, automatically shunted to a folder on the phone's desktop, the wallpaper of which was still a graphic of Grimaldi's choosing: a buxom woman in a red-white-and-blue bathing suit. Despite the grim scenario he faced, Bolan found himself smiling. Some things, he reflected, never changed. Jack Grimaldi was a constant in the universe.

Bolan supposed he was, too.

There were worse things to be.

The data files contained everything the Farm had managed to gather so far on the OPP hijacking. A complete map of the route the train was supposed to take, as well as an overlay indicating the route the Twelfth

Reich terrorists intended to use, was included. Bolan called up several photographs taken of the migrant work camp, some of which were overhead shots, obviously taken by satellite. Others were news photographs taken when the camp was first established. Scans of those articles and wire releases were included.

While Grimaldi flew them to the target zone, Bolan read through each file. He never missed an opportunity to familiarize himself with data the Farm supplied. The war he fought wasn't merely a conflict of guns and explosives, of tooth and claw and steel and fire. It was just as much a game of intelligence. There was no way to tell when a discrete piece of data might provide a crucial, missing puzzle piece; no way to predict when a seemingly unimportant bit of information would help him achieve his short- and long-term combat goals. Whenever possible, he assimilated, and committed to memory, as much of the Farm's analysis and data as he could.

The schematics for the train and, more importantly, the armored passenger unit, were included. These were of specific interest because of the challenge they represented. He would have to find a way to free the hostages, but depending on the battlefield conditions he faced, would have to do that without killing the very people he was trying to save.

The plans had been sent by OPP. Barbara Price had appended notes to the files, adding that the management of the petroleum prospecting company was apoplectic over this latest turn of events. Bolan thought it bitterly ironic that the very precautions OPP had tried to take to safeguard its personnel—at great expense in customizing an already state-of-the-art train—had made it possible for the hostage situation to come about.

Standard procedure, were the hostages under the direct sway of the terrorists, would be to treat them as already dead, or at least potentially so. As harsh as that might seem to the uninitiated, it actually increased the array of options available for counterterror response. An operation planned with that cold, hard fact as its premise could focus on the most expedient method for neutralizing the terrorists, taking into account the *possible* rescue of innocents. Once the threat was resolved, any hostages rescued alive would be a bonus.

In the case of the OPP train, the hostages were confirmed alive and likely to remain so. While Hyde and his skinhead scum were doubtless angry to be cut off from their victims, the presence of the OPP employees was serving the same purpose from the terrorists' perspective. In point of fact, the reality of the train's passenger compartment served Hyde better than if he had guns to the hostages' heads. Force response to the hijacking had to take into account the fact that the employees were thus far unharmed and could be released if the train was taken intact. Any action that might damage the train and kill the hostages would be deemed unacceptable…unless and until the conscious, deliberate decision was made to sacrifice those men and women.

Bolan would do whatever was in his power to prevent that from happening. Innocents didn't die on his watch; not if he could help it. That didn't mean that bystanders and allies, friends and loved ones, the innocent and the guilty alike, hadn't died before him and beside him.

He had learned hard lessons; he had made hard

choices. More would lie before him before the mission was done.

His thoughts returned to the assault on the second safe house. Knowing who they faced, or why—that was the most challenging aspect of the current hunt. Quantified, defined problems, even big ones, were easy enough to solve, either with force, intelligence, or both. The unknown…that couldn't be resolved until it was faced, and rarely could it be faced until it was defined.

So. That was the question.

Who did he face, and why?

CHAPTER SIX

Nuevo Laredo

Russell Troy sat on the edge of the sagging motel bed, squeezing a red rubber ball. The cracked and worn sphere was small enough to fill his palm. To squeeze it until its largest cracks touched required all the strength in his left hand. The first three fingers of that hand were numb. They always would be.

The last two fingers were missing.

They had told him at the rehabilitation facility in California that the nerve damage was severe and permanent. He was lucky, they had informed him, to retain any function in the hand at all—function that could be improved through the exercises they prescribed. There was no reason, they had assured him, that he couldn't go on to live a reasonably normal life.

They were welcome, he thought, to go straight to hell.

They had given him a ball to squeeze. It wasn't white. It wasn't gray. It wasn't really anything. It was, in fact, the exact same color of the walls of his room, the same institutional not-quite-beige that some smug puke with multiple degrees in psychology had probably determined was the least offensive to the most number of people.

Except that the residents of the San Diego rehab center weren't people at all. Not anymore.

They were treated with something that wasn't kindness but never quite dipped into indifference. The staff members were mildly solicitous of his well-being and of the well-being of his fellow...*inmates* was the word that came to mind. The creaking and many-times-converted old house was an asylum, a sanitarium. It was a kind of holding tank, as he saw it, for people who were neither dead nor alive.

Most of them had been, as he had, undercover operatives. Their departments and branches of service varied; at least one of the worst cases was a former Special Ops soldier who, somewhere in Afghanistan, had run afoul of the counterinsurgents he was training to fight the Taliban. They'd taken his tongue and his eyes, among other things. He sat slumped in a wheelchair on the front porch most days, indifferent to the sun on his scarred face.

There were half a dozen others, although two or three were rarely in residence, spending time in and out of the hospital for continuing reconstructive surgeries. There was a woman everyone called Jane but whose real name was Karen. She had told him that much, from amid the bandages swathing her face and arms. From acid, poured over her as she sat strapped in a metal chair, in some godforsaken garage.

Karen was with the Bureau and had worked a Mob case in Philadelphia. They had found her and taught her a permanent lesson. She spoke rarely, but seemed to find Troy easy enough to talk to.

The smile was stillborn on his face. Of course he

was a good listener. He never talked. He hadn't spoken a word to any of them—not the staff, not the patients and not to his sister when she came to visit from Salt Lake City. Liz hadn't known what to do with him, hadn't known how to react to what he had become. She had fussed over him, had made small talk. Finally, she simply sat with him quietly and held his right hand as they looked out the second-floor window. She had told him he was welcome to come live with her and Paul.

"Whenever you're finally ready to come home," was how she'd put it.

Home. Now he did laugh. It was a miserable bark, a sardonic, bitter bleat that bore little resemblance to mirth. There was no home for him. There never would be again.

He flexed the ball, over and over. The anger lent him strength. The cracks in the rubber skin touched. He flexed them further. The knuckles of his three remaining fingers were white. His fingertips were blue.

They had made him watch. They had videotaped it. They played it for him, explaining to him in exquisite detail exactly why everything they were doing to his wife was *his* fault, was payback for his betrayal. It had to be a video, for by the time they showed it to him, it was far too late. They wanted nothing from him; they sought no information; they were interested only in making him suffer before he died. His last thoughts were to be of loss and impotence and astonishing shame.

He hadn't been there in person because it had happened while he was being beaten a hundred miles away, while his hand was being clenched in a shop vise at the back of the decrepit garage where…where…

He stopped. It was happening again. Try as he might, he couldn't remember their names. Couldn't remember the men who had been working with him, who had been part of his undercover team. It was an ambitious operation with a large budget; he remembered that. He was given unprecedented free rein, the authorization to conduct his cover and to bend, judiciously, the laws as he saw fit. He had done his best to blend in. He had taken drugs. He had beaten other gang members, sometimes close to death. He had rutted with the whores the Twelfth Reich vermin kept around. He had lived his cover, had been one of them. Even now, he could mouth the words of their hate, read the lines of his script as if he truly despised all the "mud people" Hyde and his zombie acolytes so feared and loathed.

They had given him literature to read, at first. It was mindless drivel, written by people who were barely literate themselves. One was a charming piece of claptrap, a novel about a man whose hobby was shooting interracial couples. Another was the book reportedly the inspiration for major terrorist bombings, complete with formulas for making explosives. Still another was one he recognized, an anarchy handbook long ago discredited even in anarchist circles as containing faulty information that would get the reader killed if he tried to reproduce what the book contained.

Hyde's idiot skinheads fancied themselves geniuses. Never had so many people had such a high opinion of themselves with so little justification. In their minds, it was everyone *else* who was stupid.

It was easy to be among them, easier than it should have been. Like all deep-cover operatives, he had felt himself slipping away, felt himself starting to like the freedom. Even amid the dissolution, the depravity, the debauchery that was killing his soul and sucking the life from his eyes, God help him, he had enjoyed some of it.

Now and again he would remember that. He would feel it in his stomach, like a sucker punch deep in his guts. When those times came he couldn't escape the memories fast enough, couldn't tamp them down hard enough, couldn't displace them with thoughts of his home and his family and the wife he had betrayed and neglected for his job. He had taken hot shower after hot shower, trying to get the stink of their rat holes and their cigarettes off him. He had gone to doctors, hoping for reassurance, hoping for a rubber stamp on a test form somewhere that told him he was going to be okay, he wasn't scarred forever, he wasn't damaged goods.

It was his weakness, he knew, that had eventually undone him. One of Hyde's toadies had gotten curious and followed him. Once there, the skinhead had seen something, read something, found something out that exposed Troy for other than what he seemed. Troy never knew exactly what it was. A name on a clinic form, an incautious word on the phone to his wife…there was no way to know. He was distracted; he had thought his cover inviolable, had begun to think of himself, in unguarded moments, as one of Hyde's street soldiers. He had gone to the clinic in…where was it? He couldn't remember. Places, names, people, they swirled through his head like wisps of fog, evaporating when he tried to catch them. The doctors had told him it might be like that, especially concerning anything to do with the trauma. What trauma? Something had happened. He didn't remember. It didn't matter.

He looked down at the rubber ball in his fingers. Sara. It had belonged to Sara. His daughter.

Troy was up before he realized he was on his feet, ripping the mirror from the wall above the entertainment center, throwing it to the floor. It cracked when it landed, but he put his foot through it anyway, feeling the glass splinter under his shoe, relishing the sound of destruction. Still holding the ball, he drew the .40-caliber Glock from the holster clipped to his waistband and smashed the barrel into the television, sundering the flat screen. The telephone flew across the room when he hurled it. He kicked over the wooden chair next to the bed.

It wasn't enough. He looked around, looking for something else to break, hoping for something else to absorb the black rage that had descended on him. He heard breathing. No, it wasn't breathing, it was hyperventilating. His heart hammered in his chest. His vision started to dim. He could feel blood pounding in his head, could feel the veins in his scalp throbbing. The choking, wheezing noise was coming from him, was him, was his breathing, and the barrel of the Glock was under his chin and his finger was tightening on the trigger....

He stared down into the shattered mirror. Through the cracks and shards, his own face, livid and gaunt, stared back at him. He saw the gun in his hand. He saw the barrel pressed against the flesh of his neck. He pictured the bullet that would blow a hole through the bottom of his jaw, through the soft palette, up into the brain—

No!

Glass cracked under his knees as he fell to them, tears streaming down his face, the Glock falling to the carpet from limp fingers. He squeezed his hands together, probing at the stumps on his left hand without knowing he was doing it, rubbing at them, washing them in his mind, trying to make the memory disappear.

It would never be gone. He would never be free. He could never not know.

He wept, on his hands and knees amid the broken glass, his chest racked with deep, heaving sobs. It wasn't fair. It wasn't just. It wasn't right. No man should have to live through what had happened to him. Serial killers, genocidal dictators, monstrous villains the world over had suffered less for their crimes than Russell Troy had been made to suffer for trying to do his job in the name of law and order.

Those sons of bitches. Those miserable, skinhead sons of bitches.

The thought brought him back. The memory of killing them sank its claws into his chest and hauled him in, away from the precipice, away from the bottomless pit of insanity that yawned, deep and seductive and inevitable, before him.

Killing them.

Killing them *all*.

It had felt so good. So…equitable. There was no shame in taking pleasure from it. They had robbed him of everything. To be repaid in the fleeting jolt of nearly orgasmic satisfaction he'd felt murdering them. There could be no shame in that. There was no wrong there. Was there? Could there be? Surely not.

What was his wife's name?

He couldn't remember. Would she have wanted this? Would she have approved? Would she have told him not to...

He couldn't remember.

He pulled himself back up onto the bed, leaving blood smeared on the overbleached comforter. The briefcase containing his Heckler & Koch MP5/40, spare magazines and boxes of ammunition was open on the bed. He brushed the barrel with the three fingers of his left hand, watching curiously as blood shone on the blued metal.

Easy. It had been so easy.

He had walked away from the San Diego rehabilitation house. There was no one to stop him. What did they care? Russell Troy was a piece of meat waiting to die, to the extent that they knew or cared. They would throw up no roadblocks, send no alarm. He was a footnote in a weekly report. They would adjust their budget accordingly or find some similarly damned soul to take his place. That's what he was. He was a doomed spirit, a ghost, ravenous to fill the aching emptiness at the center of his being.

He had come, eventually, to understand this. At the time he'd left, he hadn't yet come to terms with it. Something drove him, but it had no words then. He knew only that the scales didn't balance; he understood simply that Russell Troy and his family had been murdered, and he wanted justice for them all. The only possible solution was to bring pain and death to Shane

Hyde and all who served him. Only purging them, to the last man, would satisfy the hungry ghost once known as Russell Troy.

Hyde's organization, and the Bureau's inability to deal with it effectively, had created more than a few bitter agents at the FBI. The men with whom Troy had died—what were their names?—had friends, coworkers. There were people who hated Twelfth Reich almost as much as Russell Troy hated Shane Hyde.

There were people willing to help.

It had taken time. He wasn't without resources, however. Before assuming their cover identities with Hyde's organization, Troy and his team had been instructed to memorize the locations of several drop boxes and cutouts set up for emergencies. These caches included weapons, money, clothing and identification, all of it untraceable lest the skinheads have some means, from within the Bureau, of having sensitive data leaked to them. Troy remembered little, these days, but he remembered these drops. He had gone to each one, cleaned it out, and then started making phone calls.

He had been cautious at first, then more bold, as the extent of the anger among his fellow agents became obvious. They weren't just mad. They were *outraged,* filled with righteous fury, ready to step outside the boundaries of the law once and for all in order to end the obvious threats plaguing society. Why, they wanted to know, was a man like Shane Hyde tolerated? The Bureau had more than enough firepower to take him out. Why, then, was this cancer not burned out of the body of the world?

Why, indeed.

Sooner than he would have thought possible, Troy had assembled a network of former FBI agents, some of them previously hostage and rescue personnel, all of them willing to take action toward a better world. One and all, they wanted payback, and they looked to Russell Troy as the avatar of their anger. Troy, who had suffered at the hands of the animals he now sought to stamp out. Troy, who was willing to use his resources, drain a bank account he no longer cared for or otherwise needed, to finance the operation.

Getting weapons and equipment was almost laughably easy. They hadn't even had to pay for them apart from the bribes Troy spread around; the supposedly "decommissioned" weapons were old Bureau inventory, consigned to private sales and quietly diverted to Troy's couriers. Obtaining them had been one of the first services extended to Troy by Buster Wong, his most loyal and deeply planted source within the FBI.

Explosives had been harder, but not impossible. That, too, was simply a question of paying off the right people. As for the rest—vehicles, tactical accessories, clothing—they had purchased practically all of it from local sources, in cash. There were more retail outlets than you might think for that type of thing; survivalism and "preparedness" were all the rage these troubled times.

The money in Troy's bank account, swelled by life insurance payments he couldn't and didn't think about, he had transferred through a dummy charity set up for the purpose. He hadn't spent all those years within the Bureau without learning how things worked, after all.

His trail was clean. By the time anyone figured out what he and his allies were doing, it would be too late.

What was more, Troy still had contacts within the Bureau and, to a lesser extent, within Homeland Security. Even though his DHS informant was somewhat lukewarm to Troy's cause, he was consistent, and he passed on what he could. Troy's FBI contact, by contrast, had been invaluable, funneling detailed intelligence about Hyde, his safe house network, his known targets and his prospective victims.

Between the two sources, Troy had been able to locate and plan the assault on the two safe houses in New Mexico. The operation had started smoothly enough. They had hit the skinhead bastards, had worked their way through the house. At Troy's instruction, an explosive surprise was rigged to the safe they found, to catch any stragglers who came looking for secrets, money or drugs left behind. Like rats, Hyde's racists were most comfortable in their familiar nests. Even after one of these sites was shot to pieces, it was a good bet somebody affiliated with Twelfth Reich would return. The bomb would be Russell Troy's parting middle finger, vengeance delayed but not denied.

Things began to unravel thereafter. Troy and most of his team had mobilized for the second safe house, leaving behind a mop-up crew. These men were never heard from again. The second safe house, the one farther outside town, had been hit already when they reached it. They had barely missed being discovered by what could only be government recovery or forensics teams already swarming the location.

The crushing disappointment, of course, was that

Shane Hyde wasn't there. The intelligence they had was the best that his contact at the Bureau could provide and, augmented by tidbits from DHS, it had been thorough. Troy was convinced that Hyde had been at one of the two locations, or splitting his time between both, within at least the past two weeks. Indications were that he had been there for some time. This begged the question: Where had Hyde gone? More importantly, Troy now had to worry about the competition. If somebody else had hit the second safe house, it was either an enemy of Hyde's or a government operation. Of all the times for the government finally to decide to take action against his nemesis...

But of course that made sense now. Shortly after returning to the motel, he had received the news through Buster Wong. Hyde and Twelfth Reich were moving forward with their most ambitious terrorist attack to date, hijacking a train and rigging it with explosives. Right now, Troy was waiting for his attack team to regroup with him. They would leave from the motel, make a direct course by four-wheel-drive SUV to intercept the train and attack it. Where Twelfth Reich was, Hyde would be. They would take him while he was aboard the train, and eliminate him. Anyone who got in their way would be killed. It probably wouldn't be easy, but it was simple and it was direct. Anything else was just a question of firepower. Troy and his men had plenty of that.

The news of the imminent terror attack had painted what Troy already knew in a different light. Assuming Shane Hyde and his skinheads weren't coincidentally the target of a gang hit of some kind, there could be no coincidence here. An official operation, a law-enforcement raid on one of the Alamogordo safe houses, *had* to be mounted based on the knowledge that Twelfth Reich was up to something. It made sense. Even the fools within the domestic intelligence network wouldn't tolerate Hyde forever. They would be forced to move if they received credible intel based on something big, something new. Troy and his people now knew what the Bureau and DHS knew. They were all aware of the train operation.

If they were working from the same intelligence playbook, could their paths have crossed? Was a government team hitting the second safe house while Troy and his men hit the first, their priorities reversed, their target designations opposite? Was luck the only thing that had prevented Troy from finding himself staring into the guns of FBI or DHS assault team members before he even really got started?

The possibility concerned him. He needed to know who and how many he was up against. He needed to know the odds against him, and whether it was likely his government counterparts would think to check their files for the current whereabouts of one Russell Troy, last known survivor of an infiltration of Shane Hyde's terrorist group.

He had been worried enough, in fact, to risk a direct phone call to Peter Copley, his DHS ally. Copley hadn't been at all happy about that, even though Troy was using a prepaid cell phone purchased with cash. Regardless, he had promised to check, and to call back.

The SUVs were pulling up outside Troy's motel room when the former agent's telephone began to vibrate. He took a moment to make sure his Glock was holstered under his shirt, and his briefcase with the MP5/40 was secured. Then he wiped his hands on a corner of the bedcovers. His palms were tacky with dried blood.

"Here," he said finally, thumbing his phone.

"It's me," Copley said. He sounded nervous. He *always* sounded nervous, but there was an edge of fear to his voice that Troy hadn't heard before.

"What have you got?"

"You're got trouble," Copley said. "There's an operation being mobilized right now. Joint Homeland and FBI, with priority. Their target is the hijacked train. You know about that, right?"

"Yes," Troy said. "Who's in charge? Anybody I might know?"

"No," Copley said. "That's the problem. It's the frigging Justice Department, of all things. The field office here has never seen anything like it, or so they said. Some big wheel in D.C. is making a lot of noise. They've assigned some sort of troubleshooter to it."

"A troubleshooter," Troy said. "That sounds like—"

"It sounds like a lot of Agency talk," Copley stated, his voice even more shrill. "Doesn't matter if it's really CIA or NSA. I did some digging. Turns out this isn't the first time somebody from Justice has crashed the party."

"What do you mean?"

"I got a name. Matt Cooper. Nobody can verify for me who he's with, not for certain." Copley rattled off a description. A big, dark-haired man, tall and powerfully built. It didn't ring any bells, but then, it could be any operator Troy had ever met.

"Nominally attached to Justice," Troy said.

"Yeah," Copley said. "There's a lot of funny business in the computer where this guy is concerned. Wherever there's a domestic operation and Justice gets mentioned, this Cooper or somebody who looks just like him, from the reports, isn't far behind. And there's more. Where this guy shows up, there's a body count. A big one."

"Some kind of government assassin?" Troy asked. He opened the motel room door. The SUVs were idling just outside. His people were waiting, ready and eager to take justice for themselves.

"Maybe," Copley said. "If even half the reports that sound like him are him, you've got a real problem facing you. He's good. And he may not be alone. The guy's got juice, Russ. A direct line to D.C., maybe."

"I'll be careful," Troy said. "Thank you for your help."

"Just get him," Copley said. He hung up without another word.

There was no confusing whom Copley meant. "Him" in this case was Hyde. Copley had lost a brother to border skirmishes in Arizona, a younger brother working for INS. Hyde was implicated in the unrest that had turned the Mexican border into a war zone. Whether Twelfth Reich was directly responsible or not, Copley believed Hyde was to blame. The DHS man wasn't brave enough to do it himself, but he was happy to help Russell Troy exact revenge. Troy didn't care. As long as Copley kept him informed, he was happy to be the man's sword.

That's what he was. The sword of justice. The sword of justice for—

He didn't think the name. He couldn't. He couldn't remember.

Troy bent, scooped up the fallen red rubber ball and hurried out, closing the motel door behind him.

CHAPTER SEVEN

Outside San Antonio, Texas

"You sure you don't want air support, Sarge?" Grimaldi asked.

"If we can avoid making you dodge antiaircraft missiles," Bolan said, "I would prefer to keep it that way."

"I didn't know you cared, Sarge," the pilot quipped. He grinned widely.

Bolan couldn't help but smile back. "We just need the chopper for transportation," he said.

"Touché," Grimaldi said. "You know, you could pull rank. With Hal and the Man behind you, you could direct the operation. You're on this because the White House says so."

"I know," Bolan said. "But if I do that I lose the cooperation of most of the personnel on-site. They'll see it as territorial gamesmanship. I go in there hard and start pushing people around, and I'll be making Hal's job harder while losing the only support available."

"And you'd never do that." Grimaldi grinned again.

"No," Bolan said, smiling despite the ache in his hands. "Never."

"Hal would be proud of you, Sarge."

"Take her up, Jack," Bolan said, climbing from the chopper, gesturing toward the dark blue Hummers emblazoned with Department of Homeland Security logos. The vehicles were parked near an access road that, Bolan knew, ran parallel to a rail line that connected with the hijacked train's route. "Make our fellow government employees jealous of your ride."

"I'll keep it at minimum safe distance," Grimaldi promised. "We're fully refueled from top to bottom, all the reserves. I've got your back."

"I know you do."

Bolan resisted the urge to crouch even lower as the Pave Hawk churned the air around him. As he approached the knot of men standing at the DHS Hummers, he caught snatches of conversation. The mixed group of law-enforcement officers was dominated by a DHS strike team in full battle dress uniforms and body armor. Several men and women wearing FBI windbreakers and carrying M4-pattern automatic rifles formed the rest of the force. Loudest among all of them, however, was a florid-faced DHS man whose body armor bore Team Leader tags. He had unfolded a map on the hood of the nearest Hummer and was stabbing at the document with his thumb, barking orders to the personnel around him.

"Unit One, that's Harsey and Smith, with me." He gestured to one of the vehicles. "Unit Two, Jones, Grant, Adams and Peters. Three and Four are Wood and his people." This last seemed to be directed at the Bureau group. The DHS man jerked his prominent chin at the closest of these.

"What about him?" one of the FBI agents asked. He wore a neatly pressed shirt and tie under his windbreaker and was somewhat older than the agents with him. He was pointing at Mack Bolan.

"Cooper," Bolan said, offering the FBI man his hand. "Justice Department."

"Michael Wood," the Bureau man said. His grip was firm. Bolan ignored the pain that caused in his own palm, making sure his discomfort didn't show on his face. "I'm in charge of the FBI complement here." Wood extended his other hand, in which he held a portable radio. "I assume you'll need one of these?"

"Just the frequency," Bolan said. When Wood read it off, the Executioner input the number into his secure satellite phone, which would act as a wireless relay for his earbud transceiver.

"That's some pretty smart tech," Wood said admiringly. "Who did you say you were with?"

Bolan shook his head. "I said Justice Department, didn't I?" He wanted to grin despite the situation. Wood wasn't stupid.

"Who the hell is that?" the DHS man growled.

"And that," Wood said, leaning in to speak quietly for Bolan's benefit, "is Harmon Margrave, God's gift to Homeland Security. Watch your ass."

"Margrave, Homeland Security," Margrave said, nearly at the top of his voice. He leveled an index finger at Bolan. "Let me guess. You're the golden boy the higher-ups in Washington thought we couldn't live without?"

Bolan blinked. He looked at Wood who, unseen by Margrave, rolled his eyes. Turning back to the DHS man, Bolan identified himself again. "Cooper. Matt Cooper. Justice Department."

"Yeah, yeah." Margrave shook his head. "And you've been holding up the show just to make a fancy entrance. At taxpayers' expense, too, I bet."

Bolan ignored that. "You're in charge?" The skepticism in the soldier's tone was, he hoped, lost on Margrave, whom he couldn't afford to antagonize if the operation were to move forward.

"You bet I'm in charge," Margrave said. He hooked his fingers into the duty belt around his waist, which was heavy with equipment and a pair of horizontal magazine pouches for the SIG-Sauer pistol on his belt. An M4-pattern carbine hung from a single-point sling over his shoulder. His dark blue battle dress uniform—BDU—pants were tucked into combat boots so shiny they looked brand-new.

Bolan maneuvered around Margrave, who seemed annoyed by that, and examined the map on the hood of the DHS vehicle. It showed the railway and nearby roads, with a route highlighted in yellow marker. Bolan raised an eyebrow. He glanced at the vehicles. Already, the teams were moving toward the Hummers, as Margrave waved his arms at them.

"You're…just going to drive alongside?" Bolan asked. It was possible, he reflected, that there were worse things than poisoning the well of interagency cooperation.

"What else?" Margrave said. "There's no need to overcomplicate it. We intercept the train, pace it, board it and take out any resistance. We have—" he spread his arms to indicate the men and women climbing into the Hummers "—a complete joint strike force here. Why, I can't imagine we'd need even one more man."

Bolan frowned. "Twelfth Reich is heavily armed," he said. "Well-equipped enough that we don't dare bring the chopper close without fear of it taking missile fire. You're just going to drive up and take that train? And what about the hostages? What's your plan for freeing them?"

"Once we control the train," Margrave said, "we'll release them. Simple."

"Simple?" Bolan said. "Or stupid? What if it doesn't work? And what about Shane Hyde? I need him alive."

Margrave turned red. "And just who the hell are you to say who does what?" the DHS leader yelled. "We don't *need* you, Cooper. As it is we're cutting our timetable close for the privilege of your interference." He turned and made for the lead Hummer. "Stay here if you want. We're going."

Bolan wasn't about to let that happen. There was no time to argue about it now. He climbed into the passenger seat next to Margrave, who didn't look at all thrilled. The DHS man put his walkie-talkie to his face and bellowed into it. "All units, move out! Move out!"

Bolan shook his head. Margrave shot him a dark look but said nothing. The convoy of Hummers took off, spraying dirt and gravel.

Margrave drove badly, his foot heavy on the pedal, the Hummer always on the verge of leaving the road. Bolan, and the DHS operatives in the backseat, sat in silence as Margrave found every rut and hole in the weatherbeaten gravel track. As the access road curved, following the rail section convening on the main track, Margrave sped up, nearly putting them on two wheels.

Bolan had seen the type before. He had Margrave

pegged as a desk rider enjoying the chance to stretch his "combat" legs in the field and pursue a mission at last. The only problem was that the hostages held aboard the hijacked train couldn't afford to be treated like guinea pigs while Margrave figured out the job. Bolan's mind raced with possible counterplans.

He took out his secure satellite phone and tapped a quick, encrypted text message to the Farm and to the Stony Man pilot. It read, Jack. Alert for standby. DHS/FBI plan DOA. Bad news coming. Striker. The message would also signal Grimaldi to track Bolan's phone through its GPS feature, allowing the pilot to stay close at hand while out of antiaircraft range.

Margrave shot Bolan a look. "Checking in with the wife?" When Bolan said nothing, the man smirked. "Boyfriend, maybe?"

"Jeez, Harm," one of the operatives in the backseat said. "You want to draw a reprimand?" Bolan could feel the nervous glances on the back of his neck. To most of the joint government team, "Matt Cooper" was an unknown quantity, and presumably a man who commanded a fair amount of power. The fact that Margrave had been forced to wait for the mysterious Agent Cooper of the Justice Department to join this operation obviously had rankled the man's petty sense of authority. He was pushing his luck, probably gambling that Bolan wasn't exactly the type to file a complaint with a man's supervisor.

"We're all on the same side," Margrave said slickly. "I'm sure Agent Cooper here can take a joke."

Bolan said nothing. It had been his experience that silence was more unsettling to blowhards like Margrave than any retort might be. Margrave wanted a battle of wills, wanted to reassert what he thought was a superior position. Men like that, more worried about their rank in the pecking order than in the successful completion of a vital mission... Bolan had no use for such people, who weren't "men" at all, but children playing dress-up games with guns.

"There," the man behind Bolan said. He pointed across the Hummer to Margrave's window. "I see the train."

"Right on schedule," Margrave said. His voice was close to cracking. He was either excited, nervous or both.

Bolan tugged on the strap of the FN P90 and resisted the urge to draw his 93R. He had checked the machine pistol and his Desert Eagle already. He was as prepared as he was going to be. As thin as Margrave's plan was, there was nothing to do now but power through it and make it work.

"All units," Margrave shouted into his handheld radio, driving with one fist on the wheel. "I am now ready to pace the train. Wood, you speed up, cross over in front and take the left side. We'll match you on the right. When we have them boxed in we'll take out any resistance and board from both sides at once. Let's take it to them, ladies." Margrave floored the Hummer. The vehicle's powerful engine roared in response.

"We are go," Wood said over the radio. Bolan watched as the blue DHS Hummer carrying Wood and his men charged forward, around Margrave's vehicle, cutting in front of the OPP train and bounding over the tracks. As the vehicle neared, blooms of gunfire appeared along the length of the train. Hyde's men had seen them and were intent on stopping them.

"Here we go!" Margrave yelled. He swung the wheel too hard to the left, causing the SUV to yaw on its suspension as he sent it hurtling toward the flank of the train. Only the Hummer's width kept it from flipping onto its side. As the train loomed in the windshield, small-arms fire began peppering them. Bolan ducked as a round starred the windshield in front of him and took a chunk out of the headrest of his seat.

"Excitable, aren't they?" Margrave shouted. "Let's teach 'em who's in charge!" He rolled down his window and began firing his SIG Sauer at the train. What he was aiming for, Bolan couldn't tell.

The soldier lowered his own window. Hooking one leg through the strap of his seat belt, he turned his calf in a tight circle, effectively tying himself to the belt. Then he lifted himself halfway through the opening of his window, bracing the P90 on the roof. Sighting through the weapon's optics, he lined up the closest of the terrorists, who were firing from positions of scant cover from the railings and roof of the moving train.

"This is Wood!" the voice of the FBI team leader cried in Bolan's ear. "We are engaging! Taking heavy fire!"

Bolan lined up a shot and, feeling the burn in the flesh of his hands, triggered round after round. The light recoil of the FN 5.7 mm cartridge was easy to control, despite his handicap, and his optics gave him a good view of the Twelfth Reich terrorists dotting the train.

What he couldn't control was Margrave's driving. Each time Bolan had a shot lined up, the DHS leader's erratic driving proved its undoing. Margrave kept weaving in and out, closer to the train and then farther away, angling the nose of the vehicle as if he thought he had anywhere to go besides parallel to the rails. He was still firing randomly out the window, bracing his M4 carbine against the frame, triggering shots that couldn't possibly be aimed.

"Hold it steady!" Bolan shouted down to him. "Hold it steady!"

"I'm doing my best, golden boy!" Margrave yelled back.

The Hummer lurched closer and closer to the train, coming dangerously near. Bolan could see the expressions on the terrorists' faces. They were dressed in an eclectic mixture of cast-off military clothing and gear, obviously their idea of battle-ready accoutrements. They carried weapons ranging from Kalashnikov and AR-15-pattern rifles to handguns, shotguns and even a couple of lever-action carbines.

And they were all too close to the DHS Hummer.

"Back! Back!" Bolan shouted.

The skinheads aboard the train probably couldn't believe their luck. They were poorly trained and ill-coordinated, but they caught on eventually. Margrave hadn't allowed enough time to take out enough skinheads to permit his team to get close enough for boarding. They were driving straight into a buzz saw of terrorist gunfire.

"Here we come, scumbags!" Margrave, oblivious, was yelling from the driver's seat.

Gunfire raked the roof of the Hummer. Bolan was forced to lean back, wrenching his spine as he hung out the window horizontally, avoiding the bullets that climbed in two, then three paths across the Humvee. The big SUV shuddered as more bullets struck its flanks. One punctured one of the run-flat tires. Smoke began pouring from beneath the hood.

Bolan forced himself to sit upright, though his stomach muscles burned. He sprayed out what remained of the P90's magazine in long, aimed bursts, pinning first one, then another, then a third terrorist, trying to force a hole in the Twelfth Reich defenses. The gunfire showering them lessened somewhat, but it wasn't enough. They were close enough for Bolan to see the splashes of blood streaking the train where his bullets had found their mark. As he swapped magazines from his war bag, ignoring the distress signals from his hands and slapping the magazine home, he saw another plume of smoke from the front of the train.

It was Wood's Hummer, churning up the arid soil and gravel as the FBI men fled the danger zone on the left side of the train. If they stayed far enough ahead, they could avoid all but the most sporadic of sniper fire, should Hyde's people post a gunner near the nose of the train.

Bolan touched his ear, activating his transceiver on the scanned band Wood had given him. "Wood! This is Cooper! What is your status?"

"Stay off the channel!" Margrave shouted. Bolan ignored him.

"One of my men is injured," Wood said. "And one... We have one down. I think he's dead."

"Fall back!" Bolan said. "Fall back! I have a chopper on standby. We can medevac—"

"Negative," Wood said.

"No way!" Margrave started to say. "We've got to—"

Bolan snaked his way back into the Hummer. He glanced around and realized that one of the DHS men was bleeding badly, as his partner tried to apply direct pressure. Bullets had scored the interior of the Hummer, and either those or shrapnel had taken the DHS agent in the neck. There was a lot of blood.

Bolan looked over just in time to see the side mirror on Margrave's door explode. The DHS leader swore and covered his face with one arm, slapping the barrel of his M4 against the roof of the truck.

Bolan was done tolerating incompetence. He reached over, grabbed the steering wheel and wrenched it hard to the right. The Hummer, still under close to full power, peeled away from the train and the bullets popping and cracking behind it, speeding at forty-five degrees across the arid terrain and narrowly missing an abandoned clapboard shack.

The SUV struck a deep rut, a depression in the road that might have been a gully or simply an old trench. Margrave's M4 actually flew out the window. The wounded man in the back cried out, as his partner tried desperately to apply pressure with a crimson-soaked handkerchief.

"Jack, Jack, I need you," Bolan said. "I need medevac."

"We have emergency services responding," Wood's voice replied. "Respectfully, Agent Cooper, the responders on the way to us are better equipped than your man will be. I have arranged for airlift to the nearest hospital."

"Margrave's got wounded," Bolan said. "Bad, but I'm not sure how bad."

"We're coming at you," Wood said. Through the cracked windshield of the Hummer, Bolan could see the FBI team approaching in their own smoking Hummer. The other DHS men were pulling alongside.

"Brake," Bolan said. He turned sharply to Margrave. "I said brake, damn you."

"What the hell are you doing?" the DHS leader demanded. The Hummer slowed, but his hand drifted toward the SIG Sauer on his belt.

"You touch that gun," Bolan growled, "and I swear to all you hold sacred I will make you eat it."

"Sarge—" Grimaldi's signal was strong through the transceiver "—what do you want me to do?"

"Come in, Jack," Bolan said. "On my signal. We're FUBAR here. I'm taking control."

"So much for Hal's afternoon," Grimaldi said. More seriously, he said, "I've got incoming air traffic. Medical chopper."

"Courtesy of the FBI," Bolan said. "Get as close as you can to me, but stay out of their way."

"You don't have to ask," Grimaldi said. "On my way."

"And Jack?" Bolan said.

"Yeah, Sarge?"

"Rig the door guns."

"Understood," Grimaldi said. The electric Gatling gun could be shifted to permit for the use of the stowed door gun on that side.

With the vehicles stopped and the train quickly leaving them behind, Bolan helped the DHS and FBI team members get their wounded out of the vehicles and ready for transport. The medical chopper, a Bell JetRanger, threw up a storm of dust and grit as it landed. Bolan helped the agents who were not wounded to cover the others with their bodies. The Pave Hawk wasn't far behind, but Grimaldi set the machine down farther away to avoid spraying the team further.

It was Michael Wood who found Bolan after the wounded had been loaded and flown off. He looked shaken and angry. "Now what, Agent Cooper?"

"Now we do it the right way," Bolan said. He looked at Wood and then to the FBI man closest to him. "Think you can find your way around a door gun?"

"I served in Desert Storm," Wood said. He nodded to the man next to Bolan. "Greene here wasn't in the military, but he's been to more machine gun shoots than most gun nuts can ever dream of. He's our resident fire-arms enthusiast."

"All right," Bolan said. "The two of you, come with me. Everybody else, pile into the least damaged vehicle and pursue, but don't make contact. We need a trail car, just in case, but we won't be mounting any ground assaults. Any vehicles too damaged to get far, leave them here. Margrave and anyone not up to the ride can wait here for backup. I'll have my pilot call in for support."

Margrave looked up at the use of his name. He was leaning against the fender of his bullet-riddled, smoking Hummer, looking shell-shocked. As Bolan eyed him, however, his face turned bright red. Eyes narrowed, he headed toward Bolan, clenching his fists.

This, Bolan thought, was going to hurt. A lot.

"This is still my operation!" Margrave said. "There's

no room for jurisdictional pissing matches here, Cooper! I am the duly appointed leader of—"

Bolan punched him the face.

The glove helped a little, but the starburst of pain radiated up his arm like an electric shock. Wincing, he watched as Margrave hit the ground, his nose smashed, streaming blood across his mouth and chin.

"My *nobe!*" the man bleated. "You *broge my nobe!*"

"What did he say?" Wood asked, coming to stand next to Bolan. He looked down at the DHS man with an expression Bolan took for satisfaction.

"His nose," the soldier said. "I broke his nose."

"Good," Wood replied. "Saves me the trouble."

"Yeah," Bolan said. Margrave continued to squawk in pain.

"And now?" Wood asked.

"Now we go to work."

CHAPTER EIGHT

Shane Hyde crouched in the crew car, one foot balanced against the body of a dead engineer his men hadn't been allowed to throw off the train. Hyde had taken an immediate liking to the dead man, whose coveralls indicated his name was Robert. Several times his faithful had offered to remove poor Robert, but Hyde had refused. Robert was an excellent listener and, if Hyde had learned anything at all through the long years of his struggle, it was that good listeners were, to misunderstood men of power, invaluable.

Mein Kampf, he thought. Truly, it is my struggle, as it was his.

He took the leather pouch from inside his camouflage jacket. He wore his own Army BDUs, now an iteration or two out of date, and his own government-issue combat boots, which were scuffed and worn. The M16 rifle he carried was an older model, equipped with a full-automatic fire mode rather than the 3-round-burst found on later weapons. This one had been stolen from a government armory, most likely, before making its way into the black market from which Hyde had purchased most of Twelfth Reich's weapons. America truly was a land of opportunity. You just had to have enough money…or be the right color.

The thought, as it always did, brought a scowl to his

face. As a white male, the demographic on which this biased, patriarchal society was thought to be based, he was supposed to be among the privileged. The system, he was constantly told, was stacked in his favor, as institutionalized racism and sexism forever screwed everybody who wasn't a white man. "People of color," as the current euphemism went, women, and a laundry list of other agenda-driven groups, everyone from the transgenders to the climate-change nuts and the earth-peace whale-loving tree huggers to people born with birth defects and eating disorders or injured in capitalist factories…they were all supposed to be disadvantaged, all of them standing in line behind Shane Hyde and other white males in the grand order of things that ran the country.

What a pack of lies.

America's secret shame, the knowledge of which had long ago dawned on Shane Hyde and the men and women who followed him, was that everything popular culture vomited forth about the country's power structure was a lie. It was a lie told by those in power— homosexuals, mud people, Zionists and even their collaborators among the white race—who had a vested interest in maintaining the myth. The myth of white male power was, after all, what made it okay to oppress whites, to push an agenda of hatred against those *most* qualified to be in power. It was one of life's most delicious ironies that the very men who could wield power best, men like Shane Hyde, had the least amount of power. Their ability to see the truth, their unflinching acceptance of cold, hard reality, marked them as pariahs. They were the carriers, the promulgators, of the most inconvenient truth of all: that white men *were* superior, but a corrupt society ruled by their enemies worked constantly to hold them in check.

From his suede pouch, Hyde removed rolling papers and tobacco. His hands worked automatically, the movements practiced, familiar, habitual. As he crouched, feeling the train rock beneath him, he peeked over the edge of the window closest to him. The reinforced glass was shot through in several places, but the wire mesh within had stopped the window from shattering to pebbles. Those oil company camel jockeys could build a train; he would give them that. It was just possible they had a few white men in charge at the top, in whatever third-world factory put these cars together.

He rolled a nice, tight cigarette, thinner than normal. He enjoyed smoking the little pin-joints, as one of his bedmates had called them. Which one was she? Carrie, he thought. Or maybe Tina. He couldn't remember and it wasn't important. Twelfth Reich had several women in its ranks, but neither they nor Hyde and his men harbored any illusions that those women were equal. They understood that unless they wanted to live in a world, raise children in a world dominated by black rape gangs and overseen by Zionist slave-masters, a world in which they would have to learn Spanish just to buy a hamburger at a fast-food joint, they should support Hyde and the order of power he represented. If that meant accepting their relative lack of power in a white man's world, then they would accept it.

Really, Hyde admitted to himself, such women were good for only one thing, and the best among them understood that. But he had no problem humoring them and even letting them fight and die for the cause. Especially now, in the early stages of the struggle, he needed their zeal, needed their energy. It didn't hurt that the women among his group kept his bed warm at night, either. It was one of the inducements he offered to his lieutenants. There were too few women to go around, much as they were shared. Loyal service to Shane Hyde meant more favors from among the ranks of Twelfth Reich's female members.

He removed the disposable butane lighter he kept in the pouch, and fired his cigarette. Drawing the unfiltered smoke deep into his lungs, he smiled at the familiar warmth. He adored smoking. A man, a great man, allowed himself few pleasures. Women were among them, of course; no great man denied his primal urges there. But smoking was his second vice. It was a respectable pleasure, something that at one time was not reviled by a hypercritical society obsessed with nanny state control over every habit and act in which its subjects indulged.

"There's something I'll change, Bob," he said to the dead man. The corpse in the coveralls made no reply, but then, Hyde hadn't expected one. You never knew. Occasionally the dead spoke, though only seldom were they coherent. "I'll make it legal to smoke in public again," Hyde went on. "No more sticking your nose in your neighbor's business."

He drew deeply on the cigarette again. He had gone through a period of ripping the filters from commercial smokes. Eventually, however, he'd gone straight to rolling his own. The quality of the tobacco, if he purchased with discretion, was always better. A great man understood the finer things in life.

Idly, he went through the dead man's pockets. He found some change, which he kept, and a wallet, which he emptied. The photographs there could have belonged to anyone. A fat wife, a pair of homely children. Well, at least they were white. It was a shame that the Twelfth Reich had been forced to kill whites while boarding the train, but even considerations of racial fealty had to give way to the plan.

The thought of the plan renewed the smile on Hyde's lips.

Since 9/11, Shane Hyde dreamed of making an operation of this scale work. The terrorist attacks in New York City had changed the way global society looked at revolution. No longer were small guerrilla groups presumed to be largely ineffective. Now, as the human race had learned only too painfully, a small group of armed men could move the world with the lever of their will. It was a lesson Shane Hyde had always thought to be true, but seeing the proof, hearing the wailing and gnashing of teeth that followed the successful completion of such a daring operation, had spurred him and encouraged him. He no longer had to theorize; now he knew. He knew it was possible. He knew that what a group of corrupt Arab fanatics could do, he, an intelligent and motivated white man, could do better.

The choice of target, too, was inspired by that fateful September morning. Hyde prided himself on his ability to learn from his enemies. The attackers had hoped to cripple the American economy by striking at the heart of the world of business, of banking and finance. They had done serious damage, but even this Americans had managed to absorb.

That had been the Arabs' mistake.

Hyde knew, as most Americans did on some visceral level, be they white or some lesser race, that the heart of America's economy wasn't banking and finance at all. It was fuel, the lifeblood that pushed the engines that moved the nation's economy and the people living within it. Fuel drove the trains. Fuel pushed the cars. Fuel powered the ships. Fuel propelled the trucks. Fuel kept the planes in the sky.

Take the fuel, and you took the country.

With energy prices soaring and oil more expensive than ever, the new pipeline created by the race-traitors at O'Connor Petroleum Prospecting was the key to the nation's economic recovery. The oil pumped by OPP from across the border was all that was keeping the nation's fleets of cars, trucks, planes and ships from grinding to a halt.

Hit the OPP tank field, where the shipped oil was stored and staged for processing, destroy the millions of dollars in infrastructure erected by OPP with federal subsidies, crush the flow of fuel that was all that kept the nation moving, as foreign imports grew ever more expensive and you dealt, if not a killing blow, a crippling blow to the rotted nation that was the United States.

Of course, simply doing damage to the economy wasn't Hyde's primary goal. Yes, it was true that to build a new system, you had to destroy the old one. For a new world, a revolutionary world, to rise on the blood-soaked soil of the United States, the old order had to be swept away. Everyone knew that to destroy such an entrenched system, you first had to shock it, stun it, put it off balance. Hitting the American economy hard would do just that. Thus weakened, America would be ripe for revolution, for the Day of the Rope.

Spurred by the symbolic act galvanizing sympathetic white men and women, like-minded revolutionaries would rise up and begin the real work Hyde saw as Twelfth Reich's calling: fighting street to street, house to house, hanging the inferior races from every light pole, making it clear that once and for all, the oceans of Muslims and Mexicans and mud-colored races the world over, who stormed the borders of the United States daily, would no longer be tolerated.

There were so many. There was a lot of work. In some ways, Hyde realized, now was their last chance. The population numbers were already slowly turning. Whites were no longer a comfortable majority in the United States. In many cities, they weren't even a plurality. That was, in part, why they were the only group that could still be mocked and even persecuted in public—especially white males.

Hyde believed with all his heart that the silent majority of white Americans would respond to his message. All it took, all that was needed, was an act bold enough, powerful enough and shocking enough to change the world. Just as 9/11 had done, Hyde's attack on the OPP tank field would alter the "game" forever. He would send a message to the whites of the world that there was a way to stand up to alien invaders, to Zionist power brokers, to the dark-skinned hordes swamping the shores of this once-great land. He would give them a new leader.

That leader would be Shane Hyde.

It was a far cry from his humble beginnings in the slums of Chicago. It was there that he had first learned to hate the mud races, had first been treated to the victimization of a white man by mobs of lessers. There were huge portions of Chicago where, even as a young boy, Shane knew a white man dared not go. Any fool could see that the white man had no power. He was forever a victim, forever getting the short end of the stick.

Hyde had known the pain that came from such injustices. His father had come home complaining of being fired from the plastics factory he worked for. The jobs were being given on a quota, he explained. He was white, and there were already too many white workers. So his dad had been shown the door.

Before that, Hyde's memories of his childhood had been relatively normal. He'd been blue-collar poor, sure, but they had always done all right. His mother was a dissolute alcoholic, yes, but many of his friends' parents were dependent on such crutches.

That day, the day the racial injustice of the world had cost his father a job, everything changed.

Shane's dad started attending meetings. They were held by other men like him, dispossessed factory workers, disenfranchised blue-collar workers who didn't like where the world was headed and didn't know what else to do about it. They met in the basement of the church down the street, and when for some reason the priest told them they weren't welcome anymore, they started using a Veterans of Foreign Wars hall.

The young Shane Hyde didn't understand, at first, what it all meant. Over time, however, he started to piece it together. The adults made no attempt to shield him from the way the world worked. They didn't go out of their way to teach him, either, as he was just a boy. But they let him listen.

He listened well.

He came to understand that people called "Jews," which until then he had thought were simply people who had a religion not his own, were somehow responsible for much of the evil of the world. He thought he could relate to that. Billy Goldstein downstairs was a Jew, and Shane Hyde didn't like him. Billy was a braggart and a bully.

There was more. There were people, people not from America, who wanted to come to this country and misuse it, abuse it. Shane could grasp that. He loved the American flag. He loved his homeland. He loved the idea of protecting his country. He longed, one day, to become a soldier like the ones he saw on his mother's tiny black-and-white television. He wanted to go off to war, which seemed very dashing and adventurous to him. By fighting for America, he could fight for freedom, and since freedom was good, that meant he would be fighting to make his father happy again. A free America was one where his dad could find work and wouldn't be so angry all the time. That made sense to Shane Hyde. Each time they went to a meeting at the VFW, he stopped to look at the flags and at the plaques devoted to old soldiers. It made so much sense. He didn't understand why everyone didn't talk about it, all the time.

There had been a period of several weeks when his father took Shane out with him while he looked for work. Looking for work was best done in bars, apparently, and they spent a lot of time in taverns and pubs in the neighborhood. His dad spent a great deal of his drinking time talking to women, too. Soon they were making trips to motels and to the women's houses. When Shane asked about it, his father explained that looking for work was difficult, and that when he got tired, he sometimes needed to find places to rest. Sometimes those places were with people he met at the bar.

Shane had made the mistake of telling his mother about that.

She hadn't seemed angry. She had seemed, if anything, smaller, less real than before. The news had broken something in her, something that had been in the process of breaking for a long time. When Shane's father found out that she knew, that she suspected he was sleeping with other women, there had been a terrible argument.

Shane remembered the argument because it was the first time in years he had ever seen his mother truly animated. Her rage gave her strength, briefly. As quickly as it began, it evaporated.

The trips to the bars, the visits to other women's houses and to motels, stopped. With little else to do and still no job, Shane's father fell to drinking harder than ever to pass the time.

The first beating took Shane by surprise.

He remembered that he had been playing stickball in the street with his friends. When he returned home, his father reeked of old beer and young wine. He had demanded to know what Shane had been doing with his time. When he stammered that he had simply been playing ball, his father had asked with whom.

It was then that Shane realized. One of his friends was black.

"I guess it don't matter to you," his father had raged, "that it's 'cause of *them* that we're on fucking welfare! Or that it's because of *them* that I can't find a job, because ain't nobody hiring us white guys anymore! Come here, you…you little…*race-traitor,* you."

His father had beat him with a belt that first night, and then the leg of the end table. The table his dad had smashed only hours before, while trashing most of the house in his anger.

The beatings went on like that, increasing in frequency and intensity.

The drunker his father was, the longer the unemployment wore on, the worse Hyde got it whenever he was home. He started spending more and more time on the streets, and coming home late into the night, the later the better. If he timed his entrance appropriately he could get in after his father had drunk himself unconscious. Shane would have to get up early in the morning, too, to flee the home before his father slept off the booze and woke up. He had made the mistake, once, of being home on a Saturday morning when his father woke after Friday's binge.

"Where were you all last evening, punk?" his dad had asked, before slapping him across the face repeatedly. "Where do you go? What did you do? Do you think you can hide from me? Do you? *Do you?* What's wrong with you? Why are you so stupid? You can't be no son of mine. No son I fathered would be so dumb. Is that it? Has your mother been whoring around on me? Maybe it was with one them colored fellas downstairs. Is that it, Shane? Are you part darkie? Huh? Are you?"

He wouldn't realize it until many years later, but his father had beaten him unconscious. He'd woken in his bed later with no understanding of how he'd gotten there.

He had hidden the bloody, fattened lip from his mother at first, then told her he had been hit in the face by a baseball. She had listened to his lies, nodded and gone back to the bottle of cheap wine at the kitchen table. A little bit more of the diminishing light in her eyes died that day.

The bruises and other injuries soon became more than he could conceal. His mother reacted to the beatings by retreating further into herself and drinking more. Shane's father was beating her, too, in places where the bruises didn't usually show. It wouldn't do for the neighbors to know. At least, Shane assumed that was his father's thinking. As thin as the walls of the Chicago tenement were, as close as they lived to everyone else in the neighborhood, there was no way every person in the building didn't know that Shane Hyde's father was an unemployed bum who beat his wife and child.

The situation soon became intolerable. Shane himself had become inured to the pain, eventually coming to understand that such things made a man stronger. It was during this time that he had first retreated into reading about philosophy and politics. The library became his haven from the misery at home. "That which does not kill me makes me stronger," he had read, and almost wept with relief. Discovering Nietzsche had brought him real joy and salved the ache in his soul that was growing worse each day.

One day, he decided to kill his father.

The voices had told him it might be helpful.

He had first started to hear the voices while his father was beating him. They had told him jokes, and as he laughed and smiled, his father had beat him harder, not understanding what it meant. Shane Hyde now had friends who were with him always, who never failed to offer him a kind word of encouragement. They were forever telling him things, and most of the time, when he followed their advice or listened to their counsel, he came out ahead. They whispered answers to him on tests at school. They told him what to say to his mother to help her feel slightly better, on those days when she was not so thickheaded with alcohol that she couldn't even hear him.

And now they had told him to kill his father.

He listened to what they had to say, and it made quite a lot of sense, really. He didn't hate his father. His dad wasn't responsible for his behavior; it was the darkies, the muds, the Jews, the people in power and who supported those in power, who had made him so miserable. This was obvious. His father was as much a victim as were Shane and his mother. The people responsible for the beatings were the people who had taken Dad's job.

Hate took root in Shane Hyde's heart, and that hate warmed and cheered him.

He listened to what the voices had to say about his father, then, with an open mind. The man was miserable and would likely never be able to find a job. He had, however, stayed current on a life insurance policy, which would pay Shane and his mother handsomely, provide them with several years' support, should anything happen to Shane's father.

Killing his dad would also end the beatings, which, while not the end of the world, were starting to make it difficult for Shane to go to school. The teachers were asking too many questions. Students he could ignore; teachers tended to call social services. He couldn't have that.

Having decided to act on the advice of the voices, he then had to plan how to do it. He wasn't sure if his father's life insurance would pay out in the event of a murder. He also didn't want to go to prison. Stabbing his dad through the neck with a kitchen knife, his first impulse, was therefore not an option.

He was reading Machiavelli in the library, hiding a black eye behind a pair of sunglasses, when he realized what he had to do.

He bought his father expensive bourbon, using the money he had horded from odd jobs and his mother's infrequent, but guiltily generous allowances. Flattering his dad, repeating back to him everything he wanted to hear, Shane had gotten him more stinking drunk than even he had ever seen him. Then he had led Seamus Hyde to the roof of the tenement building.

Once there, he had explained to his father what the voices wanted. Seamus was too far gone to understand the words. He listened, a vacant expression on his face, and nodded each time his son stopped talking. Finally, Shane had led his old man to the ledge of the tenement.

"The voices say you have to go now, Dad," he had

said. "I wish you didn't have to, but you do. I think they're right. Can you hear them? They're saying nice things about you."

"Yer a good boy, Shane," his father had slurred. "A good boy."

"No, Dad, I guess I'm really not."

Then he'd pushed his father off the building.

Police and an ambulance had responded, but the officers' investigation was perfunctory and the medics were far too late to perform any miracles. The broken bourbon bottle was next to Seamus Hyde's body and he smelled so badly of alcohol he could be his own refinery. It was an open-and-shut case, really. A drunk, unemployed factory worker had fallen off his own building, where his son said he enjoyed drinking late into the evening. At the son's urging, the officers had obligingly written the matter up as an accident. For the life insurance, the boy had told them. Well, what harm did it do to help out the kid and his mother? Even if they suspected Seamus Hyde had jumped himself, rather than fallen, it was no skin off their noses to make sure the insurance company didn't suspect.

Things had been considerably more peaceful for Shane Hyde for a few years after that, although never easy. His mother drank away the insurance money in short order, which meant he supported them both working part-time jobs during his high school years. When the booze finally killed her, he had her cremated, and sprinkled her ashes on the roof of the tenement. She would never leave this place. That was her destiny.

It was not Shane Hyde's.

Not for the first time, he reflected on all the hard

work it had taken to get here. Hyde regarded himself as a patriot. At eighteen, just before graduation, he had joined the Army out of a misguided desire to serve his country. He had *wanted* to serve, had wanted to fight, had been willing even to die for a land that, he abruptly discovered, no longer existed.

America had once been a strong nation, but like a hollow tree that cracked in a wind, the free nation of the United States had rotted from inside. He had seen it in the Army, where inferior races were given positions of power over white men, where women were treated as equals when they clearly were not, where homosexuals were tolerated despite whatever official policies were supposed to be in place. The Army, where he had thought he would serve his country with honor, had been terribly disillusioning for him. He had found himself in constant conflict with the inferior races who wished to lord their petty power over him. When he refused to submit to their abuse, he had been punished. Ultimately, they'd invented some faulty psych profile and sent him on his way.

Broke and purposeless, he had been standing in a bus station when a television mounted on the wall of a snack shop and tuned to an all-news cable channel had shown him the way. He had looked up and, in a single second, found his new purpose, his new reason for being. Tensions on the border, the news reported, were the result of illegal immigrants committing violent crimes against white property owners in the Southwest.

In that instant, it all made sense to Shane. He had joined the Army thinking to go to war, but America was already at war. The enemy was here, already in power. Shane Hyde was behind enemy lines, and it fell to him to mount a resistance that would free his fellow white men and women to allow them to live their lives in peace.

Given his childhood, he had, since his teenage years, been a believer in white supremacy. He had stumbled across internet bulletin board postings for white power groups and felt instant kinship with them. He wasn't stupid; he was actually quite intelligent, he had been told by his teachers, and he wasn't afraid of hard work, of research.

Soon, he had all the literature: *The Turner Diaries, Serpent's Walk, The Protocols of the Elders of Zion.* He networked, as he could, with others who thought as he did. He joined mail-order groups and subscribed to white power newsletters. As a white man, all this simply made good sense to him. How anyone could see it any other way, he didn't know. He had foolishly thought his beliefs would find a receptive home in the Army, where men fought for country and to preserve their own lives alongside their fellow soldiers. He had learned that the opposite was true. The American military was as corrupt as the American government and American society in general.

Hyde, and his fellow believers in the white race, would have to fight together if they were to survive.

He had gone to the border, to look the Mexican invaders in the eye while rallying his fellow whites to his cause. There, he had discovered something that he had always believed of himself but had not, until that moment, proved: he was a natural leader of men. He spoke from his heart of his passions, of his desire to secure a

future for white people and white children in the face
of inferior races' aggression. There, on the border, in
the minds and hearts of those who had suffered through
the violence of the mud-hordes swamping America,
Shane Hyde found his calling. People believed him.
People believed *in* him.

People followed him.

Twelfth Reich—a name he chose for its tie to the
months of the year, signaling the long struggle—had existed inside his head long before ever he spoke it aloud.
On the Mexican border, the ranks of Twelfth Reich
swelled. Supporters flocked to his cause and vowed
their loyalty to him and him alone. He, in turn, promised to lead them to a glorious future, a future in which
the enemies of the white race swung from poles while
white children could play safely in public parks again.

With people came funding, and with funding came
people. The stronger Twelfth Reich grew, the more people wished to ally themselves with and under Shane
Hyde's banner. Soon, he was traveling the world, net-
working with like-minded groups in other nations. The
Germans were his favorite—their enthusiasm was all
the more genuine because what they were doing was
explicitly illegal in the eyes of their Zionist-controlled
government—but he found the devotion of many international terrorist groups thoroughly inspiring.

It was abroad that Hyde first learned of the necessi-
ties of power and the strange bedfellows that powerful
alliances sometimes produced. In the name of further-
ing global terror and thus destabilizing the existing
order—all for the ultimate goal of instituting his own
power structure in the United States—Hyde worked

with agitators and violent groups of many races and political viewpoints.

Most of these men and women would never know that Hyde was making of them "useful idiots," nor would it matter if they ultimately discovered it. By the time it became obvious that he cared only for his own people and his own nation, his American homeland, Hyde and Twelfth Reich would have the power they wanted. The rest of the world could then see to itself as Hyde and his people worked to build the future, a future for white men, white women and their children.

Hyde reached down and stubbed out the dwindling butt of his cigarette against one of the dead man's boots.

"I'm glad we could have this little talk, Bob," he said.

"Hey, no problem," Hyde heard the corpse reply. "I'm just glad that if anyone had to kill me, it was the future führer of the Twelfth Reich's new order."

The dead were funny like that, Shane Hyde thought. Sometimes they said nothing at all. Sometimes you couldn't shut them up.

He tucked away his suede tobacco pouch, hefted his M-16 and stood. Through the blood-spattered window, he watched the terrain go by.

The operation had worked perfectly so far. The Zionist pigs in the government had, predictably, sent forces to stop him. These he and his men had easily repelled. Not for the first time, he reflected on the brilliant and interlocking nature of the defenses at his disposal.

His men, the gunners, were the first line; they had repelled the government forces with ease. Hyde himself had shot one of the jackbooted commandos, lining him up and shooting him through the rear window of his pitifully vulnerable Hummer. Hyde knew the Hummer well and he knew its weaknesses. Unless up-armored, the tough-looking vehicle was actually little protection from small-arms fire, as his gunners had proved.

The train itself was the second line of defense, coupled with the hostages. He had several men still working on breaking into their armored passenger car, but even if they never penetrated, it made no difference. The hostages were needed only as a presence, preventing the weaklings in the government from derailing the train. Making such a sacrifice, to save many more lives, would seem obvious to a leader like Hyde, who understood that violence, that war, required sacrifice. The politically correct puppets of the Zionist occupation government were unwilling even to do that.

The ammonium nitrate fuel oil explosives wired to the tanker cars were the other part of the reason no major action had been taken against the train itself. The explosion, should the train be detonated, would cause great damage to the surrounding territory. The fools in the government had missed several windows of opportunity in which the train could have been destroyed with relatively little damage to the surrounding landscape. He hadn't expected them to display that kind of strength.

He had, however, prepared for the eventuality of air attack. His men were equipped with an Iranian-made copy of the M47 Dragon TOW missile, a wire-guided, shoulder-fired antitank weapon that could, at short range, be pressed into service as an antiaircraft device. The weapon would be more than sufficient to take out low-flying helicopters, which Hyde judged to be the biggest threat. A force of men inserted by chopper could conceivably storm the train and take out his personnel if they hit hard and fast enough. With the train protected by the missile launcher, purchased at obscene expense through his contacts abroad, there was no way such a plan could succeed.

"You've thought of everything," Hyde thought he heard the dead man say.

"That's true, Bob." He nodded. "That's true."

When the OPP train hit the tent city full of illegal immigrants working the tank field, the explosion would be heard and seen for miles. Hyde was dedicated to the cause of liberating the white people, and to establishing a new order for the future of white America, but he wasn't suicidal. A plan of this magnitude was no plan at all if didn't include an exit strategy.

That, Hyde had. Staged in one of the cargo cars were several dirt bikes, which he and his lieutenants would use to flee the train before impact. His remaining men and women would stay aboard to continue protecting the train from attack; it wouldn't do to abandon control of it only to let a government force board and stop it. Hyde had found it necessary to deceive the team remaining aboard, and that he regretted. They were brave white warriors and they deserved better than to die unknowingly. Still, he couldn't risk any of them losing the nerve necessary to see the hijacked train through to its destination, and therefore he had told them that they would board cars farther down the track.

The cars were real. Several vehicles, driven by trusted Twelfth Reich operatives who knew the train's route and schedule, were trailing it even now. Hyde had received text messages verifying that they were in position. When he and his lieutenants left the train, they would use the dirt bikes to rendezvous with the cars, then travel by highway to the primary Houston safe house. There, with access to all his shortwave communication equipment, Hyde could monitor the outbreak of the coming revolution, encourage it along, and if necessary, dispatch smaller teams of Twelfth Reich terrorists to push the revolution on with selective bombings and attacks.

Yes. He had thought of everything.

Really, he shouldn't be surprised. His success was preordained, a function of the superiority of his race. While it was true that many of the government pawns who fought against him were also white, they were traitors to their race. Race treason weakened the traitor; to give in to corruption invariably destroyed the soul of the man or woman so compromised. That was why there could be no living peacefully with the inferior. Such creatures were meant to become slaves to their betters, if they weren't eradicated outright. Hyde looked forward to the day, not so far away now, when that occurred in every city and on every street in America.

They had called him unstable. They had called him unfit. They had told him something was very wrong with him.

None of that was true.

Shane Hyde was a leader. He was destined to lead. He would show them all.

"Yes, you will," said the corpse on the floor, his voice echoing in Hyde's brain.

"Yes, I will," Shane agreed. "I will. I will."

As he stood before the window, watching the passing landscape, tears of joy streaked his cheeks.

He would win, because no one dared stand against him.

Who could? Who could *possibly* be ready to face Shane Hyde, to prevent what he was destined to do?

CHAPTER NINE

"I'm ready," Mack Bolan said.

"It's been a while," Michael Wood commented. "Are you sure?"

"These—" Bolan held up his gloved hands "—aren't making things any easier."

Wood clutched the Remington M700 sniper rifle that had come from a case stowed in the Pave Hawk. It was one of several specialty weapons Grimaldi's chopper carried. Now, with Agent Greene bracing him in the open fuselage of the Pave Hawk, Wood prepared to line up the shot. The two FBI men had conferred between themselves, when Bolan explained that his hands were injured, and Wood had finally volunteered to make the attempt.

The play was a dangerous one that relied on precise timing. Grimaldi would edge the chopper in within the rifle's effective range, but far enough out to prevent the terrorists from lining up an easy shot. Grimaldi had already made several high-speed, long-distance passes by the train, effectively drawing the Twelfth Reich terrorists into position to defend it. Even at a distance, the silhouette of the wire-guided antitank missile was unmistakable.

Hyde's choice of hardware was good and bad. Wire-guided missiles were only as effective as the man guiding them. To keep a missile trained on an incoming threat, the operator would have to stand still long enough to make himself a target. Unfortunately, the missiles were fast—probably close to a hundred meters a second—with an effective range of 1,000 meters. There was no way for Grimaldi to get far enough out for Wood to take a shot, unless the Pave Hawk hovered within the range the TOW missiles could reach. The antitank rounds fired by the launcher, while not ideal for antiaircraft use, would tear through the chopper like tissue paper should one of them connect.

That meant they were gambling. Hyde's people weren't professionals, by any stretch. The wire-guided missiles required relatively little special training to operate, but the personnel firing them would be relying largely on intuition and what they could comfortably see and track. If Grimaldi could stay mobile while remaining far enough away, they might be able to take out a missile operator.

That was where Wood came in, and that was the gamble they were about to make.

"All right," Grimaldi announced. "We're making our first pass."

The Stony Man pilot brought the chopper in at an angle that would prevent the gunners stationed at the train's flanks from getting a clear shot. Small-arms fire popped sporadically from below, but it was ineffective. They were beyond the useful range of most of the handguns and light assault rifles carried by the skinheads.

The bolt-action M700 sniper rifle Wood snugged to his shoulder, as he lay prone on the deck of the Pave Hawk's crew compartment, was another matter. Firing the heavy 7.62 mm NATO round, the weapon had an effective range of 800 meters, with 1,000-meter shots at least theoretically possible. Wood was no experienced sniper, or so he had said, but he was reasonably comfortable with the weapon and had told Bolan and Grimaldi that he owned a civilian version of it.

"Just try to get me close," he said.

"But not *too* close," Greene warned.

"Yeah, that, too," Wood said.

Bolan, using a pair of binoculars to spot for Wood, steadied himself on the crew seat next to where the man lay prone. A bullet panged off the fuselage near the two of them, but Wood barely flinched. Bolan gave him a lot of credit for that. He was already focused on acquiring his target.

That target was the missile operator, who knelt atop one of the tanker cars, steadying his TOW rocket on his shoulder and against the launcher's bipod. The launcher was reusable. There was no telling how many missiles Hyde and the Twelfth Reich might have managed to purchase; Stony Man's intelligence file indicated only that Hyde had been in communication with an Iranian arms dealer known to trade in M47 Dragon missile systems and Iranian copies reverse-engineered from the American launchers.

"He's lining us up," Grimaldi warned.

"Understood," Wood said. The chopper swayed this way and that as Grimaldi tracked the train and tried to stay out of the missile operator's direct line of sight. Through his binoculars, Bolan could see the missile man shifting as he tried to judge the target, probably wondering if he should risk a shot. Grimaldi, meanwhile, tried to bring the chopper farther back, creating more distance and more reaction time should a missile leave the launcher's maw.

"That's awfully far away," Wood said.

"Distance is nothing," Bolan said. "If you can see it, you can shoot it."

"Right," Wood muttered. Bolan could hear him draw in a breath and hold it. The FBI man's body tensed. He was about to fire.

The discharge was loud within the chopper, but not deafening against wind noise.

"Clean miss," Bolan reported, spotting through the binoculars.

"High?" Wood asked.

"Most likely," Bolan said. "I didn't see a spark on the tanker."

"Uh…" Greene said. "About that. Are we risking blowing one of the tankers?"

"With a single 7.62 mm round at this distance?" Bolan asked. "It doesn't work that way."

"Just checking," Greene said.

Wood fired again. He racked the bolt, steadied himself and fired a third time. Through his binoculars, Bolan could see the missile operator, untroubled, continuing to try to bring his shot on target. No doubt the man knew he would have only one chance before a slow reload—his spare shots, if he had them, were somewhere out of sight, not on top of the train with him—and during that reload window, the Pave Hawk could get as close as Grimaldi dared while dodging rifle and handgun fire from the skinhead shooters below.

"It's too far," Wood said. "I can't get him. I'm not sure where my shots are going."

Greene reloaded the rifle so that Wood wouldn't have to change position, then slid the weapon back to him as Bolan called to Grimaldi. "Jack," the soldier said. "We need to tighten the range."

"Tighten the range, increase the risk," Grimaldi warned.

"Acknowledged," Bolan said. "Do it, Jack."

"You got it." The chopper dipped, then edged closer, as the Stony Man pilot worked the stick and pedals like a magician. Still angling the open fuselage across the bow of the train, Grimaldi started to veer closer. The missile operator began gesturing wildly, and as Bolan watched through his binoculars, gunmen climbed along the rails at the sides of the train and worked their way toward the tank car on which the missile man crouched.

"They're sending reinforcements," Greene said.

"I see them," Bolan replied. He let his binoculars fall to their strap around his neck, shouldered the P90, and squeezed the trigger.

One of the gunners went over the rail, screaming. A second sprayed Kalashnikov fire into the nose area of the Pave Hawk. The chopper dipped and jerked as Grimaldi reacted, pulling back, getting them out of the cone of fire. The movement fouled Bolan's shot as he tried to tag the shooter. Finally, as Grimaldi steadied, Bolan reacquired the target. He fired several times, knowing he was well beyond the maximum range of the little FN. There were few weapons Mack Bolan didn't know intimately, and this one was no different. He walked his shots in, over and down, almost dropping them in an arc on the gunner. The 5.7 mm rounds split the shooter's head and tore open his neck before pitching him, too, off the train.

"Score a couple for our side," Greene said.

"Jack," Bolan said, "one more pass."

He looked at Wood. "You okay?"

"Yeah," Wood said. "How far away are we from Austin?"

"Not far enough," Grimaldi reported from the cockpit. "If we don't get our act together soon, we'll be close to population."

Bolan didn't like that. The nearer they got to densely populated areas, the greater the danger to bystanders. Shane Hyde had no compunctions about killing innocent men and women to get his way. In a target-rich environment like Austin, there was nothing to stop him from firing into houses and buildings the train passed, just to cause more carnage as he traveled.

"All right," Grimaldi said from the cockpit. "Everyone get ready. Here we go again."

He pushed the chopper around in an arc that circled the train, giving Bolan a chance to assess the resistance arrayed along its flanks. Skinhead shooters moved here and there, pointing at the Pave Hawk, occasionally taking shots at it. A bullet struck the deck right by Wood's hand, causing him to flinch and cry out.

"You hit?"

"Scratched by a metal flake, I think," he said, sucking at a deep scratch on his left hand. "I'm all right."

"Take your time," Bolan urged. "Line it up."

"Got it," Wood said.

The chopper continued to buzz and hum as it took

more rounds from below. Mack Bolan had ridden in enough helicopters—and enough helicopters piloted by Jack Grimaldi—to know the experience had to be putting Grimaldi on edge. No pilot liked to take ground fire. Every round the chopper absorbed was yet another possibility that a critical system would be compromised.

"He's going to paint us sooner or later, Sarge," Grimaldi said, forgetting himself in the heat of the moment and using his nickname for Bolan. No one noticed or, if they did, neither Bureau agent commented.

Wood fired.

The round drew sparks near the missile man's foot, but was still wide of the mark. The close call made the terrorist sprawl backward, losing his fix on the moving chopper. For the moment, the deadly antitank missile in the launching tube remained where it was.

"Again!" Wood demanded. "Line me up!"

They made their way around for another pass. The terrorists below were now very aware of what was happening. One man, dressed in camouflage BDUs, was gesturing from the footholds outside the crew car. Could that be Hyde? At this distance Bolan wasn't sure, even through the binoculars, but the build and the general appearance were right.

It would be easy simply to take out Hyde, to cut off the head of the snake. Skinheads were cowards, by and large, and very reliant on their power structure and mob mentality for strength. With Hyde to ramrod them, they were dangerous, even for reckless amateurs. The planning that had gone into the train hijacking, the many different contingencies to prevent an easy counterterror insertion and recovery…that was all the proof Bolan needed of the danger the Twelfth Reich offered. But Hyde was the brains of the operation. Remove him and the others would fall apart. The soldier had seen it before.

But he couldn't. Hyde was needed alive. Bolan still wasn't sure how he would manage to extract the terrorist, but that wasn't his primary concern. The more immediate problem of taking out the antiaircraft defenses would, once accomplished, lead to the rest. Bolan was a firm believer in taking complex goals one step at a time. Getting caught in nearsighted overanalysis often led to freezing in battle, to a failure to remain flexible in fluid combat conditions.

Grimaldi changed the angle. The helicopter bobbed and then pointed, nose level, shooting sideways as Grimaldi fought to keep the ride as smooth as he could. Wood braced himself. Sweat was pouring down the sides of his face.

Greene leaned over. "I could take a door gun," he offered. "Lay down some cover fire."

"Negative." Bolan shook his head. "We don't need the extra noise and vibration, not now." The Executioner snapped off a couple shots from the P90. "This is light enough it shouldn't be a problem."

"I got you," Greene said.

"I'm doing my best," Wood said. "But there's… What is that?"

Wood raised his head from the scope as Bolan brought the binoculars back to his face.

"That's…" Bolan said, as the terrorist gunner climbed to a better vantage on the tank car, adjacent to the missile operator. "Jack! Jack! RPK, Jack! Move!"

Grimaldi banked the chopper away as the man with the light RPK machine gun opened fire. The rounds that rocked them, fed by the RPK's big 40-round stick, came fast and furious, ripping through the fuselage. One of them tagged Greene in the head, chest and throat, spraying his blood through the helicopter.

"Greene!" Wood shouted. He tried to roll, to grab the other FBI agent, and Greene's body collapsed against him. Blood was everywhere.

"Jack, we have a man down!" Bolan reported. He knelt to check Greene, moving him off Wood, but there was no pulse. As he straightened the body, he realized that part of Greene's head was gone. The heavy RPK rounds had done their work.

"He's gone," Bolan said.

Grimaldi was shouting from the cockpit. "What's the situation back there? Sarge?"

"Back us off, Jack," Bolan said. "Back us off for now. Greene is down. A casualty. There's nothing we can do for him."

Wood was silent for a long moment. Grimaldi kept the chopper moving, well away from the train. "Sarge?" he asked. "What do you want to do?"

"We can't save Greene," Bolan stated. "But we can still do our jobs." He took an emergency poncho from the kit under one of the seats, extended it and wrapped it around Greene, securing the poncho by tying its ends near Greene's feet. The plastic fluttered in the wind that whistled through the open fuselage. Bolan looked at Wood.

"I can't," the agent said, shaking his head. The chopper bucked beneath them as Grimaldi maneuvered for better position, extending the range to avoid another fusillade from the RPK gunner. "I just can't get it." Wood looked at Bolan, his face flecked with blood that wasn't his own. "I don't have the skill, Cooper," he admitted. "Not at this range while we're moving. We could do this all day, and sooner or later, he's going to shoot us down. Greene is dead. My hesitation is going to get us all killed."

"All right," Bolan said. He frowned. Wood was a good man who had done the best he could. The soldier wished he had the words to salve the man's grief, but that was combat. There was always a price. "All right. Let's go. Switch with me."

"Sarge?" Grimaldi called back. "Uh, Agent Cooper, sir? Are you sure about that?"

"It's going to have to be me," Bolan said. "You know I've got the time in."

"But," Grimaldi said, "your hands?"

"I'll be okay," Bolan answered. "Put us in position. Get us as far out as you can. I'm going to need time to get this right. Put us at maximum effective range."

"If you're sure."

"I'm sure," Bolan said.

Awkwardly, the soldier switched places with Wood, his war bag and the P90 resting on the deck next to him, as if he lay in a puddle of gear. He took a fresh magazine from Greene, slapped it home and grabbed the bolt to chamber a round.

Flames licked up his arm, centered on his palm. The pain was bad, and getting worse as his painkillers wore off. There was nothing to be done. He put the sensation out of his mind, focusing on the mechanics, on the rote muscle memory of operating the bolt and shouldering the weapon.

Mack Bolan had been shot. He had been stabbed. He had been tortured. He had been held captive and had escaped. There was little he hadn't experienced of man's cruelty to man; there was even less he hadn't seen. In his time fighting his seemingly endless war, he had seen torture, had stood witness to atrocities, that no human being could ever stomach or forget. Compared to that, the pain in his hands was nothing, was trivial, was easily ignored. He told himself this as he pressed the M700's synthetic stock to his shoulder, breathing deeply as he calmed himself to find his sniper's center.

Breathe, Bolan told himself. Breathe. There is no pain.

"He's steadying," Wood said, spotting through the binoculars he had borrowed from Bolan. "It looks like he's getting ready to fire."

The RPK gunner opened fire, but his rounds went wide or short. Bolan wasn't sure which and didn't care. His entire world was now his rifle. The sounds of bullets striking the Pave Hawk became muted, as if far away. The universe was his rifle. The center of the universe was its trigger.

Bolan drew a breath, let out half of it, held it, then fired.

"He's firing!" Wood shouted.

The missile rose on a plume of smoke, faster than Wood could warn it was coming, faster than Bolan could watch. Grimaldi reacted instantly, almost presciently, jamming the stick and pedals, ripping the helicopter around in an arc that lifted its tail and dipped its nose toward the earth. The plume of the wire-guided rocket shot past the Pave Hawk's rotor assembly, jerking as the man below tried and failed to track Grimaldi's evasive action with the missile.

The target assembly on top of the TOW launcher had exploded.

Wood was staring through the binoculars, trying to find the missile man. Grimaldi steadied the chopper, doubtless ready to hit the controls again, keenly aware of their vulnerability.

"You…you got him!" Wood said. "He's down. He's shot through the face. You shot him through the optics on the launcher!"

Bolan lay curled against the stock of the M700. He heard Wood's words, and through the haze in his vision, saw the dead missile operator fall from the train. The launcher tumbled off with him, bouncing and crashing on the arid soil as the train sped by.

"You did it!" Wood said again.

Bolan shuddered. The pain in his hands was so great that he almost felt nothing. It reminded him of the warm, numbing sensation produced by enduring great cold. His vision started to gray out.

"Cooper!" Wood shouted. He grabbed Bolan by the shoulders and turned him over, careful to safe the M700 and set it within its padded case. "Cooper! Stay with me, Agent Cooper. We're still in this."

"I'm…" Bolan said. He shook his head. The electricity crackling from his hands became a sharp sting and then a dull ache. "I'm okay." He pointed to the door gun. "We have some unfinished business."

Wood caught the look in Bolan's eye and his own

expression hardened. He nodded. "You're damned right we do." He handed the binoculars back to Bolan and positioned himself behind the weapon. Grimaldi pushed the Pave Hawk forward, then turned, bringing its opposite flank to bear on the moving train. The FBI agent yanked back the charging handle on his 7.62 mm door gun. It would give them a level of precision Grimaldi wouldn't have been able to manage with his electric Gatling, for he had to both pilot and fire when using the automated weapon.

"Time for some payback," Wood said.

Bolan nodded. Using his binoculars, he sighted along the length of the train. He found what he wanted.

"Third car back, Jack," he said. "Bring us in low and slow, from the rear. I want him to see it coming."

"Roger," Grimaldi said. His voice was deadly serious.

From his vantage in the fuselage, looking over Wood's shoulder, Bolan watched the steady stream of jacketed bullets hose the roof of the train. The bullets ripped the RPK gunner in two from crotch to neck, spreading him over the top of the train and punching him off the side. The deadly RPK tumbled with him, lost in the dirt and blood along the tracks.

Wood gave the door gun a workout as Grimaldi changed speed to fall slowly back. The stream of bullets made deadly work of several of the terrorists, who were pinned between the exterior of the train and the railing against which they were braced. Bodies collapsed and littered the track behind the OPP train.

Bolan nodded in grim satisfaction.

As horrible as it was, the body count was about to get worse.

CHAPTER TEN

"Go!" Grimaldi shouted. "Go, go, go!"

Bolan dropped. The rope ladder secured within the Pave Hawk spun wildly, turning him with it, as the soldier was lowered violently toward the top of the train. They had finished another sweep of the train's flanks to give Hyde's men something to think about, then brought the chopper to the middle of the tanker car section, where coverage by Hyde's men was the lightest.

Response was faster than Bolan would have credited the skinheads for managing. He couldn't hear them over the chopper, but he could see them swarming from car to car ahead of his position, waving their weapons. When they thought they had a shot, they would begin firing on him and the Pave Hawk.

The chopper was already showing signs of the pounding it had taken. Grimaldi had reported several warning lights active. None were critical...yet. If the Pave Hawk were to continue to function, however, Grimaldi couldn't continue to hang around, having it absorb bullets. As Bolan's boots hit the top of the tanker car, the Stony Man pilot pulled the chopper up and away, quickly putting distance between them.

The Executioner was on his own, for the moment.

The P90 would be perfect here in the close quarters of the train, and given his aching hands, Bolan was

grateful for the light-recoiling, high-tech little submachine gun. He dropped to his knees to steady himself
on the moving train, then lay flat, extending the P90 in
front of him and aiming through the optics.

True to form, the skinheads came on without disci-
pline and without planning. Bolan was struck by a moment's disbelief that Hyde and his racist Twelfth Reich
punks could have planned and executed an operation
like this with such poor coordination evident among
them. He could only chalk it up to Shane Hyde's leadership, which was seeming more formidable with each
encounter.

Bullets began to ricochet off the tanker car as the
skinheads, firing blindly, emptied their weapons in his
direction. Lying prone, Bolan pushed himself along,
inch-worming across the rusting metal grates of the
car. He would run out of tanker shortly, and would be
most vulnerable to enemy fire in the gap between cars.
Based on the muzzle-flashes and the sounds of gunfire, he didn't believe there were skinhead shooters in
the first gap, unless they were lying in wait, silent and
cagey, hoping to catch him unaware.

As he crawled, he noted the wires connecting each
car to the next. Dotting these were bundles, each about
the size of a field pack, shrouded in canvas. They had
to be the ANFO bombs. The design of the explosives
had been determined within reasonable limits by satellite photography, enhanced and processed by the Farm
and transmitted with his intelligence package for the
mission. The cable harness connecting the bombs was
believed to be an antitamper fuse. Separating the cable,
such as by blowing the connector between the cars to

reduce the size of the train and its explosive impact, would cause the bombs to detonate immediately.

Bolan reached the first gap and, without exposing himself, pushed the snout of the P90 over the edge and triggered a short blast. There was no answering fire. He rolled into the gap, caught the handhold and hoisted himself to the next car, cursing the spasms that made his thumb twitch. He was paying the price for a clear head.

As he climbed the ladder connected to the rear of the tanker, making his way to the top of the next car, a bullet struck rust and paint from the corner of the tank near his face. He dropped back and, one-handed, raised the P90 and triggered a burst. The little 5.7 mm rounds skimmed the top of the tanker and struck the prone, almost hidden skinhead in the forehead, blowing his brains through his nape.

Bolan pushed to his feet. Crouching low, stabilizing himself against the rolling movement of the tanker car, he crept forward, the subgun up and seeking targets.

He saw the tattoos first. As one of the skinheads threw a hand over the edge, pulling himself up the ladder, the tiny lightning bolts on his knuckles gave him away. Bolan didn't waste time. He tracked with the P90, settled the optics over the fingers and blew the guy off the train.

The hideous scream of the terrorist was cut short as he was pulled under the tanker car's spinning wheels.

There were two more gunners waiting. They climbed, hand over hand, firing blindly as they lifted their weapons above their heads. One man had a revolver; the other held a 1911. The revolver went dry first. As the automatic pistol's slide clicked open, Bolan

stuck his P90 forward and pulled the trigger, stitching
the man with the pistol across the neck. He toppled. The
skinhead with the revolver, hanging on the ladder on
the opposite end of the tanker car, swung his weapon in
Bolan's direction and pulled the trigger several times.

The cylinder advanced and the hammer fell on already fired rounds.

"You should have done the math," Bolan said. He
pulled the trigger once, punching a 5.7 mm round
through the skinhead's brain. The dead man fell from
the train and was ground underneath the wheels.

Bolan kept going. He needed to work his way to the
front of the train. It would have been helpful to insert
closer to the engine, but there were too many men waiting there. The skinheads would have shot Grimaldi's
chopper to pieces. That left the soldier with the unen-
viable task of slowly fighting his way from car to car.
There were a couple crew and cargo compartments in-
terspersed among the tankers, but he would avoid those,
sticking to the tops of the cars to avoid being boxed in.

He made the next gap, then climbed up, the stinging
in his hands a constant throb in time with his pulse. He
could feel, beneath the rocking of the train, the vibration
of footsteps somewhere on the car. There were men on
at least one side, perhaps two. Bolan went prone again,
determined not to make an easy target. In the distance,
out of small-arms range, he heard the Pave Hawk pacing the train.

He didn't count the tanker cars ahead of him, which
lay between him and the armored passenger car containing the hostages. He would take them one at a time, as

they came. There was no point dwelling on the length of the journey, or the number of obstacles.

Each would fall in turn.

Two cars ahead, skinheads began climbing up on top. They were learning, if slowly. Directly attacking a tanker while Bolan held the high ground had done them no favors, so they were mounting one at a distance in an effort to get a bead on him. Bullets began to pound the steel just ahead of his position.

Bolan rolled over, then slid down the outside of the curved container, landing heavily on the soles of his combat boots. There were men climbing up the same tanker car on this side. When they saw him they began firing.

Bolan pressed himself against the metal as close as he could. Swapping magazines in the P90, he charged the weapon and extended it with one arm. His right hand screamed in protest, but he was getting used to ignoring it. The subgun, fortunately, wasn't terribly heavy, even fully loaded.

The Executioner fired. His rounds buzzed through the air, bouncing off the tankers forward of his position as the train cars rattled and bounced and rolled. The nearest skinhead among the oncoming terrorists was cut down first, taking a round through the knees and then the chest, folding over himself.

Bolan shot down the man behind the first, punching rounds through his chest, and then dropped the third with a well-placed burst to the head. He continued to move along the side of the car as he fired, always shuffling toward his goal, never stopping. The skinheads were shouting to one another, calling for reinforcements, and now the men on top of the train were massing to concentrate their fire on Bolan's position.

Sparks and shrapnel filled the air as he neared the next gap. The skinheads were pumping the space full of hot lead, hoping to create a fatal funnel through which he would have to move if he were to advance.

Bolan was pinned down.

At least, that's what his enemies thought.

The Executioner reached into his war bag and produced a stun grenade. He pulled the pin, released the spoon and counted through most of the less-lethal bomb's fuse. Then he tossed the orb overhand toward the gap before bending back, covering his ears, squeezing his eyes shut and opening his mouth.

He was good with the timing. The stun grenade exploded in midair, close to the center of the gap, scattering the skinheads near the edge of the connecting tanker car. One man fell off the train, unconscious or simply too stunned to cry out. Another fell from the top of the tanker onto the walkway, managing to topple the remaining two men coming up that side with the weight of his body.

Bolan leaped the gap, landing on the walkway, and threw a kick that snapped the stunned man's head back. The skinhead rolled through the gap in the railing and off the train. Still firing the P90 with one hand, the soldier raked first one remaining terrorist, then the other, using his bursts to shove the skinheads aside.

"Jack!" Bolan shouted. His earbud transceiver would carry his words to Grimaldi. "Warn the vehicles behind us. We're leaving a trail of wounded or dead. They'll need to keep an eye out along the tracks, pick up any stragglers." The trailing Hummers would be out of range of Bolan's transceiver, but not of Grimaldi's chopper.

"Will do, Sarge," Grimaldi said in response.

Bolan checked his position. "I'm midway to the personnel car and still mobile."

"Roger. I've got you covered." There was a pause. "Sarge, something strange here. The Farm reports that real-time satellite imaging of the area shows a convoy headed in our direction. Several vehicles, moving quickly."

"No chance it's a coincidence?"

"You haven't started believing in coincidence, have you, Sarge?"

"Can't say I have. Keep an eye on them for me."

"You think it could be more of Hyde's boys? Maybe an extraction team?"

"Possible," Bolan said. "Not sure yet. Going topside. Keep a lookout for me."

"On it," Grimaldi said.

"Out."

Cautiously, Bolan pulled himself up to the top of the next car. He met little resistance as he crouch-walked from one end to the next. Once there, he again sprayed a burst into the gap, but there was no response. Leaping once more, he landed on the next car and traversed it similarly. Now he was very close to the personnel carrier.

Something was wrong. There weren't enough enemies.

Too late, he realized what that meant. The hand that shot up over the side of the tanker car grabbed his ankle, toppling him. He fell, hurtling into the gap between the two cars, the spinning wheels too close below.

He was hanging upside down.

The pain in his shoulders was so intense that it blotted out the pain in his palms for a moment. He was hanging from the strap of his P90, his legs against the side of the tanker car, all his weight straining against the subgun's single-point sling. Dust and grit, kicked up by the spinning wheels of the tanker car, pecked at his neck and scalp.

The skinhead who had grabbed him reached out with one hand. He held a switchblade. He was going to cut the sling.

Bolan reached behind his hip, pulled the Desert Eagle and pointed it.

"No—" the skinhead said.

"Yes," Bolan said, and pulled the trigger.

Despite the glove, the recoil of the .44 Magnum hand cannon was broken glass against the flesh of his hand. He considered shoving the gun back in its holster but discarded the idea. Instead, trying to take as much weight off his shoulder as he could, he hooked one leg in the ladder on the end of the tanker car. Then he drew the Beretta 93R with his left hand. He could hear footfalls on either side of the tanker.

They came around the corners of the car, certain of what they thought would be an easy kill, and Bolan let them have it. The pain in his hands fouled his aim, but he compensated with raw firepower. With the Beretta in 3-round-burst mode, he sprayed out its 20-round box magazine. He almost emptied the Desert Eagle as well, feeling the recoil punish him as he threw heavy slug after slug into the skinheads coming at him.

They had been hiding on either side of the tanker, waiting for him as he'd thought they might, just slower on the uptake than he'd expected. They fell to either side along the tracks.

Bolan was stuck, caught upside down, and he was slipping. He holstered his guns and tried to right himself, but the angle was all wrong. The strap of the P90, which was holding him in place, was preventing him from swinging to the side, where he needed to be to extricate himself. Whipping the double-edged Sting boot knife from inside his waistband, he cut the sling free. The P90 dropped to the tracks below and was gone.

The momentum of his sudden drop allowed Bolan to push off with his free leg. He hit the coupling on the opposite side of the gap, hard, and managed to haul himself up the next ladder without pitching over the side.

At the top, he went flat again. Gunmen clustered at the far end, between the tanker and the personnel carrier, were shooting from behind cover, reluctant to come out and aim their shots. As long as he stayed low, he was relatively safe until he reached the midpoint of the car. Once there, however, he would be wide open, and a few bursts would be all it would take to blow Bolan off the train and into the unwritten history of covert operatives.

He considered his options while swapping magazines in the Beretta and readying the weapon. He could toss another grenade, but anything other than a stun canister would detonate the ANFO bombs nearby. He wasn't certain he could time a stunner from this distance across the top of the tanker. Well, there was nothing to lose in trying it.

He did so, pulling another stun bomb from his war bag, judging the count and snapping out the pin. The spoon flew free and he waited for a few moments before chucking the grenade along the tanker. It almost made its mark, but the jostling of the train car sent it bouncing unpredictably. It finally detonated to one side of the tanker, too far off target to have any real debilitating effects.

The skinheads reacted, though. Angered by the noise and brightness of the blast, they started firing furiously, emptying their guns.

Time to improvise.

Bolan pushed off at a dead run, ignoring the unsteady footing, making as much progress as he could. He was nearing the gap when he saw the gunners frantically reloading, trying to get their assault rifles and pistols back into play.

He fell flat at the end of the car, on his chest, his weapon extended. With only his head and arm exposed, the soldier pushed out his Beretta and pulled the trigger, moving it left and right, hosing the gap with 3-round bursts of 9 mm hollowpoint ammunition. The skinheads dropped, some of them dying where they were, others falling free of the train.

Bolan got to his knees and leaped the gap. He was at the armored personnel car.

He lowered himself to the sealed, armored door. The hostages inside had apparently lined the reinforced window with newspaper. He tried rapping on the glass, but received no response. They either couldn't hear him through the thick barrier, or thought he was one of the terrorists and were ignoring him.

He paused and, Beretta at the ready, removed his secure phone. He checked the schematics for the train that were loaded into the device, paying special attention to the personnel carrier itself. Yes, there was supposed to be a two-way camera relay at the head of the car, nearer the engine and its computerized control compartment. He would need to work his way to that end and see if he could use the camera setup to make contact with the hostages.

He stuck to the narrow side walkway, checking each window as he inched along. They were covered in magazines and more newspapers, whatever had been at hand. He had to give the OPP employees credit. Preventing the terrorists from monitoring them, while they were relatively safe within the armored train car, was very smart. It's what he would have instructed them to do had he been trapped with them.

He caught movement from the corner of his eye. Peering more closely, he saw that the paper over one window had been peeled up slightly. There was someone peeking out. Judging from the lashes, it was a woman.

"Miss!" Bolan shouted over the noise of the train and the passing wind. "Miss! I am with the Justice Department! I'm here to help!"

The woman made no sign that she could hear him, but didn't take her eye from the window. Bolan tried pantomiming to her, but couldn't convey the message that he was an official of the government sent to assist them.

This, he thought, is really no time or place for charades.

The woman's eye shifted. She blinked. Then she ripped back the paper and pointed.

She saved Bolan's life.

The woman had seen what he hadn't: the skinheads near the engine were peering around the corner of the armored car and, seeing Bolan, they opened fire.

He had nowhere to go, and no option but to overpower them. Leveling the Beretta, he fired again and again, hearing the shells clatter against the side of the car. The skinheads were driven back. None of their rounds came close to Bolan.

He was like a fish in a barrel at the end of a metal pipe. It would take almost nothing for his enemies to put several rounds through him unless he kept the pressure on. As quickly as he could, he retracted his elbow, angled the Beretta, popped the empty magazine and slammed home another one, doing his best to rip the slide off the gun as he chambered the next round.

It was almost not fast enough. The skinheads' gun muzzles were just creeping around the corner again when he laid down another curtain of fire. While he was shooting he was relatively safe, but even though he had plenty of loaded magazines for the machine pistol, he couldn't keep this up indefinitely.

He was pinned down.

The woman in the personnel car, a pretty brunette, had peeled the paper from the next window and was looking at him.

From somewhere farther off he could hear a furious exchange of gunfire.

"Jack, Jack," he called. "Striker to G-Force. What the hell is that? Who's doing that shooting?"

"Striker, I have unknown hostiles in black SUVs coming up on your six," Grimaldi reported. "They're engaging Hyde's forces at the rear of the train, behind your point of entry. It looks like they're working their way up to you."

"Government reinforcements?" Bolan asked. He continued firing. His earbud had smart sound technology built into it, similar to ear protection used for recreational shooting that permitted conversation but screened the higher decibels of gunfire. It prevented his earbud from inundating Grimaldi with the deafening noise of his shots.

"Negative," the pilot said. "They're not answering on any channel."

"It's the competition," Bolan guessed. "Whoever hit the safe house. The .40-caliber shells. That's them. It has to be."

"Do you want me to engage?" Grimaldi asked.

"Negative," Bolan said. "I have a more immediate problem. I'm pinned down." He emptied the Beretta, swapped magazines and continued shooting. Through the window, the wide-eyed brunette was moving her arms frantically. He couldn't tell what she was trying to communicate.

"Oh, that," Grimaldi said. "Hang on. Wood and I can fix that."

The Pave Hawk danced in then, moving aggressively and under full power. Grimaldi's expert touch brought the door gun to bear just in time for Wood to hose the knot of skinheads with it. Bolan could hear the screams

of his enemies as the heavy 7.62 mm rounds chewed
up the terrorists. Blood and flesh splashed the front of
the armored personnel car. The woman at the window
flinched and turned away.

When the Pave Hawk pushed skyward again, avoiding return fire from the front of the engine and from
farther down the train, Bolan turned to the window. The
pretty woman behind the glass threw him a tentative
thumbs-up. Bolan, grinning, returned it.

At the end of the car he crossed over the front, peering along the opposite side. The camera array was there,
but had been destroyed by gunfire. He watched the Pave
Hawk ascend. It was hard to be disappointed, given
that Grimaldi and Wood had cleared the road for him.

The door to the engine stood before him. He decided
it was time to bring the train to a halt, here and now.
Bolan checked the Beretta, reloading again, and made
ready to breach the door. There would be plenty of resistance on the other side. Once he had fought through
that, he could—

The black SUV that shot up alongside the train was
missing a door. In the open space on the driver's side,
a man holding what looked like a canvas satchel was
reaching out with the device in his hands. The SUV
was closing on the armored car.

A satchel, Bolan thought. A satchel charge.

It had to be a bomb.

CHAPTER ELEVEN

It was a bomb.

The thought echoed through Russell Troy's brain. He knew, on some level, that the bomb would do what bombs do. It would explode. When it did, like fish in a pond, the OPP employees inside the armored, pressurized, sealed personnel car would be blown to jam. The bomb had to be powerful enough to pierce the armored car, giving Troy's people a means to board the train. Once inside, they would have a reinforced staging area from which to make their way forward and back, killing Hyde's men as they went.

He had worked the plan over and over in his mind. Each and every time, he had come to the conclusion that the entry point *had* to be the armored passenger car. It was the only portion of the train not potentially crawling with Hyde's men, and once Troy's men were in it, it provided the best cover for them to work their way through the OPP train.

The fact that he didn't care if the hostages died—or whether the train ultimately derailed and exploded, for that matter—meant he wasn't hamstrung as any official response would be to the hijacking. He had the option, the luxury, of keeping his plan simple. They would just drive alongside, force their way in with the magnetic satchel charge, board the train and fight the terrorists using overwhelming force. He had more than enough trained men, all of whom understood the sacrifices necessary. The nation was in the sorry state it was in *because* the powers that be gave in to the slightest threat against the smallest number of people.

The reality was that the O'Connor Petroleum employees were dead the moment Shane Hyde and Twelfth Reich had hijacked the train. Troy was sad for them, and sad for the loss their families would suffer. Certainly he was no stranger to suffering, because... He couldn't remember. But it didn't matter, because just as the nation had learned, only too painfully, that it could not let the lives of passengers prevent violent response to an airline hijacking, Hyde and his racists couldn't be allowed to use the OPP passengers as human shields in killing still more human beings. The hostages would die no matter what. Hyde possessed neither mercy nor, as far as Troy could tell, human emotion. The idea that a man as capable of casual violence as Shane Hyde would simply let those hostages go free was laughable.

American law enforcement, military and government agencies had learned the hard way that the only possible response to a hijacking of an airliner was to blow it out of the sky. The train was no different. The men and women held within the armored personnel car were sealed in their own tomb. If anything, they should be pleased that their deaths, already preordained, could occur quickly and cleanly while affording some means of paying Hyde back for his crimes.

This wasn't a rescue mission. Russell Troy knew that well, and had made sure his people understood it. To the last, they had agreed. The war against monsters like

Shane Hyde required monstrous resolve. If you weren't willing to meet a predator on his own battlefield, speaking a language he understood, you were doomed to fail. There was too much at stake to risk failure. Shane Hyde and Twelfth Reich were far too dangerous to be captured or imprisoned.

They had to die.

Every last one of them.

Troy felt the anticipation building deep in his stomach. It was like the safe house all over again. Storming that building with the MP5 in his hands, feeling the submachine gun buck as he sprayed Hyde's skinheads with its lethal contents... In those few seconds, he had felt whole again. Killing those pitiless bastards, gunning them down like dogs, had for the briefest of moments stemmed the ache that threatened to eat him up inside.

Now he had his chance, once and for all, to end Shane Hyde's miserable existence. He only hoped Hyde didn't die too quickly. He would welcome the opportunity to kill the terrorist leader himself, after first explaining to Hyde, in great detail, exactly why he hated him so.

Troy looked to the man in the driver's seat before him, then to the other two men, one in the passenger seat of the SUV, the other seated next to him in back. They wore black BDUs and combat webbing, looking as official as any military or law-enforcement agency could have managed. That was important, for should they encounter a real government or police presence, they might be able to brazen it out by claiming to be a special response team. Really, though, Troy wasn't worried about being caught or about being killed.

He just didn't care.

Troy tried to remember the names of the men in the truck with him. He couldn't. He had made contact with each of these men himself, had recruited them to his cause, had verified, to his satisfaction and the satisfaction of other members of his rogue operation, that they held the same enthusiasm for justice, the same need for revenge, that he himself did.

Why couldn't he remember their names?

He held the satchel charge in a white-knuckled grip. They were approaching the train. It would soon be time to attach the bomb. He reached out and pulled the release they had jerry-rigged to keep the rear driver's-side door in place. The door was wrenched free by gravity as soon as the release was thrown, and fell away. The SUV behind Troy's own was forced to dodge to one side to miss it.

"I'm ready," he told his driver.

"Something's wrong," the driver said, pointing. "That's gunfire!"

Troy did a double take. As they approached the train from the rear, they could see the muzzle-flashes of a furious firefight going on. The terrorists were already engaged with some foe.

The walkie-talkie mounted on the shoulder of his web gear crackled. "This is Sloane," the voice said. Sloane was the man in the rearmost SUV, Troy thought he remembered. "We've got eyes on what look like Homeland Security Hummers, bringing up the rear and trailing the train."

Troy and his convoy had to have intercepted the train at a point between it and the pursuing vehicles, blundering in between the two. That was, possibly, a complication. They would have to contend with the government operatives while escaping. He hoped it wouldn't be necessary to shoot any of them, but they would if they had to. Anyone who stood between his people and Shane Hyde was a collaborator, someone who furthered the problem of terrorism, with all its terrible costs, by perpetuating the status quo.

Troy reached up and keyed his mike. "Leave them for now," he said. "The action is up here. Pull up and get ready to board. We're going to have to act fast."

"Roger."

The SUVs weren't armored, but his men had lined the inside of their doors with bulletproof vests for greater cover. As the convoy closed in on the moving train, bouncing and jostling over the rough landscape, they began to take fire from the skinheads. The terrorists were on top of the cars and, in several cases, braced on the walkways running alongside each tanker.

Troy was exposed, and for the first time, the thought occurred to him that he might take a bullet through the open doorway of the SUV before they reached the passenger car. He placed the satchel charge carefully on the seat, brought up the MP5 slung across his chest and aimed through the door hole. As the first of several skinheads came into range, he squeezed the trigger, sending long bursts of .40-caliber rounds rattling and blasting across the tanker cars.

The strength of Twelfth Reich's forces amazed him. Hyde had nothing short of a small army aboard. It explained how he had been able to take the train and defend it so effectively. That was, of course, coupled with the knowledge of explosives needed to rig the conveyance. One of Russell Troy's team had previously worked in bomb disposal, but whether they would be able to defuse the devices remained to be seen. Troy honestly didn't consider that a factor in the operation. If the bombs eventually went off, obliterating the entire train and the territory surrounding it, that was okay, well, as long as Hyde was taken with it. Troy didn't care if he himself died in the process.

"Go," he urged the driver. "Speed up. Let's get this done."

The man gunned it, guiding the SUV along the length of the train. Bullets punched the hood and roof, but no one inside the truck was hit. The taillight on Troy's side exploded. He returned fire almost at random, not really aiming. When his magazine was empty, he shucked it and rammed home a fresh one, slapping the cocking handle of the MP5 to chamber the first round.

He couldn't wait to kill more skinheads, up close and personal.

"What's that?" the driver asked.

Troy let his MP5 fall to the end of its sling, and grabbed the satchel charge again. He leaned out the open doorway, ready to plant the bomb, ready to make the entrance his team would need to board the train and end this matter once and for all.

"What's what?" he heard the man in the passenger seat say.

Troy heard it, then. He had been ignoring it, but the sound grew so loud that even his fevered brain had to acknowledge its presence.

A helicopter.

The massive chopper—some kind of modified Black

Hawk, from the look of it—was so close that Troy could feel the rotor wash beating furrows into his cheeks. As the chopper came in, he could see the machine gun in its open door. He also recognized the man behind that gun: Michael Wood, highly placed within the FBI, and a man Russell Troy had known well in a previous life. As close as the chopper was, Troy thought he saw a flash of recognition in Wood's face.

Then the machine gun opened up.

Troy's driver hit the brakes, falling back, as sustained automatic gunfire sprayed terrorists across the front of the passenger car. Bodies fell left, right and center. As quickly as it had come, the big chopper withdrew, rising with a roar of its engines.

"Now," Troy said. "Move in now."

The driver obeyed. He put his foot to the floor, causing the SUV to surge ahead. The V8 engine screamed. White smoke or steam was starting to billow from under the hood. One or more of the terrorists' bullets had apparently struck something vital. Troy was no auto mechanic, but he figured that meant they had only a short while before the truck stopped working completely.

He reached with the bomb. It was time to do it.

"Closer," he urged the driver. "Get me closer."

Then he saw him.

The big man with the dark hair moved like a panther. He was crawling along the front of the passenger car, on the walkway that ringed the armored car and was protected by a metal railing. His description matched the one Copley had given over the phone. This was the troubleshooter, the covert government operative with the high body count.

Seeing the man, Troy could believe it.

They were close enough to lock gazes. Russell Troy stared into the face of the soldier in black. He couldn't quite see the man's eyes, not at this distance, but he didn't like what he *could* see. This was violence made real. *This* was vengeance, if vengeance had form and flesh.

Troy had no idea why he thought such things.

He ignored the fear that welled within him. The driver was edging closer to the moving train, struggling to avoid a collision that would roll them over. As the satchel came within range of the metal skirt below the side railing, Troy stretched to his limit. At the last possible moment, he pulled the nylon strap that trailed from the top of the satchel, activating the bomb's timer.

The charge leaped from his hands, pulled by its powerful magnetic base to the side of the train.

"Back off!" Troy yelled. "It's set!"

The SUV immediately pulled away.

Troy had set the timer himself. He had been concerned about leaving enough time to get to safety. Now he wished he'd risked more. As he counted off the numbers in his head, he saw the big man, the government commando, running along the side of the car toward the satchel charge.

"No," Troy whispered. "No, no, no, no!" He was shouting by the time he stopped.

The driver whipped his head back, then to the left, and saw what was happening. "What do I do?" he asked.

"Take us back in!" Troy yelled. "I've got to stop him!"

The SUV churned dirt and gravel, trailing more

smoke, as they nosed back toward the train. The man in black was leaning over the railing now, grabbing the satchel charge. Troy raised his MP5 and prepared to fire.

Except that he couldn't. The satchel charge was comprised of rigged dynamite, procured from a construction broker Troy had bribed. It wasn't like C-4 or some more modern explosive. A bullet through the satchel would detonate the bomb, and at this range, it would destroy the men in the SUV, too.

Troy didn't care about his life, but he needed to live long enough to see Shane Hyde killed.

The SUV paced the train, scant feet from where the man in black held the charge.

The big man's eyes met Troy's.

The commando jumped.

He had ripped the satchel charge free and he threw himself through the air, hugging the bomb to his chest as he collided with Troy. The two men rolled into the rear footwell of the SUV, causing the vehicle to veer wildly. The driver was losing control.

"The bomb! The bomb! He has the bomb!" Troy shouted.

The SUV started to drop back, still parallel to the train, losing speed. Tanker cars shot past as the vehicle shed its momentum. The engine was dying. Metal ground and shrieked as the driver desperately attempted to push it onward.

Troy caught an elbow to the face, then another, jarring him. But the close confines worked to his advantage, as did the teammate riding with him. The man in the front passenger seat lowered his seat back, allowing him to scramble into the fray. Now all four of them were flailing, throwing punches and clawing for the satchel charge.

"I need backup!" the driver was calling into his walkie-talkie. "This is Car One. I need backup now!"

Troy grabbed the commando's hands, trying to peel them off the bomb. He was rewarded with a grunt of pain. Not knowing what that meant, he kept trying. Soon the two men were fighting in earnest, as the other rogue operatives hammered away at the big man with their fists and knees.

The close confines were preventing them from doing any real damage. Troy suspected that the man in black, were he not fighting for possession of the satchel, would make short work of them all. He had guns holstered on his body....

The guns. Troy let go of the satchel and snaked his arm around, trying to draw the pistol from the big man's shoulder holster.

"I don't think so," he thought he heard the commando say. The big man used the crook of his elbow to capture Troy's arm, pinning it.

"The bomb is going to blow!" Troy screamed. "It will kill us all! We've got to get it out!"

A second SUV pulled up alongside Troy's faltering vehicle. Both trucks were now even with the last car in the train. There was no skinhead resistance here. Hyde's men were either all dead in this portion of the train, or they had opted to regroup closer to the hostages and to the strategic target that was the engine.

The two SUVs weaved and swerved as their drivers tried desperately to jockey for position. Finally, Troy's open doorway came within reach of one of the hand-holds of the last tanker car. He let his arm go limp and yanked it free, no longer trying for the commando's gun. Then he turned and jumped.

He caught the handholds and crashed into the lip of the railing, knocking the breath from his lungs. And he must have cracked his ribs. But knowing he had only seconds before he lost his grip completely and fell from the train, he hauled himself up.

He looked back. His smoking SUV was still pacing the train, but now the second truck was between it and the tanker car on which Troy crouched. As he watched, gunfire erupted from within the vehicle. The muzzle-flashes were drowned by crimson washes of blood that coated the windows from inside. The truck began to wheel back and forth, completely out of control.

From the open window, the man in black poked the muzzle of the biggest handgun Troy had seen in a while. It wasn't a handgun at all, he realized; it was a machine pistol. He didn't believe he had ever seen one like that, not even during his time with the FBI.

The two trucks crashed together, then rebounded, maintaining their speed. The driver of the damaged SUV, it seemed, was still alive, but what he thought he was accomplishing, Troy couldn't say. It was possible that shock and fear were simply spurring him to drive on in the hope that something would change.

Troy had lost count in his head; he didn't know when the satchel charge would go off. He only knew it could be any second.

The man in black began exchanging fire with the operatives in the second SUV. As the angle changed,

Troy could see that the commando had a second gun, a big hand cannon of some kind, which he'd jammed into the back of the driver's seat.

That explained it. He had taken the driver captive and was now directing the man's actions.

Troy extended the stock of his MP5 and braced it against his shoulder. Lowering himself to one knee, he did his best to line up the commando in his sights. The jouncing, swaying train made it difficult, but when he thought he had the shot, he took it, squeezing off first one and then several .40-caliber rounds.

He could see the bullets strike the door frame of the vehicle, but none scored a hit. The commando— was that a look of irritation?—sent a couple of 3-round bursts in Troy's direction, causing him to flatten himself to the walkway.

He should have seen that coming.

Troy raised his head slightly, in time to see the SUV with the missing door clip the rear panel of the second truck. The commando was leaning out the window now.

He had the bomb in his hands.

"No!" Troy had time to shout.

The bomb flew through the air as the man in black threw it. It landed on the rear of the second truck, sticking fast to the tailgate. The SUV in which the commando was riding suddenly jerked left and right, like a ratter dog thrashing prey. Troy could see the muzzle-flash and even hear the shots as the commando put three rounds through the back of the seat. The driver had apparently tried to knock his carjacker out of the vehicle and had paid the price for failure.

The smoking SUV, now bearing what Troy guessed

was the man in black and several corpses, rolled to a crawl. The train quickly left it behind. The second SUV was close still, but now braking, the men aboard frantically trying to stop and get clear before—

The second truck exploded in an orange-and-black fireball.

The heat washed over Troy, causing his breath to catch in his throat. Hot shrapnel peppered the rear flank of the train. As he struggled to clear his head from the concussion, he saw the remainder of his team veering off, driving away.

The plan had failed. They hadn't made their insertion. They weren't in position to board and clear the train.

But Russell Troy was.

He stood, patting himself down, as the train rocked beneath him. In the distance, the man in black, the government commando, the fearsome "troubleshooter," was faded from view.

That meant there was nothing to stop Troy from killing as many of Shane Hyde's skinheads as he could. Maybe, just maybe, he would get lucky and find Hyde himself.

He could hope.

Steeling himself, shouldering the MP5 once more, Troy crept along the walkway, working his way forward. He was going to find justice. He was going to find vengeance.

He was going to murder Shane Hyde.

CHAPTER TWELVE

Outside Fort Worth, Texas

"We're clear of the Austin area, Sarge," Grimaldi reported. "Coming up on Fort Worth. Closing in on the train's position now. They've traversed the populated areas so far without major incident, but there have been reports of gunfire."

"The terrorists are shooting at civilians?" Bolan asked.

"Doesn't look like it," Grimaldi said. "Real-time heat satellite imaging, including thermal analysis, shows the there are still firefights going aboard it. They're spotty, but they're there."

"Got to be our party crasher," Bolan said.

"His name is Russell Troy," Michael Wood said from his seat near the door gun. "We used to work together. He was captured during the Bureau's infiltration of Twelfth Reich. His family was killed."

"Yeah," Bolan said. "I've read the report." He had, in fact, recognized Troy the moment he saw him, from the photo included in his intelligence files. Russell Troy, the FBI man who had suffered at Shane Hyde's hands, now apparently head of his own detachment of what? Mercenaries? Vigilantes?

In the confusion, at least two trucks that were part of

Russell Troy's force had escaped. The Farm's satellite scanning of the scene had tracked the vehicles to nearby Austin, where they were lost in the crush of city traffic. That meant Troy still had people on whom he could call, who were, at this moment, at large and well armed.

There was little Bolan could do about that, for the moment.

The interior of the Pave Hawk had been hastily cleaned. Greene's body had been removed and sent back with most of what remained of the joint DHS-FBI detachment. Bolan had invoked his authority again as Agent Matt Cooper, detailing a single Hummer—the least damaged among them—to act as trail car, picking up any bodies and securing any live terrorists that might be thrown or fleeing from the train as it moved.

Predictably, Margrave had made a lot of noise when the Pave Hawk returned to pick up Bolan. Grimaldi had used a private Austin airfield to top off his fuel tanks and make hasty repairs. By the time he got back, the support teams had converged on Bolan's position and a bloody-faced Margrave had worked himself into a lather.

A glare from Bolan, who looked ready to put Margrave down a second time, had silenced the man. By the time Grimaldi, Wood and Bolan had taken to the air, Wood having elected to lend himself to Bolan's cause for the near future, the rest of the men on the ground were doing all they could not to laugh at Margrave to his face.

Bolan's secure phone buzzed. He checked it. The text message from the Farm included a data attachment. The documentation was summarized in the message. The shell casings Bolan had recovered from the safe house had, at one time, been part of several supply caches distributed for the use of deep-cover agents.

That made sense.

"It doesn't make any sense," Wood said. "The last I knew, Russell Troy was a wreck, living in a convalescent home in California. How could he be running an independent counterterrorist operation? He'd be in no shape to do so."

"He got better," Bolan said. He eyed the FBI man. "Listen, Agent Wood, this is something I understand only too well. The evidence is staring us in the face. I've seen the kind of damage Troy can do, along with whoever is helping him."

"It couldn't be something official?"

"No," Bolan said. He had received confirmation from the Farm on that very point. No known government agency, no matter how covert, was employing or had empowered Russell Troy to run an operation relative to Hyde. Troy's official status was "missing." The recovery home in which he'd been living had no record of him checking out, no forwarding address and apparently no reason to care. After checking various channels, Barbara Price reported that scant record of Troy's absence existed. It was as if nobody had bothered to notice he was gone until government agencies, acting as proxies for Stony Man Farm, came asking.

"Troy is hurting," Bolan explained. "He's lost everything. In his pain, in his hopelessness, he's reaching for the only thing he can think of that will ease the ache. He thinks revenge will plug the hole in his soul. What he doesn't know is that it won't help. Not really."

"You sound like you know."

"I've seen it before," Bolan said. "A few years ago, in upstate New York, I hunted a man. He was just an ordinary guy who had lost his daughter to drugs, to the gangs that ran those drugs. He declared war on an entire crystal meth–producing operation and he didn't care who got in his way. He was one man, but motivated, and all the more dangerous because he didn't really care if he lived or died. Hate is powerful fuel, Agent Wood. It drove that vigilante farther than you or I would believe possible. He got put down, hard, more than once, but he got up again, and he killed innocent human beings. Men. Women. Even an infant, caught in the crossfire, DOA in its crib."

"That's horrible," Wood said.

"It was. And it was all because he wanted revenge for his dead daughter more than he wanted to be alive."

"You're guessing. You can't really know."

"I'm guessing," Bolan said. "But I do know, because I've seen it. Troy is like that vigilante, and in some ways to be *preyed on* forces a choice."

"What do you mean?" Wood asked.

"Every man, confronted with the need to correct a terrible wrong, to strike back at those who've taken his family, who've destroyed his life, has to choose. He can choose the path of revenge or he can choose the path of justice."

"But revenge on Shane Hyde. Isn't that justice?"

"It could be," Bolan said, nodding. "But if I'd let Troy plant that satchel charge, how many innocent people would have died? Revenge makes a man blind. He stops caring about the innocent. He starts using terms like 'collateral damage' and 'ancillary casualties.' He thinks that what he does, no matter the cost, is justified in the name of his vision of justice. But what he wants isn't justice at all. It isn't about what's right. It's about payback, about what *he* wants."

"And justice?" Wood asked.

"Justice I know very well," Bolan said. "When you lose loved ones and when you face the predators who have taken them from you, you have be able to look into the darkness in their souls without becoming tainted yourself."

"'When you stare into the abyss,'" Wood quoted, "'the abyss also stares into you.'"

"Yeah," Bolan said. "You can let the desire for revenge rot your soul, or you can hold to a moral code, do what's right, while fighting to bring predators down."

"That's a mighty fine line sometimes, Cooper," Wood said.

"It can be," Bolan agreed. "But it's still a line, and it's not hard to see if you're looking for it."

The FBI agent was quiet for a long time. Finally, he turned back to Bolan.

"Exactly who are you, Cooper?" he said.

"I'm a man who chose justice over revenge."

"Thar she blows, gentlemen," Grimaldi interjected. Bolan looked out the open doorway to find the train was below. He grabbed the rope ladder and prepared himself. He had taken what few painkillers he dared, which had cut the ache in his palms slightly. The rest was up to him.

"Ready to go," Wood said. He shifted his position and cocked the door gun.

"I'll give it a couple of passes, clear them out a little," Grimaldi said.

"Mind the explosives," Bolan warned. "We don't dare hit any of the ANFO bombs or the fuse cables."

"I didn't hit them before, did I?" Wood asked. He threw Bolan a thumbs-up.

"Right," Bolan said.

Grimaldi pushed the Pave Hawk as fast as he could while giving Wood a chance to target the skinheads crawling across the train. As they neared, Bolan could see the muzzle-flashes of a gunfire exchange near the last third of the tanker cars. Troy had made it onto the train. That had to be his position, unless the skinheads had suddenly taken to fighting among themselves.

"I need to take Shane Hyde alive," Bolan reminded Wood. "If you see him, don't put a bullet in him."

"No pressure, though," the agent said.

"Hyde has intelligence," Bolan explained. "Knowledge of terror cells here and abroad. I have to have him alive and talking. That's my directive. He can't die during the assault."

"Nag, nag, nag," Wood said. He shot Bolan a lopsided grin. "I understand, Cooper. Shall we?"

"Let's," Bolan answered. He returned his full attention to the train below.

Wood began firing in short, aimed bursts. The skinheads they passed hit the deck as the chopper skimmed by. One or two men went down. The sizable force that Hyde had brought onto the train was being whittled away, however slowly. It was too bad that Bolan and his allies couldn't afford to continue the war of attrition. The train had to be stopped before it reached its destination at the tank field. Dallas was less than forty miles from Fort Worth by car. They were running out of time.

Bolan tucked his arm through the rung of the rope ladder. As he stepped out into space, he let himself drop, riding out the jolt in his armpit as the rung took all his weight. Grimaldi began lowering the chopper near the midpoint of the train, where armed resistance seemed lightest. Skinheads farther up and down the cars began shooting at the Pave Hawk.

Bolan hit the tanker car, released the ladder and rolled, nearly spilling over the side. He caught himself, got to his feet and crouch-walked down the length of the tanker. He spent, he reflected, entirely too much time on top of trains rather than in them. This wasn't the first time, and it probably would not be the last.

The Pave Hawk circled the train from above, high enough and far enough out that the danger from the terrorists' weapons was minimized. Grimaldi and Wood had strategized with Bolan before this new drop. They would continue to provide air support as required, hosing out areas of strong resistance Bolan couldn't reach with his guns.

He had only his Desert Eagle, his Beretta and his Sting knife. It would be enough.

There was a crew-and-cargo car between two tankers at the next connection. A couple of them dotted the length of the train. One was farther back, and Bolan suspected very strongly that Troy was now inside that very car. The firefight raging before his arrival had seemed centered on that area.

Troy would keep, for now. Bolan was determined to get to the engine.

He dropped down to the walkway outside the rear door of the cargo compartment, which wasn't locked. He threw the door open and stepped inside.

A skinhead tried to crush his skull.

As the door closed behind him, Bolan ducked. The steel bar, some kind of breaker bar used aboard the train or to throw connecting equipment, whistled through the air and struck the metal bulkhead behind the soldier. The interior of the small compartment rang like a gong.

Bolan had bent at the knees. When he came up, the Sting was in his fist. The little double-edged blade went in quickly and deep. The Executioner grabbed the back of the skinhead's neck, pulled him in and pumped the knife blade in and out, spraying the punk's blood across the floor of the car. He finished the terrorist with a deep cut to the throat, shoving the blade through to one side before withdrawing it.

The soldier knelt, wiped the blade on the calf of the dead man's pants and sheathed it. The action hardly hurt his hands at all. Perhaps the painkillers were kicking in, for whatever they were worth.

The cargo-and-crew car was divided, according to the plans he had studied, into several subcompartments, each separated from the others by a sliding door. He had deliberately avoided cars like this one during his first run at the train. Now, with many of Hyde's men dead or at least off the train, fighting his way through this car was more of an option. That didn't make the prospect of clearing it any less dangerous.

He leveled his Beretta, hit the foot pedal and watched the door slide open. The skinhead standing on the other side was naked from his waist down. The tattoo-covered

woman lying on a rumpled wool blanket wore even less.
She screamed when Bolan entered the car.

The pantsless skinhead opened and closed his mouth
like a fish. When he remembered the pump-action shotgun leaning against the compartment bulkhead, he went
for it. Bolan simply angled the Beretta and pulled the
trigger, blasting the man from below with a triple burst
that punched up under his chin and blew off his jaw.
The half-headless corpse toppled. The woman screamed
louder.

He saw her make a move for a fold of the blanket,
and he was ready for it. When she tried to drag the old
snub-nosed revolver out from hiding, he stepped forward and kicked her in the face. His heavy boot made
her jaw click as her teeth slammed together. Bolan saw
the whites of her eyes as they rolled into her head.

She collapsed on the blanket.

He paused just long enough to zip-tie her hands and
ankles together. He was getting good and tired of the
lady friends these skinheads counted among their number. This one, at least, would live—provided the train
didn't detonate.

The thought spurred him on. He hit the foot pedal to
the next compartment and pressed himself against the
wall without stepping through. The shotgun blast that
peppered the opposite door with double 0 buck pellets
didn't shock him. He shoved the snout of his Beretta
through the opening, underhand, and pulled the trigger
four times. A body hit the floor.

Bolan checked quickly, exposing only one eye and
jerking his head back as fast as he could. Satisfied that

the man on the floor was really dead and not shamming, he swapped magazines in the Beretta and kept on going.

The soldier had been counting as he went. The next compartment was the second to last. He paused and listened, hearing breathing and the shifting of body-weight on the opposite side. It was loud enough that he suspected there were more than one of them.

He rapped on the door with the snout of his gun.

"Who the hell is it!" a voice demanded.

"Housekeeping," Bolan said.

"It's him!" he heard someone say. The door shot open and a skinhead stuck his head through the doorway, eyes wide. When Bolan smashed the butt of his Be-retta into the man's left temple, the scream he made sounded inhuman.

The door closed immediately as the half-blinded ter-rorist pulled his head back.

When the door opened again, Bolan wasn't fooled; he threw himself to the floor of the compartment.

The skinheads, predictably, didn't fire through the doorway, but tried to shoot through the wall, think-ing themselves clever. The ricochets were loud, like deadly leaden wasps that chewed through whatever they touched. Bolan made things worse for the men within, firing his Beretta at an angle through the doorway, add-ing to the carnage.

The skinheads knew, as Bolan did, that most bullets, from either handguns or rifles, would penetrate an or-dinary wall, especially a drywall barrier within a home or commercial structure. What they hadn't counted on was that the compartments of the OPP train were made of reinforced steel, even in the crew-and-cargo cars.

This was due precisely to O'Connor Petroleum's previous experience with terrorists and hijackers. It was the reason the firm had provided the hardened, mobile "panic room" that was the armored passenger car forward on the train.

Bolan reached out with the toe of his boot, touched the floor plate again and fired several more times through the opening door. Again the ricochets chewed through the compartment beyond. There were no more cries.

Blood oozed out from under the door, soaking the floor plate.

Bolan's combat boot left a print in the crimson puddle as he stepped forward and made his way through the charnel house he had created. The last compartment awaited. He hit the floor pedal for the door and dodged aside, after catching just a glimpse of what he faced.

The skinhead on the other side, wearing camouflage pants, a leather jacket and a chain mail shirt, held a Glock pistol under his own chin.

"I'll do it, man!" he shouted. "You come in here and I'll blow my brains out."

"Okay," Bolan said, pressed against the bulkhead near the doorway. "I'm coming in."

"Come on, man!" the terrorist shouted. "I got information! You need me!"

"I don't," Bolan said. "And I've heard this song before."

"Just who the hell *are* you, man? What do you want? I'm serious. I'll kill myself. I won't go to jail."

"Don't worry," the Executioner said. "I don't intend to take you to jail." He came through the doorway low, near waist height. The skinhead pulled the gun from his head and tried to track Bolan, who shot out the terrorist's kneecaps and dropped him to the soldier's level.

The Glock spun away on the metal deck.

The skinhead cried out in agony. "You son of a *bitch!*"

Bolan pistol-whipped him in the face, knocking him unconscious. Then he zip-tied the terrorist's arms behind his back, leaving him to live or bleed out as he was wont to do. His wounds weren't immediately life-threatening, provided the train did not remain in Hyde's control. Were the train liberated, a cleanup crew could find the kneecapped man, the woman Bolan had knocked out, and any other survivors, gathering them for treatment and trial.

But if they died, well, that was the price you paid for signing on with violent terrorists like Shane Hyde.

It was rough justice, but it was *justice,* not the mindless revenge that Russell Troy sought. Bolan had spent a lot of years thinking about, and acting on, the difference. He reloaded his Beretta.

It was, as Wood had said, a fine line. He had learned to walk along its edge and not falter. It was what made the Executioner who he was, what he was capable of being. It was what drove him.

It was long past time to end Shane Hyde's reign of terror.

Bolan exited the cargo car. Drawing the Desert Eagle by reaching across his back, he stood with a gun in each hand, mindful of the side rails of the tanker car before him. Hyde's men were there. He could hear them.

"Hey," he called out. "Who wants to hear a joke?"

There was no response. He thought he heard the low murmurs of conversation, but it was difficult to tell over the wind and the noise of the rocking train.

"Hitler, Shane Hyde and Pol Pot walk into a bar—" he began.

The screams of outrage were followed by footsteps on the railing. Men with submachine guns and pistols stopped short of the edge of the tanker, drawing down on him. None of them got off a shot. Bolan was already standing in position, one gun pointed to either side of the tanker car. He triggered the Desert Eagle and the Beretta 93R in tandem, shooting first one man, then another, punching holes in chests and necks and faces, knocking back three men each on either side.

In moments, six men had died.

CHAPTER THIRTEEN

Russell Troy was in hell.

He had pressed himself against the wall of the first compartment, at the edge of the sliding doorway that would take him farther into the cargo area. There was a side door here, and a bay holding four all-terrain motorcycles.

The floor was covered in blood.

The woman lay at the center of the spreading pool. He had gunned her down as he entered the car. He had no choice; the Uzi submachine gun was still gripped in her bloody hands and she'd meant to take him out. She was one of the Shane Hyde's people. Her blond hair was cut short. Her features had been fine, her chin pointed, her eyes blue and clear, the spitting image of...

His wife.

He was frozen in place, stricken. It wasn't supposed to be like this. It wasn't supposed to feel this way. He was an avenging angel. He was the spirit of revenge. He was payback. He was righteous anger. He was the wages of sin.

Troy clawed at his web gear, fighting to get under it, fighting to reach the pocket inside his shirt. The rubber ball came out in his mutilated hand and he squeezed it furiously, pumped it, crushed it, as if the familiar motion would somehow purge the sin, purge the shame, cleanse the memories that even now threatened to—

Memories!

No! He didn't want to remember! He had tried so hard not to recall any of it, not to picture it, not to see it! But he could. He could, and he couldn't make it stop.

They had held him down, had butchered his hand, had laughed and told him that they weren't going to cut him up any more. They stopped because they didn't need to take pieces of him. That's what they'd said. They didn't need to because they were going to show him something that would take so much more from him, something he would feel deeper and for a lot longer than any couple of fingers.

He had tried to turn away, but they'd put a knife beneath his eye and made him watch. With horror, he'd realized after only a few moments that he couldn't stop, that he couldn't turn away.

The things they had done to her. The abominable, unthinkable, degrading things. To know she had died as they did it, that her last feelings, her last thoughts, were thoughts of unspeakable abomination and helplessness…that was worst of all. He clutched the rubber ball in one hand and his MP5 in the other, pressing the gun against his chest, sobbing uncontrollably. Sinking to his knees, he looked up, helpless, as the sliding door opened.

The skinhead looked down. "Uh-oh," he said, clawing at his waistband for a revolver.

The face was coarse, the head shaved, the skin rough. The terrorist was everyone who had ever harmed his family, every piece of human trash who had ever taken from Russell Troy the things that were rightfully his. He dropped the rubber ball as he stood and, reversing the MP5, brought the shoulder stock down on the fumbling skinhead's skull, over and over again, crushing the bone, pulping the face, spraying himself with the skinhead's blood.

There were more men behind the first. Troy was a man possessed. He stepped into the next compartment, lowered the MP5 and triggered a full-auto burst, spraying out the entire magazine. The floor at his feet was littered with brass shell casings and the air was suddenly thick with the smell of fired cartridges. A skinhead toppled at his feet. The others were scrambling for cover in the next compartment, trying to dog the door shut from the other side.

He shoved his empty MP5 through the gap, using it like a lever, and wrenched the door open. As he did so, he popped the magazine free, using his injured hand to replace it. There were crates and supplies here, things he didn't recognize, stored in metal drums that were proof to his gunfire. The terrorists hid behind them, denying him the justice he sought, forcing him to hunt them, to shoot them, to fight them....

"Get him!" his wife shouted. He turned and saw her face. She became his daughter. She became a snarling wolf. She became a terrorist he recognized, a skinhead with a pair of pliers, the man who had taken his fingers.

"No! Stop! No!" he barked.

He couldn't breathe. He couldn't draw the air he needed to scream long and loud, to rend his throat, to roar his fury. His chest hurt. His hand ached. His face was bloody and he didn't know whose blood it was.

The MP5 was empty and he used it as a club again, smashing, crushing. The skinheads roared and squealed and cried, and he didn't hear them. Every one became his wife, became his daughter, became some monster, some memory he couldn't crush.

There were more of them, climbing overtop of one another, getting in one another's way in the close quarters. Some remaining part of him, some tiny corner of his mind that was still rational, processed that this wasn't normal. The terrorists, the skinheads, were moving as one through the compartment, moving as a knot. They had come not with weapons ready, not prepared to face down Russell Troy and kill him as the invader he was to them. No; they had been surprised.

They hadn't been expecting him.

He couldn't fix his place in time and space. Everything was a blur. But he understood, at the very back of his brain, that something had changed. The skinheads, the terrorists, were trying to…trying to…

Escape!

They were fleeing!

He wouldn't let them go. As if walking through water, he fought on. He drew his Glock, fired, punched a hole through the face of a tattooed man who turned and came at him with a knife. A second man with a pistol fired and missed, fired again, scored a graze that burned Troy's ribs. He shot the man in the stomach, again and again. Then he shoved the Glock in his waistband and took up the MP5 once more, feeling its weight, enjoying its heft.

He began to shake. He began to sweat. His face felt hot. His scalp crawled. He saw creatures, alien bugs, half recognized and only partially resolved, creeping up his arms, from his shirt, out of his ears, from his mouth.

He screamed.

And he remembered everything.

It washed over him and he fought with his fingers, with his teeth, with the MP5 club, trying to smash and splinter and destroy, to flee what was coming for him inside his own head. His daughter.

His daughter was dead and it was his fault.

Troy remembered the long hours. He remembered the look on his daughter's face, each and every time he'd told her he had to work, he had to go, he couldn't stay. He remembered the expression of betrayal on his wife's face, the first time she'd suspected, the first time he didn't want to go to bed with her for fear he might pass something to her. She knew about the drugs. She knew about the violence. Now she suspected the whores.

He had lost himself. He had become the Twelfth Reich, and they had discovered him, had turned on him, and if it weren't for his failure, for his weakness, his loved ones would still be alive, happy and beautiful and alive, and he would be with them even now—

"It's my fault!" he screamed. "It's my fault! They're dead because of me! Me! Because it was my job! Because my job was more important than my life! You bastards took my life! Took my life!"

He crashed into another terrorist. This one was a woman. He didn't look at her, but crushed her throat with the MP5, ramming it into the hollow, pressing it home, bending her neck backward and down. A man came up behind him, tried to stab him, cut his shoulder. He couldn't feel it.

The skinhead with the knife fell under Troy's swinging MP5. The sound the man made was like the whimper of a whipped dog, cut short by the second blow. The barrel of the MP5 streamed red. Troy hit again. And again.

Bone cracked. Far away, he could hear the gibbering of a madman. It was the garbled language of a man gone insane.

It was him. The noise was coming from him.

The man beneath him was dead and Troy hammered away at him anyway, chopped at him with the MP-5 as if he would chip him in two with his bloody, blunt, makeshift hatchet, clubbed him as if killing him would take away the terrible knowledge that was now boiling to the surface.

He had fought it.

He had tried to crush it.

He had tried to suppress it.

But he couldn't, and now that it had broken free, it was a serpent in his mind, coiling through his brain and puncturing him with its venomous memories and pumping him full of its poison.

He stopped at the last door of the crew car, stopped because some sense, some otherworldly knowledge, some foreboding froze him.

Someone was on the other side. Another monster. The greatest monster of them all.

The door opened, and Shane Hyde stepped through.

Troy tackled him.

He smashed Hyde in the face with the blood-soaked MP5, pulled him to the ground, hammered him with his good hand balled into a fist. He rained slashing elbows across Hyde's face, crushing his nose, blackening his eyes. He dropped the MP5 and tore with his fingers, clawed like a demon, like a tiger, like a rabid animal.

He felt blows landing, felt his jaw giving, saw stars as each powerful punch and kick crashed through his oblivious lack of defense. It didn't matter. Nothing mattered. The monster was in his hands and he meant to kill it, to choke it, to take its head, to end its evil.

He crawled for position. His skin was bloody and slippery, as was Hyde's. The monstrous racist leader wasted no breath on words, offered no explanations. He fought, and fought viciously, cracking ribs, making nerve clusters spasm, grabbing and digging in with his fingers as if each portion of Troy's flesh were a bowling ball he might rip free and roll away.

Troy wasn't stronger. He wasn't meaner. He wasn't more skilled.

But he was winning.

He got Hyde on his back, mounted him, punched him again and again. The exercises, the strength of the fingers of his injured hand—he felt it now. He curled his remaining fingers into the flesh of Hyde's throat, around the cord of muscle there, and brought his good hand over the other side. He squeezed.

Hyde became his wife. His fingers were wrapped around *her* throat now. She stared up at him, despair in her eyes, and when she raised the pistol to try to shoot him, he barely noticed. He wrenched it free from her grip, breaking her finger, smashed her in the face with it and threw it across the bloody compartment.

"You," she said.

"Don't you…don't you…" Troy said. "You recognize me, don't you? I'm so sorry. I'm so sorry for everything that they—"

"God, you're pathetic," his wife said. She wiped her face and became Shane Hyde. Then she was his wife, then she was Hyde.

"Stop doing that!" Troy shouted. "Stop it!"

"What the hell are you talking about?" Hyde asked. He looked confused. Troy's wife look confused. Hyde look confused again. The shapes, the images of the terrorist leader and Troy's dead wife, kept melding and changing and becoming each other.

"I've lost it," Troy said. "I've…I've lost it. It's gone. I'm insane. Kill me."

"With pleasure," his wife said. She reached for the Glock in his belt.

Troy reacted without thinking. He looked down at his bloody, scratched hands, now empty, and willed them to move. He pulled the Glock from his waistband and leveled it at his wife, who was Shane Hyde, who was his wife again.

"Stop," he pleaded. "Please don't do that anymore."

"You really are unhinged, aren't you?" Hyde looked closely. "It *is* you. I'm sure of it."

"My name is Russell Troy," the former agent said, slowly standing, keeping the gun trained on Hyde. "You murdered my family and took part of my hand."

"Of course I did. Of course."

"Tell me," Troy said. Hyde remained Hyde, and for that Troy was grateful. He gestured with the gun. "Tell me it was nothing personal. Tell me it was just… business."

"Oh, but it was personal, Russell," Hyde said. "It

was never anything but personal. You betrayed me. You came into my halls of power and you presumed to dupe me. You didn't just betray your race, Russell. You betrayed yourself. For that, you had to suffer. That's why I took your family. That's why I killed the other agents' families."

"How could you do this?" Troy shrieked. His finger tightened on the pistol's trigger.

The switchblade snapped open and came up seemingly out of nowhere. The sharp edge caught Troy's wrist, shocking him, causing him to drop the .40-caliber Glock. Hyde was on his feet and charging in, making up for in aggression what he lacked in technique. He very nearly speared the rogue agent through the stomach.

Troy barely knew who he was, but his muscles remembered. He sidestepped the clumsy thrust, chopped at Hyde's knife hand, managed to ward off the cut. The two began circling in the tiny compartment, Hyde lunging and thrusting with the knife, Troy barely intercepting each attack.

You have a knife, his daughter said. Her disembodied voice seemed to be floating above and behind his head. You have a knife in your pocket.

He did. He had forgotten it. It was only a lock-back folder, the type of thing any trucker carried on his belt twenty years ago. He dug in his pocket and pulled it out, managing to do so before his opponent could leap again. The blade of Hyde's switchblade dug skin from the fingers of Troy's mangled hand. It seemed like adding insult to injury.

I've gone mad, he thought. My thoughts make no sense.

Who was he? Who was he fighting?

Oh, yes. His wife.

She came for him, her knife sharp and long and terrible, and it was all he could to fight her off, to bring himself to strike her, to kick at her, and finally, to gouge at her with his own blade, which he snapped open using only one hand and a snap of his wrist. Some informant, a recidivist piece of criminal trash who carried a knife because he was many times a felon and dared not rack up another gun charge, had shown him that trick when Troy was a green FBI agent.

Strange that he should remember it now.

They came together, hand to knife, grabbing each other's wrists, locked in deadly combat, rolling around and around in the compartment. Lucidity descended on Troy like a curtain, and with it came cold detachment. He needed to know. He wanted to know.

"Where were you going, Hyde?" he asked as they struggled together. "Where were you headed?"

The man smiled, briefly transforming into Troy's wife before becoming his daughter and then himself again. Troy shook his head as if to clear it, his wrist cracking under Hyde's brutally strong grip. His own death grip on Hyde's knife wrist was obviously painful, for his enemy was pale and sweating.

"You really don't understand at all, do you?" Hyde asked. "Did you think I was going to die for the great and glorious cause? What am I, a mud person? Do I look stupid? The tide has turned. Government action was always a given. We could only hope to hobble them, slow them. And now, now I'm leaving. Certain actions have been set in motion. I don't intend to be here when they play out. It will be enough to see it on the news and ride the wave of revolution that it brings about."

"You're insane," Troy said. He pushed, and the two parted, backed against opposite walls of the compartment, their knives at the ready.

"And you're not?" Hyde said. "I should introduce you to my friend Bob. You could tell him all your problems. He's in the crew compartment farther forward."

"I'm going to kill you," Troy said.

The rocking train beat with a curious rhythm as the two men stared at each other, breathing heavily. Troy thought he heard a helicopter. He wondered if the commando would find them, if the man in black would come to kill them both.

He thought that might be better.

"No," Hyde said. "You're not going to kill me. Look at you. Look at what you've become."

"You took everything from me!" Troy gritted.

"I gave you life," Hyde replied.

Troy's jaw dropped. "What…"

"Think about it, Troy," Hyde said. "What were you when you were a pawn of the government? You played at being one of us. You wore a mask. You pretended to believe as we did. You mouthed the words of our pledges. You paid lip service to loving your race, to protecting and preserving a future for white men and women in the face of the inferior hordes swamping this country. You drank with us. You slept with our women. You snorted our drugs. And what did that do for you? You died inside because you wanted to be one of us and couldn't be! You betrayed us because you had no choice!"

"No!" Troy said. "I wasn't one of you! I wouldn't ever be!"

"Lies," Hyde said smoothly. "Lies that you tell yourself. Tell me you never felt the stirring of pride when we glorified the accomplishments of the white race, *your* race. Tell me it wasn't your desire, your primal manhood, that made it possible for you to sleep with women you told yourself were beneath you and your lofty government ideals. Tell me you didn't even once wish that you could leave your past life behind, join us once and for all, and stop living the deception that was not your choice. It was inflicted on you!"

"You're a monster," Troy whispered. "I could never be like you."

"Then if I am a monster," Hyde said, smiling broadly, "I'm a monster who has breathed life into you. I am the golem of Zionist mythology, a dread creature made living by the breath of will. Or is it you, Russell Troy, who are *my* golem? For I have forged you in torturous fire. You have been reborn a man of action, a man of will, because I gave you the hatred to find your true heart. People say that hatred is wrong, Russell. Why? Hate is what makes us strong. Don't you hate evil? Don't you hate what is wrong? I know I do."

"You didn't…you didn't make me anything but…but dead. I'm dead inside."

"Who stood with you?" Hyde asked. "Who were those men?"

"My… The… They want to help me. They want to kill you."

"They aren't with the government? You aren't part of a counterterror action? It's not that I need you to tell me. I doubt you could pass a psych profile any more than I could right now. But I want to hear it. I want you to say it."

"They're helping me because they hate you!" Troy shouted. "I'm no pawn of the government! I'm my own man, and I'm going to make you pay!"

"There," Hyde said. He sounded smug, satisfied. "There, don't you see? Does a dead man forge a private army? Is a dead man a leader of men? Does a dead man fight through my lieutenants like a demon warrior, beating them to death with his bloody hands?"

"Your lieutenants?"

"These were my leaders," Hyde said, spreading his hands to indicate the dead men and women scattered through the compartment and its connecting segments. "These were the best Twelfth Reich had to offer. You killed them."

"Then it's over...." Troy said. "It's over when I destroy you."

Hyde laughed, a sound of genuine mirth, perhaps tinged with madness. "You don't really believe that, do you? My organization is huge. Even now I have men waiting to rendezvous with me. I have more troops staged nearby. And this train hasn't yet completed its task, either."

"You haven't killed all my people," Troy said. "Nor has he."

"'He?'"

"The man in black. The commando. The big guy with the dark hair."

"Ah," Troy said. "Well. It hardly matters, does it? Soon the train will reach the tank field and explode.

And there is nothing you, nor anyone else, can do to stop it."

"I could kill you."

"Have you considered what your life will be like without me to hate?" Hyde asked. "To whom will you turn? Where will you go? Do you have a home? Do you think you can reach it? What would be the fun in that?"

Hyde very slowly closed his switchblade and put it back into his pocket. Throwing Russell Troy a salute, he fled the compartment, heading for the motorbikes and the cargo ramp. Troy slumped against the wall of the car.

Tears began to stream down his cheeks. Through the roaring in his ears he heard the ramp open, heard one of the motorbikes roar to life, heard Shane Hyde leave the train.

"No!" he shouted. Grabbing up his Glock, he ran for the motorcycles, determined to follow.

Shane Hyde had to die.

Russell Troy had to kill him.

CHAPTER FOURTEEN

Outside Dallas, Texas

"Jack," Bolan said. "I have a problem."

"What is it, Sarge?" Grimaldi asked through Bolan's transceiver.

"Things have gotten quiet," the solder said. "I have a feeling the rats are leaving the sinking ship."

"You got that right," the pilot replied. "We've been watching the skinheads jump off the train for the past few minutes. A couple of dirt bikes have made the jump from the rearmost crew car, too. Any one of them could be Hyde, but we can't get sufficient satellite imaging to tell. You want me to patrol and eyeball, pick up Hyde if we see him?"

"You can't," Bolan said. "We're approaching the tank field. We'll be there soon."

"I don't follow you, Sarge."

"Jack," Bolan said. "I'm going to take the locomotive. There are three chambers, per the plans. All will likely be sealed. Resistance unknown. But if I'm put down while trying to make the play there won't be anyone left."

"I still don't follow you."

"Jack, I need you to shoot out the ANFO bombs and start the chain reaction," Bolan said. "If I don't come out of this, if I can't stop the train, you've got to blow it before it gets to the tank field."

"The hostages…" Grimaldi said.

"They'll be dead anyway, when we hit that field," Bolan said. "And with them the migrant workers, all the equipment—everything we're fighting to protect. You read the same briefing I did. If that tank field goes, the price won't be tallied in human lives alone. The damage to the economy will cripple us. We can't take it, Jack. Not with things like they are."

Grimaldi was silent for a long moment. "I don't have to like it, Sarge."

"No," Bolan said. "You don't. You just have to promise me you'll do it."

"Affirmative. You know I will."

"Good man." Bolan checked the sealed computer lock on the high-tech locomotive's outermost hatch. "Wish me luck. I'm going in."

"Good hunting, Striker," Grimaldi said.

"Thanks. Out."

Bolan removed the small C-4 charge from his war bag.

Armed resistance had evaporated almost as if a switch had been thrown. One moment the Executioner was trading fire with the many terrorist skinheads who guarded the train. The next, all was silent except for the rolling, rumbling train itself and Bolan's own inner warnings. He had the distinct impression of being had, and worse, he was almost certain that meant Shane Hyde would have abandoned the train.

That left only the problem of the enormous and complicated bomb the Twelfth Reich terrorists had created.

The C-4 bomb was about the size of a digital recorder and equipped with both magnetic and adhesive mounts. He peeled the backing off the adhesive, ran his hand across the plastic surface of the computer lock's number pad and rammed the bomb against it, making sure it caught fast. Then he flipped the protective switch off the timer, punched the button with his index finger and swung himself out of the way, using the corner of the locomotive to protect his body.

The bomb exploded.

It created a small plume of black smoke and orange flame, a scattering of plastic and metal shrapnel. The sealed door burst open, and from inside the compartment, screams began. Screams belonging to a single male.

They were punctuated by Kalashnikov fire.

There was no more distinctive sound in the world of weapons than that of the Kalashnikov. The empty space within the receiver, under the metal cover atop the weapon, created a drum that gave the assault rifle a hollow clang like a deadly gong. In the course of his war the Executioner had stood, crouched and run downrange of thousands of rounds from Kalashnikov pattern rifles. He would recognize the sound anywhere.

The skinhead in the first compartment of the locomotive was bleeding from the ears. The concussion of the C-4 charge had battered him senseless, but to his credit, he fought on. He held a folding-stock AK at the waist, squeezing the trigger back and spraying the weapon like a garden hose. Several of the rounds caught on the lip of the hatchway and ricocheted, very nearly chewing up the terrorist himself. He was oblivious to the danger, swinging his weapon back and forth as if he were trimming a hedge.

The weapon cycled dry.

Bolan leaned in the doorway and put a single 9 mm round through the man's face. There was no way to miss the head shot at this distance. The mild recoil of the Beretta 93R was warming up his palm again, which meant the weak painkilling drugs in Bolan's system were already starting to dilute.

The man in the first compartment was very dead.

Bolan stepped inside. The locomotive was maintaining its speed, the cars behind it rolling and vibrating. Above, the thrum of the Pave Hawk reminded Bolan of a score of different battlefields. War-torn landscapes the world over shared certain universal sounds, certain ever-present smells. Smoke, blood and heated steel.

There was an intercom connecting the inner hatch to the second compartment. Bolan thumbed it. It buzzed, but there was no response.

"Open the door," Mack Bolan said. "It's over."

"Nothing is over!" another male voice shouted, this one cracked and hoarse. "We will secure a future for the white race and a place in the world for white children!"

Monitors on the wall of the second compartment, which appeared to be a navigation station, were alive with close-circuit camera pictures of the rail before the train and the terrain distant from it. Peering at them through the reinforced glass panel in the door, Bolan could see what he thought might be the beginning of the tank field and the tent city surrounding it. The doomsday clock was about to run out on the migrant workers and the facility in which they toiled.

The soldier removed his phone and consulted the schematics it contained. The control room was between this navigation station and the engine room of the locomotive, which meant he had to pass this chamber to stop the OPP train. He reached out and pressed the intercom again.

"I have a bag full of grenades," Bolan said. "I'm going to pull the pins on all of them and leave them here. Then I'm going to step out. The concussion will rip this train open like a cardboard box. Guess who'll be the creamy center? That's you, pal. Over."

There was a pause. It was a complete bluff on Bolan's part. He would no more set off grenades here, at the center of the locomotive, than he would risk shooting one of the ANFO bombs. The explosion would set off the chain reaction he was trying to avoid. All he needed, however, was for the dimwitted skinhead on the other side of the door to want to try to—

"I want to negotiate!" the man on the intercom said.

"I will negotiate," Bolan said. "Open the door so that we can talk more clearly."

"Don't you try anything!" the skinhead said. "You try anything and I'll blow this train!"

Bolan didn't think that likely. Chances were the means to blow the train were held in the final compartment. If he was Shane Hyde, that's how he would set it up. The fact that the rest of the surviving skinheads seemed to have abandoned the train pointed to an Egyptian pharaoh's approach. Hyde had locked his men in the locomotive, creating a layer of fail-safes through which counter-terrorist operatives would have to fight. It was exactly what Bolan would have done, in Hyde's position.

Everything the soldier had seen and experienced so far pointed to the fact that Shane Hyde wasn't stupid, no matter how evil he might be.

The hatch slid open a few inches. Through the gap, the skinhead inside stared wild-eyed at Bolan. "Don't you try anything!"

"What are your demands?" Bolan said. He busied himself screwing the custom suppressor on the threaded barrel of the Beretta 93R.

"I...I want a helicopter," the skinhead said.

"Helicopter, right." They always wanted a helicopter.

"And I want...I want twenty million, no, fifty million dollars in used twenty-dollar bills," the skinhead said. "And I—"

"Do you have any idea," Bolan asked, "just how heavy fifty million dollars in twenty-dollar bills would be? Do you have any concept how much space that would take up?"

"Huh?"

"Let's just say, that you'd have to settle for a larger denomination. Is your friend in the engine room listening to all this?"

"What?"

Bolan jerked his chin at the walkie-talkie on the skinhead's belt, which had its microphone button taped down with red electrical tape. "Bet you thought that was pretty clever. I have to admit I wouldn't have given you credit for it."

The skinhead looked nervous. "What are you getting at, man? You gonna get me my helicopter or what?"

"Don't you hear it?" Bolan said. "I already have one."

"Yeah," the skinhead replied. "Okay. Yeah. Have him bring it close."

Bolan looked at the monitors tracking the train's progress. There was almost no time left.

"Look," he said. "I'll let you in on a little secret."

"Yeah?"

"Yeah. I'm in a really, really bad mood. My hands are killing me and, frankly, they're not going to get better soon enough for my attitude to improve. And that means, kid, that I'm really in no mood for this garbage. You have five seconds to put any weapons on the deck and step out. If you manage to persuade whoever's barricaded in the engine room to do the same, that might work in your favor."

"What do you mean, work in my favor?" the skinhead demanded.

"If you do as I ask, I won't shoot you in the stomach."

"Screw you—"

Bolan shot him in the stomach.

He had been holding the Beretta low, underneath the skinhead's line of sight, trusting the conversation, which Bolan was largely ignoring, to keep him distracted. The weapon smacked his palm only a little, and the suppressed shot, while louder than the absurdly hushed sound one saw in movies, was sufficiently muted by the suppressor that it wasn't deafening in the enclosed space.

The Executioner's hand shot through the gap in the door, grabbed the stricken skinhead's dirty T-shirt and yanked him through the doorway. He threw the gut-shot man to the floor of the outer compartment and started to step past the sliding door.

"You don't get to win!" the bleeding skinhead whined. "You race-traitor bastard!"

Bolan turned and looked down. With shaking fingers, the kid was pulling a ballistic knife from his belt. The tubular blade could be propelled from the handle on powerful springs. Bolan could see his death in the terrorist's eyes. Blood was spreading across his T-shirt, but the skinhead was fixed only on striking back at the source of his torment.

"Put it down," Bolan said.

"Yeah? Well, you can—"

Whatever it was Bolan could, he wouldn't know. He raised his leg at the knee and brought the heel of his combat boot arcing down in a powerful, deadly ax-kick that laid open the skinhead's forehead and bounced his skull off the deck. The gut-shot man went completely limp.

Bolan dropped to one knee, rolled the bloody skinhead over and zip-tied his hands. The man might never regain consciousness, but the soldier didn't leave live, mobile enemies behind him. He hadn't fought as long as he had to end up shot in the back.

Now he stood before the last hatch.

The deck swayed and rocked beneath him, reminding him of how little time he had left. The train had to be stopped. He took the walkie-talkie from the skinhead's belt, ripped the tape from the mike switch and keyed the device a few times.

"Ripper?" said a voice from inside the engine room.

"No," Bolan replied. "Ripper's not feeling well. He

caught lead poisoning, probably brought on by a case of early onset stupidity. Now open this door or I swear I'll blow it. The concussion will hammer you into paste."

The door opened.

Bolan could hardly believe he was facing a reasonable terrorist, for once. The soldier stepped through the doorway, his Beretta held low, ready for anything.

Great. That was just great.

The skinhead was soaked in sweat. He wore a pair of jeans tucked into scuffed, untied combat boots. Naked from the waist up, he wore only the canvas straps of a suicide vest over his bony shoulders. In his hand, wired to the sticks of dynamite in the loops of the vest, was a dead man's switch, which he was holding down with his thumb.

"Why don't you do it, asshole?" The skinhead smiled. His cheeks were hollow, his face gaunt. The light in his eyes danced at the edge of madness. That, too, made sense. Hyde was, per his files, not exactly sane. With his charisma he would be able to spot a fellow traveler, the sort of person who would welcome blowing himself to bits in order to strike a blow for the master race or whatever.

"If I let go of this switch," the skinhead said, "the bomb explodes." He looked up at the ceiling. One of the ANFO devices had been planted here, at the head of the train, within the engine room. Wires trailed from it through a ventilation grate. From there, Bolan knew, they connected with the interlaced bombs running the length of the train. An explosion here would end everything. They might even be close enough to the tank field now that Shane Hyde's plan would prove successful.

"Easy," Bolan said. He took the Beretta, with its suppressor still attached, and slipped it into the custom leather shoulder holster he wore. He snapped the retaining strap deliberately. "Easy now. There's no need to get crazy. Your buddy out there wanted to negotiate. You and I can do that."

"So you can kill me, race-traitor?" the skinhead demanded. "I don't think so."

"I'm *really* getting tired of being called that," Bolan said quietly.

"Sarge," Grimaldi said in his ear, "the Farm calculates that you're almost at the redline of safe distance. If you want me to blow the train, it's got to be now."

"We have a problem," Bolan said.

"What?" the skinhead said.

"What, Sarge?" Grimaldi asked.

"I'm staring at a man wearing a bomb and holding a dead man's pressure switch," Bolan said.

"It's worse than that, Sarge," Grimaldi told him. "The track curves near the tank field, to clear the pipelines. You're moving too fast. If the train isn't slowed, it's going to derail when you get there, and then it's going to blow."

That had been Shane Hyde's plan all along. He had set the train in motion, protected it until he got close to the tank field and then abandoned it, leaving his handpicked pawns and this bomb-carrying madman to guard the engine until the train eventually derailed.

Smart.

"Jack," Bolan said, "it's been good knowing you."

"Who the hell is Jack?" the skinhead demanded.

"Don't worry about him," Bolan said. He had been

holding his hands high in a sign of nonaggression. Now he lowered them to his belt line.

"You're gonna die, you jackbooted thug," the skinhead said. "You government goon."

"You know," Bolan said, "your ignorance is matched only by your complete inability to grasp irony."

"What?"

"Jackbooted thugs," Bolan said. "Hitler. He was known for that kind of thing."

"Don't you talk about the progenitor of the white race like that!" the skinhead shrieked. He gestured with the dead man's switch. "This is it! We're going!"

"Then we're going."

"Sarge—" Grimaldi's voice sounded in Bolan's ear "—I'm sorry."

"I'm not," Bolan said. "It's been a good run."

"Who are you talking to?" the skinhead demanded. "Who *are* you?"

"My name," the soldier said, "is unimportant. It's enough for you to know that I've killed as many predators that walk the face of the Earth as possible. I've fought the Mafia. I've fought international terrorism. I've fought racist and separatist thugs. And there's one thing every last one of them had in common, no matter how confident they were that they had the upper hand. There's something that every criminal, predator scum has in common."

"You shut the hell up!" the skinhead screamed.

"Preparing to fire," Grimaldi stated.

"They all," Bolan said, "bleed."

The Sting knife flashed from Bolan's waistband. The double-edged blade bit deep, cutting across the skinhead bomber's throat, washing the soldier's forearm in the man's blood as one of his carotid arteries was laid open. Gurgling and gasping, the terrorist reached out, as if he would hold himself up using Bolan as a crutch.

The body fell in slow motion.

Bolan saw the hand on the pressure switch begin to release. He dived for it, grabbed the switch and kept it pressed closed. As the skinhead hit the deck, paralyzed by shock and bleeding out all over the floor of the control room, Bolan wrapped a strip of tape from his bandaged hand around the switch and rubbed his thumb along the plastic surface, sealing the bond created.

"Firing," Grimaldi said in his ear.

"Abort!" Bolan cried. "Jack, abort! Abort!"

"Affirmative!" the pilot shouted. He sounded surprised, concerned and jubilant all at once.

There was no time to celebrate his near-execution at his friend's hand. Bolan busied himself with the locomotive controls, the computerization of which made them simple. He found the throttle and yanked it back. The brakes were prominently marked, a red, rubber-coated swivel switch, which Bolan turned. Warning lights filled the control room and a woman's recorded voice announced, "Brake applied. Brake applied."

"Jack," Bolan called, "is she slowing? Are we going to make it?"

"She's backing off," Grimaldi reported. "You are entering the curve."

Bolan felt the deck shift beneath him. The brakes were squealing loudly now, throwing up sparks that he could see on the monitors. The terrain around him was full of tents and drill equipment, pipelines and wells. On the monitors he could see throngs of workers pointing. True to form, they had apparently stayed right where they were, or left and returned again. They would never know just how close they had come to dying.

The train continued to slow. Bolan made sure the controls were set and locked before stepping from the engine room. The skinhead wearing the bomb was dead. In the outer compartment, the man he had gut shot was dead, as well.

"Scramble cleanup crews," Bolan said into his transceiver. "Tell the Farm to send bomb disposal technicians. A lot of them."

"Roger, Sarge," Grimaldi said. "Anything else?"

"I'm going to sweep the train, make sure Hyde's not here," Bolan said. "Then there's a very pretty young lady whom I'd like to meet and thank in person." He was thinking of the brunette in the personnel car.

"Get a phone number for me," Grimaldi said. "I'm getting intel through the feed from the Farm now. They've identified two properties, outside Dallas and near Houston, that are linked to Hyde's shell companies."

"No rest for the weary," Bolan said. "It looks like we'll be doing more house hunting, then."

"Got it," Grimaldi said. "Stand by, Sarge. Your ride is on the way."

"Yeah," Bolan said.

From the railing of the train, now slowing to a crawl, he watched the tent city and the gaping migrant onlookers go by. One of them waved. Another cheered. Soon the entire crowd was smiling and clapping. They might not understand exactly how dangerous the threat had been, but they understood, on some level, that Bolan had helped them, had stopped the train before it did them harm.

What the hell, the soldier thought.

He broke out in a wide grin.

CHAPTER FIFTEEN

The Outskirts of Dallas, Texas

The sun was a blood-orange disk dipping into dark, wispy clouds, tinting the Southwestern terrain a warm shade of red. Mack Bolan paused outside the Pave Hawk to admire it. The M4 carbine he had borrowed from the chopper's stores rested on the end of a single-point sling. Grimaldi, busy stowing supplies from which Bolan had obtained loaded magazines and other munitions for his war bag, stopped to look at the sunset with the soldier.

"It's been a hell of a day, Jack," Bolan said.

"It sure has, Sarge," Grimaldi replied. "It sure has. And it's not over yet."

"No." Bolan shook his head. "But I've always been a night owl."

Grimaldi chuckled at that. "Yeah. Night owl."

According to Stony Man intelligence, there were two places Hyde and his people might choose to go to ground. The first was a structure, formerly a set of self-storage units, that Bolan presumed was now a safe house of sorts. The next one, a sprawling house outside Houston, was isolated and, judging from satellite imagery, possibly fortified. Grimaldi and Bolan had opted for the methodical approach, tackling the nearer site first.

It was all eerily familiar.

Shane Hyde had, of course, been nowhere to be found when the train was checked. Follow-up sweeps had turned up no trace of him, nor had Bolan expected them to. The mission continued. The soldier's priority was, as it had been from the start, to pin down and recover Shane Hyde, to bring him in alive.

"I'm going to miss Agent Wood," Grimaldi said. "He was good on the door gun. And you never did get me that girl's phone number."

"She was half your age, Jack."

"I'm as young as I feel."

"Well, I feel like hell," Bolan said, chuckling. The woman, Danyelle Smith, was one of O'Connor Petroleum's junior executives. When he had finally opened the armored car, she had been the first to rush out and hug him in gratitude. Grimaldi had been teasing the soldier about it during the subsequent chopper flight.

Wood had stayed behind, opting to help oversee the cleanup crew. There was a heavy blacksuit presence amid the tank field already, and the Farm was sending in more people, but a lot of the personnel on hand were also Bureau, Homeland Security and even INS agents. Bolan was pleased to have someone on-site, besides the Farm's handpicked people, who could be trusted to exercise sound judgment. He had no idea where Margrave had ended up, nor did he care.

The ache in his hands was still there. It had gotten slightly better, and he was still chewing light-dose painkillers to ease it, but the pain wasn't going away anytime soon. It had him on edge. He really *was* in a bad mood. His old friend Grimaldi helped lighten it, but the fact was, Bolan was angry, and he was sick and tired of the damage done by Shane Hyde and his murderers. Bringing the racist leader to heel would be a service to humanity, not to mention a source of great personal satisfaction to Mack Bolan.

Of Russell Troy, there was also no sign. Satellite tracking of the vehicles and personnel fleeing the train had lost those that entered highly populated areas, including the motorcycles Grimaldi had seen. Bolan was willing to bet that at least one of those bikes had carried Shane Hyde away from the scene of his ultimately failed terrorist attack. Had Troy escaped the same way? Had he been killed, his body stretched somewhere along the train tracks, as yet undiscovered by the mop-up crews policing that area?

"I keep asking this," Grimaldi said. "Do you want air support?"

"I shouldn't need it for this," Bolan replied. "Just stand by to bail me out if it comes to that. You're getting pretty good at saving my bacon."

"Don't think I'll let you forget it, Sarge," Grimaldi said.

Bolan shouldered the M4. "All right. I'm going in."

"I'll be here."

Bolan hoofed it from Grimaldi's landing spot. Finding a staging area close enough to the safe house, but far enough away that they could land, insert Bolan and keep the Pave Hawk's presence a secret, had required a bit of tricky navigation. Finally, Grimaldi had settled on a salvage yard within a reasonable hike to the suspected terrorist property. The area was sparsely populated, though not as isolated as the fortified Houston location was supposed to be. Bolan suspected very strongly that before this was over, he would have personal experience of the second site, too.

It paid to be thorough.

Every one of the terrorist rat holes he cleared out, every one of their safe havens he burned to the ground, was one more location denied Hyde and his people. It was a process of elimination. As Bolan tightened the noose around the terrorists' necks, he made it that much harder for them to evade his grip.

He *would* find Hyde and make the terror-master pay. He would bring him in alive.

There was no alternative. Bolan refused to fail. He refused to be defeated.

The storage complex was nearly collapsing in on itself. The soldier reached it after twenty minutes' hike through the rugged terrain, grateful for the concealing darkness. He stopped to scan it through his light-amplifying binoculars, crouched on one knee, surveying the battlefield to come.

The storage units were arrayed in three different blocks, each a row of perhaps twenty garage-size containers. Many of the overhead doors on them were open, and several showed signs of habitation. There were electric lights, furniture and plywood used to form makeshift barriers in lieu of doors. There was plenty of chicken wire, and other barriers, too, including some sections of chain-link fence that had been salvaged from a perimeter fence and used to reinforce the center storage block.

Bolan spotted sentries, too. Hyde's people were on alert, and rightly so. If the leader was there, he would be licking his wounds, reeling from the defeat of his organization's most elaborate operation to date. He would more than likely be expecting retaliation. He knew about the Alamogordo raids, and therefore knew that whatever he thought had kept him off the grid, kept him hidden from authorities, wasn't working so well.

That was good, in that it would keep the terrorists off balance. A nervous man was a man who made mistakes.

Something about that center block of storage units bothered Bolan. He focused his attention on it, adjusting the binoculars, squinting against the monochrome green glow of the light-gathering technology. What was the purpose of the fencing bracing the walls? It didn't look like something that would keep enemies out, which ruled out fortification of some kind. He would have thought the center block the most likely location for the skinheads' armory. It might even have been Hyde's personal quarters, guarded by his faithful minions.

The layout was wrong, though. The fences, the boards over the overhead doors, the oil drums, possibly filled with concrete or other heavy material, used to brace the corners and bolster the perimeter—everything about that block said it was containing something.

He went prone when he saw more movement near the center of the storage compound. It was unlikely he would be spotted, but he dared not silhouette himself against the night sky. It was a fact of night fighting that darkness was never total, no matter how much it seemed so, and the sky was always lighter than the terrain below. Crouching, putting that sky behind the objects in his path, a man could spot what was coming, and thus possessed far greater "night vision" than he might have thought possible. It was a trick sometimes attributed to the mythological ninja of feudal Japan, but the concept dated much further back than that.

The movement resolved itself into a line of skinheads, moving single-file with rifles over their shoulders. They were carrying something among them. It took Bolan a moment to realize it was a chain, and dangling from that chain were heavy manacles.

As he watched, the skinheads rolled several of the drums away, clearing the center entrance to the reinforced storage block. With two terrorists standing guard, assault rifles at the ready, the others entered the structure.

They emerged a while later towing the chain. Connected to it were half a dozen human beings, their ankles manacled, their steps shortened by the bonds restraining them.

Slaves.

It was a chain gang of slaves.

Bolan felt his teeth grate together. The skinheads weren't satisfied to spread their murderous hatred for "inferior" faces. They weren't content merely to plot the deaths of those they considered beneath them. They had actually turned back the clock to a time when people worked in chains under the guns of other men. While it happened all over the world, even to this day, to see it on American soil made Mack Bolan's blood boil.

The slaves were all people of color, all of them male. All of them were limping, as if they'd been ill-used. Judging from the number of hand-built structures on the storage property—plus trenches for latrines, piles of gravel, stacks of wood for the bonfire that crackled near the resident blocks of the compound—it was obvious what they spent their time doing. This was no plantation, however, and there was little enough work for so many men to do. Bolan suspected the real reason the skinheads kept slaves was because it gratified their sick sense of superiority to do so. Sadism was its own reward, to minds mad enough to revel in it.

He scanned the skinheads he could see. None of them was Shane Hyde. The soldier felt no disappointment, however. The injustice he was witnessing was more than sufficient reason to hit this facility, to put down every last rabid monster occupying it.

The skinheads were handing out shovels to the slaves. Halogen lights mounted on the storage buildings provided enough light for them to see, and Bolan avoided the flares of these light sources as he scanned the darker shadows with his binoculars. What could the terrorists possibly be trying to do or build at this hour of the night, working in the dark?

He watched as they led their prisoners under guard to the perimeter of the storage units. Several skinheads marched sullenly from their residence units, most carrying large rechargeable spotlights. Those would be used as portable work lights, Bolan guessed.

The slaves wore rags, most likely the remnants of the clothes they'd had on when imprisoned. If Bolan had to guess, he would say these were probably indigents, homeless people taken because no one would miss them. Those who lived on the fringes of society were often victimized by that society's more violent predators. Such marginalized prey had little recourse and almost no advocacy. They fell through the cracks and ended up here, without so much as a single relative to file a missing person's report on their behalf.

Several dozen yards from the perimeter of the compound, the slaves were ordered to stop and to begin digging. Bolan didn't like where this was going. When each was ordered to carve out a trench six feet long and several feet deep, he knew what was happening.

Graves. The slaves were being made to dig their own graves.

They would do it, too. They walked like zombies, inured to the pain and misery of their circumstances, doing as they were told to avoid the beatings or torture the skinheads no doubt meted out to secure compliance.

Bolan had seen enough. It was time to put a stop to this abominable display.

He flattened himself against the ground, ready to fire the M4 from the prone position. The rifle had a red-dot sight and he lined this up on the first guard, silhouetting him against the night sky exactly as he had prevented himself from being exposed. The skinhead was laughing, smoking a cigarette, joking with the guard nearest him.

How's this for a punch line? Bolan thought, and fired.

The light-recoiling 5.56 mm rounds pummeled his injured hands but did him no great harm. The same wasn't true for the guard in Bolan's sights. The rounds punched through his neck and under his jaw, burrowing out the back under his ear. He dropped immediately, spraying blood, dead before he stopped moving.

It took a moment for the other guards to realize what had happened. Bolan tracked right, settled his optics over the next one, and dumped a 3-round burst into his chest, walking the shots up through his neck and head.

The return fire started. The skinheads were shooting blindly into the night. Bolan's M4 had a flash suppressor, but he didn't kid himself that this made him invisible. He got to his feet and, at a crouch, began to circle the encampment.

He took out the rest of the guards first. They were farther from cover and concealment, more easily picked off, and he needed to make sure they didn't get any ideas about shooting the slaves in order to simplify matters. One of the racists was just turning his gun on his prisoners when Bolan's bullets found him. He joined the other dead terrorists in the dirt, close to the shallow graves in which he had sought to put innocent men.

"Jack," Bolan said quietly. "No sign of Hyde, but I have prisoners here. Slaves of some sort. I need you to call in the cavalry, get me support and medical teams. I've got a fair number of tangos left here."

"Do you need assistance?" Grimaldi returned.

"The day I need help taking down this trash," Bolan said, more angry than ever as he contemplated the near mass murder of the imprisoned civilians, "is the day I'll hang up my guns for good."

In the dark, moving silently among the running, screaming, frantic skinheads, Mack Bolan became a terrible wraith, emerging from the shadows to end life after life, mowing through the hay like a sharp blade through weeds. Soon he had them running for their lives, circling in and out among the storage units, emptying their weapons by shooting at shadows.

He detoured to where the slaves were. They had

stayed near the graves, the chain connecting them making escape nearly impossible. Most of them barely noticed Bolan, but one or two still had bright eyes. The youngest of these called to him.

"Hey, man! Hey! Can you help us out?"

"That's why I'm here," Bolan said. He searched first one dead terrorist, then another. Finally, he found what he presumed were the keys to the manacles. They were roughly the same size and shape as handcuff keys.

"Can you use a gun?" Bolan asked him.

"I served in Afghanistan, man."

"Then here." Bolan plucked an AK from the dirt next to the closest dead guard. "Take this and look after the others. I have backup and medical on the way, but it will take time."

"I got you, man," the veteran said. Bolan gave him a quizzical look, and the younger man shrugged. "Drugs, man. Ended up on the street because of drugs. Then, you know. Picked up by this trash. They worked us hard for no reason. Beat us, too. Just because they could."

"Yeah," Bolan said. "Well, there won't be much left of them by the time I'm through."

"I hear that."

The firefight among the skinheads had taken on a life of its own. They were shooting at one another now, between the storage units and even inside the structures, fighting phantoms. It would be laughable if not for the homeless men who had suffered at these terrorists' hands.

Bolan bent and detached a pair of leg cuffs, using his recovered key. Hefting the chain and the heavy cuffs at either end, he tucked them into his war bag. Then he turned to go.

"Hey, man," the vet said.

"Yeah?"

"Kick some ass for me."

"You got it," Bolan promised.

He reentered the compound. Slinging his M4, he used the suppressed Beretta, shooting and sniping in relative quiet. Due to the din created by the terrorists firing back and forth, they had no idea he was among them until, in each case, it was too late. He left a trail of bodies from one end of the storage units to the other. Finally, he was down to only two or three men. He had lost count of how many were dead; he needed only to remember how many live targets remained.

The last skinheads were nearly apoplectic with fear. They had heard and seen their comrades die in the dark. They knew they were next. They shot out their guns without thinking, without aiming, reloading and firing and reloading again, not realizing that this panic fire was what would doom them.

"I'm empty!" one said finally.

"Me, too," his partner added.

"I've got spare mags," the third said. "Here, lemme—"

Bolan had stalked up right behind the man. He pointed the barrel of the Beretta at the back of the terrorist's shaved head.

"Keep those spares to yourself," he said, and pulled the trigger.

He shifted his point of aim and drilled the next man through the heart. The third tried to run and watch

Bolan at the same time. He succeeded only in colliding with an oil drum. The impact sent him sprawling in the dirt, where the cones of light created by the mounted halogens picked out the fear in his face and the spreading wet stain down one leg.

Bolan holstered the Beretta. "Slaves," he said.

"What?" the skinhead bleated. He tried to prop himself up. Bolan planted a boot in his chest, pushing him back.

"Slaves," Bolan said. "The most horrible thing a man can do to another man—take his freedom, make him work, hurt him if he won't. Wars have been fought to end it. Men have died to escape it. You were keeping slaves here." Bolan withdrew the manacles from his war bag as he said the words.

"Up yours, cop!" the skinhead screamed. The pistol in his waistband was an old, rusted Colt. He never had a chance to draw it.

The end of the manacle caught the terrorist across the jaw, breaking it. He moaned in pain, then abruptly went still.

Bolan knelt and chained the unconscious racist, using the manacles.

"Hardcore, man," said a voice behind him. It was the homeless veteran. The other former slaves stood with him. "You should have beaten that guy to death."

"I could have," Bolan said, "but I'm not like Shane Hyde or the people who follow him."

"Me neither, man," the veteran said. "But if you want to hit him just once more, I'll look the other way."

CHAPTER SIXTEEN

Route 90, Texas

The Crown Victoria sped down Route 90, one of a trio of cars carrying the Twelfth Reich reserve force and the survivors of the OPP train raid. Heavy metal music blasted from the stereo. In the backseat, Shane Hyde stared out the window as the stars became visible. He was thinking dark thoughts. The two men in the front seats—the last of his lieutenants, Carter, and a street soldier named McGloon—were afraid to speak, so no one talked. That suited him.

His body was a roadmap of aches and pains and wounds, none of them immediately life-threatening, but some requiring care. He would need stitches for the worst of the cuts, he knew. His only option was to have Lerner, who had trained as a male nurse, stitch him up when he reached Houston. Checking himself into a hospital or a twenty-four-hour urgent care facility would be no better than walking into a police station and announcing his identity.

Even if he wasn't immediately recognized—he was not certain what media coverage of the train might have revealed, or whether he had been identified as the leader—Hyde's body showed obvious evidence of violence. The medics would report it, and when the police came to follow up, they might know he was wanted, that he was at large and dangerous. There was too much risk. His wounds would have to wait.

The pain he could stand. The scars he could wear.

The shame, he couldn't endure.

Swept away. All of it. The culmination of a life's work. Money. Connections. Favors. The lion's share of his manpower, though there were plenty of his soldiers still stationed at the Dallas and Houston safe houses.

The plan had worked save for the detonation. He had watched on the news in a dingy truck stop near Fort Worth. The government forces had managed to stop the train within the tank field, somehow preventing the explosion that would have touched off Hyde's revolution of race. He didn't understand how that was possible.

He had met up with Carter and McGloon at the preset coordinates, using the GPS application on his cell phone to lead him to precisely the right spot. The plan had been to retreat a safe distance, sit back and watch the fireworks start. Instead, he got to listen to smug, empty-headed news anchors and on-site reporters spewing forth about the heroic efforts to save an army of illegal alien squatters.

It turned Hyde's stomach.

He tried to remind himself that great men, even the leader himself, had faced setbacks. The voices in his head agreed. Robert, the dead man from the train, seemed always to be about, somewhere, and there were others. Hyde didn't usually pay them much mind, but he appreciated their support now. Nice as it might be to focus on their fawning compliments, he had to remind himself that there was work to be done. He couldn't afford to act defeated, to seem defeated. He had to maintain the position of strength that enabled him to lead.

Weakness was death.

From the truck stop, he had placed a call to the Dallas compound, instructing them to make preparations to break camp and consolidate outside Houston. He estimated he had perhaps ten percent of the manpower Twelfth Reich had once boasted, and while that was no small number of street soldiers and enforcers, it wasn't enough to maintain multiple sites as he had before the train raid. He had been extremely disappointed to see just how few of his people from the train had managed to escape. He had thought perhaps the numbers recovered would be greater.

He still didn't understand how it could be possible for the bombs to fail. He had hand-selected the fighters to leave behind, including his chosen suicide bomber, a willing volunteer. Among Twelfth Reich the man's given name had ceased to matter; he was known only as Berserker, and it was on Berserker that Hyde had pinned his hopes. He had been equipped with a dead man's switch and enough explosives to start the chain reaction, not to mention obliterate the OPP locomotive itself. How was it that he hadn't completed his mission? Was it hidden cowardice? Equipment failure? Some other factor?

The presence of the traitor, Russell Troy, had at first amused Hyde. Clearly, Troy had suffered at his hands. Hyde wasn't unsympathetic to the man's mental break, nor had he been lying when he allowed that the disgraced agent might, in fact, still find a place within the

Reich. Troy had fought amazingly well, even if he had collapsed at the end.

But the resistance Hyde had encountered on the train had been more than Troy, and whatever malcontents such an agent could assemble, should produce. The big bastard, the one in black that Troy had mentioned... Who was he? Obviously he was some sort of government agent. Hyde supposed it didn't truly matter which.

Between Troy and the official counterterror response, then, Twelfth Reich had been dealt a serious blow. It was time to regroup, to consolidate, to pool their resources and maximize their strength. They would make themselves the hardest target possible, so that if anyone *did* find them, they could fight back effectively.

The idea of being found also bothered Hyde. He had been very careful about the paper trail, real and electronic, that led back to the resources of Twelfth Reich. If someone was capable of penetrating that, it meant none of what he thought was hidden truly was. The Houston safe house, the Dallas compound...anything left to Shane Hyde might be compromised.

All the more reason to draw in and prepare for war. If they had to fight their way out again, at least they would be free to do so, able to continue the battle another day.

The struggle. His struggle. It was all there was. It had to go on. Hyde wouldn't rest until the danger posed to white Americans was eliminated.

"Leader," Carter said tentatively from the front seat, turning down the volume on the radio. "There is a problem."

"What problem?" Hyde asked suspiciously. He was forever vigilant for power plays among his men. It was one of the reasons he was so selective in choosing his lieutenants. Should one of them decide his leadership was insufficient to the cause, his life would be forfeit, and he couldn't have that. On two different occasions he had put down, violently and permanently, challenges to his authority. After so great a failure as the aborted train mission, he wouldn't be shocked if some of the men under him questioned his abilities.

"There's someone following us, sir," Carter said. "Two cars. Trucks, actually."

"Black SUVs?" Hyde asked. He turned, staring out the rear window of the Crown Victoria. At first, in the traffic, and at a distance, he didn't see them. Then he recognized the headlight configuration. They were the same model as those that had been part of the counterattacks on the train. He couldn't be sure of the color, not at night, but in the reflections from other vehicles' headlights, he thought they were the trucks he remembered.

"So," Hyde said. "They've found us." Bothersome as that was, potentially dangerous as it was to them, he couldn't help but feel blessed. Robert's voice in his head echoed the sentiment. "Thanks, Bob," he said.

"Sir?" Carter asked.

"Nothing," Hyde said. "Speed up. We must find a suitable location."

"Leader," McGloon said. "I wonder if I might say something, sir."

His skinheads were street trash, but they had learned how to address him, how to speak to him formally. That pleased Shane Hyde. It was a sign of things to come, once he was established as the man in charge of the new order. Just the thought of that power, and the respect in McGloon's voice despite the failure at the train, was enough to shore up his confidence.

"Yes?" Hyde said. "What is it?"

"Sir, I want you to know that we understand the difficulty you face. The hard battles you fight every day. We are with you, sir."

"We would never challenge your authority, Leader," Carter interjected. "Others have tried and failed. Yours is the strength that binds us together."

"Yes," Hyde said. "Yes, it is."

"Sir?" Carter asked.

"I said, mine is indeed the strength that binds us," Hyde said.

"Uh…" Carter nodded. "Right, sir."

Something about the confused look on the lieutenant's face prompted Hyde to examine the conversation in his mind. Carter had alerted him to the vehicle following. Then McGloon had said…had said…

Had he?

Hyde wasn't sure now. He thought he remembered McGloon's glowing words of support, but the fact was, neither Carter nor McGloon had ever been nearly so poetic or earnest with their words.

Could he have imagined it?

That didn't seem like him.

"That doesn't seem like you," said the voice of Bob, the dead rail worker.

"No, it doesn't," Hyde said aloud.

"Sir?" Carter asked again.

"Nothing," Hyde said. He shook his head quickly. "I didn't say anything."

How odd. His voices had never betrayed him before. Perhaps McGloon and Carter were self-conscious, nervous in the presence of greatness. Perhaps that was why they acted as if they hadn't said such nice things about him.

"That must be it," said Bob the corpse.

"That must be it," Hyde repeated. Carter and Mc-Gloon exchanged glances.

"There's a rest area ahead," McGloon said, pointing to a road sign.

"Yes," Hyde said. "That will do. But go faster. We must gain enough of a head start to set our trap. I'll tell car three to continue on. Car two will accompany us." He used his prepaid wireless phone to call the men in the other vehicles, apprising them of his intent. The other skinheads were only too eager to strike back at their hated foes, whoever they might be.

Nearing the rest area, the last of the cars sped on, while the first two pulled off. On Hyde's orders, the drivers made sure to park with the back ends of their Crown Victorias out, near the small building that housed restrooms. This would make it seem they were unconcerned about pursuit, and had just stopped for a break.

"Your knives," Hyde said to Carter and McGloon. "Make sure we aren't seen. The cars first, then the restrooms."

The two men crept into the darkness. There were a few other cars parked here. The two enforcers would cut the throats of whoever might be in them, then make short work of anyone in the building. The hour was late enough that there shouldn't be too many, which meant they could get the job done quickly.

Hyde went to the trunk of his Crown Victoria and

signaled the trio in the second one to do the same. Each vehicle was fully loaded with weapons and ammunition. Removing a folding-stock Kalashnikov from the trunk, Hyde moved along the car and crouched near the engine block, where the cover afforded was greatest. He braced the assault rifle on the warm hood.

"They're coming," he whispered. From the car next to him, his men hissed an acknowledgment. "Wait for them to leave the trucks," Hyde added.

The two SUVs were indeed black. They were fully visible now under the streetlights illuminating the rest area. Hyde couldn't see the men inside, but he knew what had to have happened. The forces from the train, be they official government or Troy's people, had followed him. They hadn't given up on the idea of capturing him or bringing him down.

"Get ready," he said. "As soon as they leave their trucks, strike them."

The nearer of the black SUVs slowed to a crawl. It turned, as if it would park next to the two Ford Crown Victorias. Hyde snapped the selector switch on his Kalashnikov to full-auto.

The truck accelerated.

They had seen him, or they knew a trap when they saw one. The black truck came rocketing forward, and Hyde was forced to duck behind the neighboring vehicle as the SUV crashed into his with an explosion of paint flakes and screeching metal. Rapid gunfire poured from the windows, striking one of Hyde's soldiers in the head, splitting his crown.

Hyde threw himself over the trunk of the second Crown Victoria, rolling to the pavement on the other side. Only a few bullets touched the vehicle; it was the first that took most of the onslaught. Bullet holes collected in the Ford, puncturing it again and again, flattening the tires, shattering the windows. Its horn began to sound as the hood popped open.

The rear SUV began to back up in an arc, searching for a better angle of fire on Hyde and his men. Hyde aimed his Kalashnikov from the hip, spraying 7.62 mm soft-nosed bullets across the flank, the hood, through the windshield. In the harsh lights of the rest stop he saw blood splatter the interior of the truck's window. The front tires went flat.

He emptied his magazine, dropped it free and slapped home another one. His rear pockets were full of loaded 30- and 40-rounders. These goons might take him, but it wouldn't be for lack of firepower on his part.

The first Crown Victoria was a ruined mess now. Gunfire continued to erupt as each of the fighters sought to dominate. Hyde, who knew something about combat with an assault rifle, began to move around the rear of the SUVs. Shoot-outs often induced paralysis in the combatants. The man who stayed most mobile was most frequently the winner.

One of the passenger doors of the SUV Hyde stood behind began to open. He shoved the barrel of his AK into the man's stomach and pulled the trigger, blowing his guts all over the figure behind him. He kept the trigger back until he had hosed the interior of the truck, satisfied that all within had to be dead. He would never see the faces of the people whose lives he had just ended. He preferred it that way. He needed no more voices to trail him.

With nowhere else to go, he ran for the restrooms. The door yielded to his urgent shoulder, swinging back and forth on rusted hinges. Inside, there were several bodies on the floor. One was an old man; another was a woman, possibly his wife. There was a younger couple lying dead near the rack of tourist brochures. Pools of blood welled from the wounds cut in the victims' throats.

Hyde ignored his men's handiwork. He also ignored the men's bathroom, which was accessed through the front of the building. The women's bathroom had an entrance on the opposite side. He made for it, passing two dead women sprawled in the stalls.

He could hear the gunfire from the battle still raging outside. It was a stalemate, for the moment. Both forces were entrenched; both forces were, thanks to Hyde's assassination of the men in the second truck, roughly equal, or so he assumed.

The rear exit accessed a smaller parking lot. He worked his way around one of the cars sitting here and tried the door; it was open. The car was a late-model Lexus, comfortable and luxurious. Strange that it hadn't been locked. Some people were far too trusting.

"Mmm," said a woman's voice. "Are those firecrackers?"

He looked up in the rearview mirror. The middle-age woman had been asleep in the backseat. Clearly, her husband was inside the rest stop, or she thought he was. Probably he was dead in the men's bathroom.

When she realized Shane Hyde wasn't her husband, she opened her mouth to scream.

He threw himself between the front seats, into the

back, on top of her. It felt good to have a woman wrestling to free herself from beneath him again. He punched her, lightly at first, and then with all his strength when she wouldn't be subdued.

"Get off me!" she screamed. "Get off me!"

He punched her again. Suddenly, his face was on fire and he couldn't breathe. She had hit him with pepper spray.

He clawed for the door handle, spilling out onto the asphalt of the parking lot. He nearly lost his AK. It skittered across the pavement.

"You bitch," he snarled. "I'll send you to hell along with—"

She was pointing a gun at him.

She had a small automatic pistol, of the type that citizens carried concealed, a little pocket model with a metal clip intended for stowing the gun on the body without a holster. He didn't know where she'd had it, but it had to have been on her somewhere. She screamed again and began shooting, popping off rounds that sounded anemic compared to the gunfight at the front of the building.

He scrambled out of range, scooping up the AK as he did so. Once closer to the restroom door he sprayed a long, low burst from the Kalashnikov that punched holes in the Lexus's hood and shattered its windshield into safety pebbles. The woman inside, so quick with her pepper spray and with her gun, screamed one last time and then was silent.

That would show her.

How *dare* she?

He marched back through the building, raging.

Didn't these whites understand he was trying to *help* them? Didn't they have any grasp of the cause? The Jew-run government, the thugs in the police, the men who fought for the rights of inferior races to bully and enslave white men, white women, white children...*they* were the enemy. It wasn't Hyde and his freedom fighters!

Staying low, he worked his way back around to the second Crown Victoria. Bullets raked the air above him. The firefight would draw local law enforcement, if nothing else. He couldn't afford to stay here, didn't dare get caught and end up in some county jail. If he did, they would eventually figure out who he was. Once processed by the American "justice" system, he would never escape it.

He had no choice.

"Leader!" Carter called from his position by the bullet-pocked Ford. "Where are you going?"

"Keep up the fight, my brave white warriors!" Hyde shouted. The words rang contrived and false even to him. He threw himself into the second vehicle, fired its engine and roared out of the rest stop.

The absence of the second car gave one of the attackers the shot he had been trying to line up. McGloon was riddled with bullets, taking shots in the head, the neck and the chest. He sprawled on the pavement.

He would be remembered as a hero. Hyde would see to it that all the men and women martyred this day would be remembered, with respect and pride. He would call on his people to create a fitting memorial to them.

Once he was safe, of course.

He looked at his watch. He needed to get to Houston, and fast. Palming his phone, he dialed the number for the Dallas compound. It rang, and rang, and rang.

Finally, someone picked up.

"Hello?"

"It's me," Hyde said. "Rhenquist? Is that you?"

"No," the voice replied. "It's not Rhenquist."

"Then who is it, damn you? I've just left behind me martyrs to our cause, fighting for their lives against the oppressors of the Zionist Occupation Government! Would you spit on their memories? Identify yourself!"

"My name is Agent Damon Harris," the voice said. "I'm an employee of the…well, the Zionist Occupation Government, I guess. This phone was in the pocket of a dead man. Is this Shane Hyde?"

"Damn you!" Hyde shrieked. He cut the connection. The phone rang several times, every few minutes, driving him insane. Finally, he picked it up to talk again and realized they could track him through the phone. The prepaid wireless was untraceable as long as no identity was associated with it…but an operative of the government had just identified him by that number.

As if the device were on fire, Hyde pitched the phone out the open window, into the night.

He pressed his foot to the floor. The Ford sped on.

He had to get away.

CHAPTER SEVENTEEN

"We have a team on-site, Striker." Barbara Price's voice was surprisingly clear through Bolan's transceiver. "The prisoners are being treated, and we'll make every effort to place them with their families or get them further assistance."

"That's good, Barb." Bolan nodded.

"There's more," Price said. "One of the blacksuits just took a call. The team leader on-site, a Damon Harris. He said the man on the other end sounded suspiciously like Shane Hyde."

"Tell me you got a trace."

"We did," Price said, "although the signal is now stationary on Highway 90, which means Hyde probably wised up and dumped the phone. There's been a report of gunfire at a travel rest stop in that vicinity. I'm sending Jack the coordinates now. You'll want to check it out, I assume."

"You assume correctly."

"I wouldn't expect to find Hyde there," Price cautioned.

"No," Bolan said. "But I want to follow up every lead. My bet is that Hyde will go to his fortified Houston location, if he's not there already."

"He may assume we know about it," Price suggested. "He might go somewhere else entirely."

"No," Bolan said. "I don't think so. I know the type. Hyde's an animal, and now he's a wounded animal, psychologically if not physically. We've hurt him. We've bloodied him. He'll be looking for something familiar, somewhere he feels safe. He'll go to ground at a familiar location, where he believes the precautions he has taken will enable him to fight his way back out should anyone attempt to beard him in his lair."

"It's your call," Price said.

"I've got it," Grimaldi announced from the cockpit, interrupting them. "Diverting now. ETA, uh, really, really soon. We're close."

"Understood," Bolan said. For Price's benefit, he added, "I've got to go to work."

"All right, Striker. Over and out."

Bolan cut the connection, then stuck his head forward to look over Grimaldi's shoulder. "Are we coming up on it?"

"We are," the pilot said. "There!" He pointed. "That was a muzzle-flash. There's another."

"That back lot," Bolan said. "Put me down there, with the building between you and the fight. I'll go in on foot."

"Roger," Grimaldi said.

Bolan jumped out of the chopper with his borrowed M4 in his gloved fists. He yanked the plunger back to chamber the first round, shouldered the weapon and moved forward in a half crouch, ready to acquire and terminate targets of opportunity. The movements, the strategy and tactics behind them, were as natural to Mack Bolan as breathing. He hardly had to think about them.

The Lexus with the shot-out windshield caught his attention first. He approached, weapon ready, and saw the dead woman in the backseat. Surprisingly, she held a pistol in her hand. The fight, for this armed citizen, was over, but Bolan gave the handsome woman credit for going out fighting. Her murder was a waste, an atrocity.

He continued on and entered through the rear of the restroom building. It was a fatal funnel and he took the door carefully, mindful of traps and ambushes. The scene within appalled him; there were dead civilians all over. Their throats were cut, their eyes and mouths open in expressions of pain and horror.

Bolan added the death toll to the tally of wrongs for which Shane Hyde would answer.

The rattle of gunfire from the front of the rest area was diminishing. He came through the doorway at the opposite side of the building, staying low, and immediately drew fire from the men near a crippled Ford Crown Victoria. Bolan skirted their position, only to take fire from someone using a pair of black SUVs as cover.

The vehicle looked very familiar.

It was Troy! He and his men had somehow tailed Hyde and engaged his people here. It was the only explanation.

Bullets ripped the building near Bolan. He braced himself and returned fire.

"Justice Department!" he called out. "Lay down your weapons!"

More bullets struck the facade behind him. He fired again.

"I'm pinned, Jack," Bolan said into his transceiver. "It's ugly out here."

"The Farm is having the locals shut down exits at either side of the rest-stop stretch," Grimaldi reported. "That'll keep the passing civvy traffic down. You want Death from Above?"

"No," Bolan said. "It's nothing I can't handle."

"I figured."

The soldier analyzed the tactical scenario before him. He couldn't go left or right. There was no high ground to seek. The combatants had one another effectively locked in a stalemate, each one awaiting an act of fate or the hand of God to change some factor that could give them the advantage.

Bolan was neither fate nor God, but he had a knack for changing combat variables.

He couldn't go left or right, and he couldn't go up, but he could change his altitude negatively.

The soldier lay flat on the pavement before the restroom structure. He pushed his M4 to full extension and aimed sideways, so the ejection port faced up. Beneath the Crown Victoria he could see the feet of two skinheads still mobile.

He picked one and blew off his foot.

The skinhead screamed and hopped from behind the car, his foot trailing chunks of flesh and bone. Immediately, a burst of fire from one of the SUVs cut him down. The second skinhead stood and ran, going straight for the trucks, unloading his Kalashnikov into the windshield. He turned and fired backward, too, hoping to keep Bolan's head down while he made his break.

His fire came nowhere near the soldier.

Bolan calmly shot the running skinhead through the back of the head, before the murderer could find any more innocent victims to claim.

The Executioner waited.

The night was suddenly quiet. He thought he heard, very distantly, police sirens, but that might have been his imagination. He was so accustomed to law enforcement materializing after his firefights that he could easily be anticipating the familiar sound.

"Jack," he said.

"G-Force here."

"I've got dead civilians all over the place. Hyde and his monsters have been killing bystanders like there's no tomorrow."

"I understand," Grimaldi said. His tone was sober. "I'll have the Farm send another team."

"Make sure they realize just how bad it is," Bolan said. "I can't afford to get jammed up and detained by the locals before they sort things out."

"We could lift off," Grimaldi said. "Get out of Dodge before things get hairy."

"I need to check the opposition first," Bolan said. "Something's funny here."

"Ready when you are."

Bolan reloaded his carbine and, using his combat light, swept the area around and behind the Crown Victoria. When he was satisfied that no more skinhead gunners were lying in wait, he moved on to the two bullet-pocked SUVs.

The interior of both trucks was a mess. The two forces had managed to wipe each other out thoroughly.

Bolan put two fingers to the neck of the man in the driver's seat and was able to feel a weak pulse.

His eyes fluttered open.

"Who...who are you?" the man asked. He was dressed in combat webbing bearing no logos or insignia. He had no weapons. The pistol on the seat next to him was empty, its slide locked back. Broken glass and blood covered the seats, his pants and his combat gear.

"Matt Cooper," Bolan said. "Justice Department. Who are you?"

"My name is...Powell. Aden Powell."

Bolan examined his wounds. "I won't lie to you, Powell," he said. "It's bad."

"I know," the man replied. "I'm never leaving this truck, am I?"

"No," Bolan said.

"I...I didn't want to die in a rest stop in Texas," Powell confessed.

"I'm looking for Russell Troy and Shane Hyde," Bolan said.

"Hyde...was here," the wounded man replied. "He lit out when we engaged. Abandoned his people."

"And Troy?"

"He was in the other truck. I thought he was... I thought... I don't know."

"What's your story, Powell?" Bolan asked. "You don't have much time. Tell me what's going on."

"Troy," Powell said. "He was...he was the glue that held us together. A network of former agents. Disillusioned. Screwed over. Some of us lost family. Some of us just got eaten up by the job, by the hours. When Troy told us his story, we wanted to help. It didn't seem...it didn't seem that hard. Take direct action. Finally shoot down some of the bastards. Take them out. You can understand that, right? The need to…to finally put an end to people like Shane Hyde?"

"Yeah," Bolan said. "I can understand that."

"We didn't see it at first," Powell said. "We didn't know. We saw only what we shared with Russ. His pain. His need for…for payback. You know?"

"I know," Bolan said. "Very well."

"He's sick," Powell stated. "I started to see it when we hit the train. It wasn't…wasn't really *real,* what he wanted to do. Blow up all those people to board the train. He made it sound so simple. Like when they shoot down a hijacked jet to prevent terrorists from crashing it into a building. Like that. They were dead already, he said. Sacrificed. We were just going to give them a fast death."

"When you start sacrificing innocents," Bolan said, "there's no telling where the slope ends. It'll take you farther down than you'd ever dream of going."

"Yeah," Powell said. He coughed weakly. "I just…I know what I did was wrong. But please… Somebody's gotta know…I thought it was the right thing. I really did. I just…" He started coughing again.

"Easy," Bolan said. "What can you tell me about Troy's operation? How did he know about the safe house in Alamogordo? How did he know about the train operation?"

"Troy's connected," Powell said. "He's got people in the Bureau…and at Homeland Security. I was Bureau once myself. I know the guy."

"I need a name."

"Buster Wong," Powell said softly. "His name is Buster Wong. He's highly placed with Intelligence. We needed him to feed us what the government knew."

"And the DHS link?"

"I don't know," Powell said. "I'm sorry. Russ would never share that."

"What happened to you?" Bolan said. "Why did you do it? Why throw in with Troy?"

"My son," Powell said. "He got mixed up with a neo-Nazi group. Not Hyde's, but…no different. It ate him up. He started repeating their propaganda, skipping school, getting in trouble. Then the drugs and the booze. I'll never know why he finally did it. He didn't leave a note. But he killed himself. My son, dressed up like some little Hitler Youth asshole. It's my fault. His mother died having him. I was…all he had…and the job took all of my time."

"Powell," Bolan said. "I need you to concentrate for me. You're going. Do you understand that? You're leaving. You've got to focus while there's time."

"I…can do that…." Powell said.

"Did you see what happened to Russell Troy?"

"He…got out," Powell said. "Took one of the…one of the cars. One of the civilian cars. Went after Hyde."

"How long?"

"Fifteen…fifteen, maybe twenty minutes after Hyde."

"All right," Bolan said. "That's what I needed."

"I was wrong," Powell said sadly. "I'm so sorry. I just wanted…I just wanted justice for my son. You can understand that, can't you? Can't…you…"

Powell's eyes stared into nothing. He was gone.

Bolan looked at the dead man for a long time, thinking about his own family, victims to predators like Shane Hyde. Justice would be served. The Executioner would see to that.

He took out his secure satellite phone and dialed the scrambled feed for the Farm. When Price acknowledged his call, he said, "Barb. Give me Hal. Right away." When Hal Brognola picked up the line, Bolan didn't greet him.

"If Shane Hyde dies," the soldier said, "what happens?"

Brognola, doubtless caught flat-footed by the abrupt question, did not respond immediately. "Striker," he said. "I don't understand."

"You said we need Shane Hyde alive," Bolan said. "That we need the information he holds in his head. But what if we don't get it? What happens?"

"If we can't debrief Hyde," Brognola said carefully, "then we lose a possible toehold on several domestic and foreign terror groups. That puts us at a disadvantage."

"We don't know what Hyde knows," Bolan said. "Not for sure."

"No," Brognola said, "we don't. But we have reason to believe the intelligence he can offer justifies the difficulty of bringing him in alive."

"And if he doesn't come in alive?" Bolan said. "If he dies before he gets there?"

"Then I guess we just continue on the best we can. Striker," Brognola said, "what's going on?"

"Shane Hyde deserves to die, Hal," Bolan said. "He doesn't deserve to draw breath on this planet. Every moment he's alive, every second he exists, is an insult to every single human being who has suffered and died to try to bring him down. They're good people, Hal, and they don't deserve that insult. They don't deserve this mockery."

"I don't disagree, Striker," Brognola said. "You know as well as I do that there are exigencies that force us to do what we don't want to do. To take the more difficult road."

"Yeah," Bolan said. "Yeah. I get that. I understand that."

"Striker, are you all right?"

The soldier thought about that for a moment. "Yeah," he said. "I'm all right. I'm just in a very bad mood, Hal. Out."

"Striker—"

Bolan cut the connection.

He walked slowly to the chopper, thinking about killing Shane Hyde.

CHAPTER EIGHTEEN

Russell Troy wiped sweat from his eyes.

He was suffering from fatigue and blood loss. Intellectually, he understood that and could analyze the symptoms of it. Emotionally and physically, he didn't feel it. He felt, in fact, as though he were skimming across the surface of his body, traveling outside himself, carried along for one last wonderful ride.

Everything made sense now.

Everything fit.

It had been so hard, trying to keep all those feelings contained. Standing in that compartment, grappling with and then failing to kill the man responsible for everything that had happened to him, had helped Russell Troy finally accept who was truly to blame.

He was.

His family was dead because he had been too selfish, too involved in his work to draw a line and get out while his soul was still his. He had sold himself to the Bureau in the name of some abstract concept of justice.

There were those who might think what he had paid—the cost for his crime against his family—was the greatest toll a man could pay. He had lost everything he valued, and in losing it, he had known the much worse pain that came with realizing he had taken his wife and daughter for granted.

He had failed to appreciate them, to love them, to cherish them, while they were his…and now they would never be his again.

He would never have a family again.

He would never know peace. He would never feel satisfaction. He would never be happy. He would never have purpose.

This realization, as bleak as it was, had freed him. He had fought it for so long, believing, however deeply buried in his fevered brain, that he could fight his way back to "normal" if only he tried hard enough.

Now he knew that was ridiculous.

There was no normal for a man who had murdered his family. That was what Russell Troy was. He was a murderer who had taken the lives of his loved ones, had tortured them as surely as had Shane Hyde and his racist excrement. Troy had spent so much time, in fact, blaming Shane Hyde and formulating his elaborate plan for revenge, that he had completely refused to accept his own responsibility.

Fighting that understanding, that knowledge, was what had buried his memories so deeply. He had been too weak, too cowardly to face it, and so he had built walls of defense around that awful understanding in his mind. That was all gone now. That was finished.

Chasing Shane Hyde atop the stolen dirt bike, he had begun to frame that new knowledge, to taste it, to roll it over and over from his brain to the pit of his stomach and back again. The hallucinations had stopped. The memory lapses were gone. When he used his walkie-talkie to call the rest of his forces, to regroup with those who had survived the disastrous raid on the train, he was still in pursuit of Shane Hyde and completely at one with his ultimate fate.

His foolishness had been in ever believing he hadn't died with his family.

He had. He had died when they did. The moment their suffering was recorded, the second those images touched his retinas, his soul had left his body. He was the walking dead now, an animated corpse. Small wonder, then, that when they had taken his fingers and left him for dead, they hadn't managed to kill him. You couldn't take life from someone who no longer had a life to take.

He saw his wife and daughter now. They were waiting for him. He hoped they would forgive him. He thought perhaps that his final, decisive actions might redeem him in their eyes.

Troy hoped so.

It was so wonderfully crystal clear.

He had to die.

That was all there was to it. In order to fix everything, to rejoin his family, to correct what had been incorrect until now, he had to end his life. There was no more logical way to do that than to murder Shane Hyde, putting the racist terrorist out of everyone else's misery once and for all. With Hyde dead and suffering eternal torment in whatever afterlife awaited skinhead offal, Troy could finally put the barrel of his gun under his chin and send himself home—provided he didn't die before then.

He felt so relieved.

The pursuit, until the rest stop, had been easy. When Hyde had rendezvoused with the men in the Crown Victorias, Troy and his reassembled team had hung back, waiting out the transition. Their plan was to follow Hyde all the way to whatever nest the skinhead leader sought to hide in. Once they had found that, Troy and his people could bring the fight to Hyde, killing all the terrorists. That would end the affair. That would be the signal for Troy to take his life.

But something had gone wrong. They had been too obvious in their tail, or some other mistake, something he couldn't identify, had exposed them. Hyde had set a trap and, realizing that, Troy had tried to bust that trap with an aggressive and direct approach.

The skinheads were largely untrained and undisciplined, but their ferocity in combat had ultimately given them the advantage. Hyde's presence may have had something to do with it, too, although the skinhead leader had seemed more concerned with saving himself than he did with coordinating the attack.

As if to prove Troy right, fate had denied him a death at Hyde's hands. So Troy had stolen a car and continued on.

He was too far behind, however. He had lost his chance to tail Hyde, and without that link, he didn't know where he was going. He had simply stayed on the highway, driving as fast as he dared, hoping to see some sign, some example of divine providence. He had no other options. He was confident, though. The universe, if it wanted to see him die, to heal the rift between his soul and his body, would have to give him something he could use.

And then it did.

The roadside truck stop could have been any one of

a hundred others just like it. The trucks and the cars, the customers, the food offered, the almost subliminal country Muzak playing from overhead speakers. What this roadside stop had that none of the others offered, however, was a white Ford Crown Victoria parked directly under one of the lot lights.

He had hoped, initially, that it would be Hyde himself, that his search would be over almost before it had begun. When Troy pulled up and got out to examine the car, however, he knew it had to be the third vehicle, the one that had gone on ahead. It had no bullet holes in it, none at all, but there was a baseball cap on the backseat on which a lightning bolt SS symbol had been drawn in permanent marker.

Troy needed some time to think through his options. He took a long walk around the parking lot. Each time he passed the white sedan he paused to examine the hat through the window. Yes, that was a neo-Nazi symbol. No, he wasn't wrong. He wasn't mistaken.

Finally, he decided that, even if he were to make a mistake, the worst thing he'd be doing was committing an act of vandalism.

There was a large, heavy chunk of asphalt broken free from the parking lot, lying near the base of the light pole. He picked it up, looked left and right, checking for bystanders, then smashed out the passenger-side window.

Once inside, he found the trunk release and pressed it. He also rifled through the glove compartment and searched under the seat.

He found a folding-stock Kalashnikov and loaded magazines for it, as well as a duffel bag in which to put them, so he stowed everything. There was a large hunting knife, too, which he took. He wasn't entirely certain what had become of his .40-caliber Glock or his MP5, but that no longer made any difference. That was behind him. The way forward was clear.

The glove compartment proved to be the most providential of the places he searched. It contained a stack of road maps and a set of computer-printed directions containing hand-drawn notes—all pointing to a location outside Houston. If he had any doubts about the property's purpose, the words *SAFE HOUSE,* scrawled in childlike block letters, dispelled them.

That had to be it. The route the skinheads were traveling took them in that direction. It was the most likely destination, given everything he knew.

Also, Troy had no other prospects.

He hated to admit that, for it seemed terribly pragmatic. The old saying came to his mind: when the only tool you have is a hammer, every problem looks like a nail. Well, he had only one tool and only one nail. If it wasn't this, then he had no clues, and he'd be back where he'd started.

He refused to accept such a notion.

That left only one question: Leave immediately, or make a clean sweep of Hyde's gang members to the best of his ability? That seemed like no choice at all. His new revelation, his newfound knowledge of his purpose, precluded anything but eliminating the skinhead trash wherever he found them.

Troy transferred the bag with the Kalashnikov to his stolen car, taking only the hunting knife, which he tucked into his waistband, under his BDU blouse. With-

out his combat gear, his dusty, torn and bloody clothing
didn't exactly make him inconspicuous, but in the dead
of night at an all-night truck stop, he likely wouldn't
be noticed. He pulled the hems of his pants outside his
boots, hoping he looked simply like a slovenly driver
whose clothes were a few days overdue for a wash.

The interior of the truck stop was just dirty enough,
just quiet enough and just busy enough that he escaped
scrutiny. Working his way to a booth in the back, he ordered coffee from the bored waitress, who never once
made eye contact with him. Sipping the coffee, which
had sat on the burner for far too long, he had a perfect
spot to watch the two skinheads in the booth across
the room.

They were slouched where they sat as if they didn't
have a care in the world, drinking coffee and picking
at the remains of burgers and fries. He had scarcely
brought his chipped mug of coffee to his lips a second
time when one of them got up and made for the restroom in back. His buddy was faced away from Troy,
engrossed in a news program on the television mounted
to the wall in the corner. The report was of the "run-
away" O'Connor Petroleum train.

It was another sign. Troy got up quickly and quietly,
circling the dining area and moving to the restrooms
from the opposite side, where the skinhead still seated
wouldn't see him.

Troy didn't hurry. He simply crossed the dining
room. He felt as if he were walking on a glass ceiling,
beneath which the people of the truck stop went about
their lives oblivious to his presence.

A deep sadness grew within him. It was sudden,

overwhelming, almost painful. But it was also *clean*. It wasn't tainted, as his grief had been before now. It wasn't burdened with the corruption that was his guilt, his evasion of his responsibility for the terrible things that had happened to him, to his beloved wife, to his beautiful little girl.

The weight of it descended on him like a leaden cloak, familiar and warm, comfortable despite its gravity. He embraced it, let it come. Tears streamed down his face, without sound, without racking sobs. His grief poured out of him in one incredible burst, bleeding him of his sorrow, lightening his load.

Yes, his family was gone.

Yes, it was his fault.

Like a fugitive from justice who decided to turn himself in, Russell Troy no longer knew fear. There was nothing left he could lose. There was no reason he should flee, no purpose to his life but to die in completing the last tasks before him.

Feeling not the slightest bit of apprehension, he pushed the restroom door slowly and silently open.

The bathroom stank of old urine. The walls were grimy, the mirror cracked and clouded. Whistling tunelessly, the skinhead stood at the urinal, one hand braced against the wall above the fixture.

There were two urinals. The other one was shrouded in a plastic trash bag and bore a hand-lettered sign in blue marker: Out of Order. Troy came up behind the skinhead, easing the big, clip-point hunting knife out of its leather scabbard. The rosewood handle was warm in his good hand.

"Hold your fucking horses already," the skinhead complained. "I'll be done in a minute."

"Yes," Troy said. "You will."

He grabbed the skinhead by the throat and rammed the hunting knife into the man's kidney from behind.

The neo-Nazi punk crashed forward into the urinal, slamming his head against the porcelain. He tried to grab hold of something as Troy dragged him back, but succeeded only in flushing the urinal as the rogue FBI agent dragged him down. On the floor, with Troy on top of his hip, he made the strangest squealing noises Troy had ever heard.

The hunting knife went in and out, in and out. Unsure of himself but determined to do the job thoroughly, Troy stabbed the skinhead repeatedly, then brought the heavy blade to the man's neck. He dug the remaining fingers of his mutilated hand into the skinhead's eye sockets, peeling the head back, listening with an almost awful detachment to the hideous noises the terrorist made. When he pushed the blade in through the side of the man's neck and then rammed it forward, the dirty tiles beneath them were abruptly, hotly, thickly red.

The skinhead whimpered and gagged, making bubbles through the gaping wound in his throat.

"I want you to know," Troy said, "that I hope you die suffering. I only wish it would take longer."

He stood and cranked the dented paper-towel holder. With the sheets it dispensed, he wiped the hunting knife clean. Then he did his best to clean his blood-soaked hands.

He was still washing his hands when a short, bald

trucker entered the bathroom. Troy didn't turn; he simply looked up at the mirror before him.

"The urinal on the left is out of order," he said helpfully.

The sleepy-eyed trucker looked down at the blood on the floor, then back up to Troy. He took in the pink water in the basin and the knife sheathed in Troy's waistband.

He nodded once, as if in polite greeting, and backed out the way he had come without a word.

"Smart man," Troy said quietly.

When he was as clean as he could manage to get, Troy stepped back out into the dining area. The trucker was nowhere to be seen, nor did anyone appear to have raised an alarm. The skinhead sitting at his booth was still there. He hadn't stopped watching the television.

As Troy moved closer, he thought he felt a presence by his side. He wondered, briefly, if it might be some new hallucination, some fleeting unreality. It wasn't. The man nearby wore a navy blue uniform.

"Put your hands where I can see them!" the cop ordered.

Troy looked up, marveling at this. "What seems to be the problem, Officer?" he asked.

"Put your hands where I can see them!" the policeman repeated. He was young, maybe in his early twenties, and his issue automatic pistol was in his hands. He stood in a textbook-perfect isosceles stance, nose over toes, pointing the weapon with authority and poise.

The academy was either doing a great job, Troy thought, or this police officer took his firearms training very seriously.

"I'll be with you in just a moment, Officer," he said.

"Don't move!" the cop ordered.

"This dude is crazy," the skinhead said. He didn't recognize Russell Troy, nor was there any reason he should. But he could obviously sense something was wrong. It was an almost preternatural sense, a kind of animal cunning, Troy mused. Most living creatures knew when something dangerous existed in their midst. It was the same reason that serial killers were almost immediately murdered when they were released into the general population in a prison.

"You stay put, too," the cop declared.

"That's him," said a voice. It was the trucker. Troy felt even more respect for the man. He wasn't the sort to decide murder wasn't his problem, after all. He was simply cool and collected enough to handle the encounter with aplomb.

Troy felt like applauding. He suppressed the urge.

"You lie down on the floor," the cop said.

"I can't do that, Officer," Troy replied. "I have to kill that man."

"What the hell?" the skinhead said.

"You stop that right now!" the cop ordered. "Down on the floor!"

Troy sighed. The young officer seemed likeable enough. He didn't want to hurt him, even a little.

"Stop right there!" the cop cried.

Troy picked up the nearest chair and swung it.

There was a shot, and another, and another. The rounds missed Troy. Whether by fluke, luck or miracle of divine providence, he would never know. His wooden chair smashed into the cop and knocked him flat. The young man's head bounced off the floor. His eyes rolled into his head. He was out cold.

Troy turned to the skinhead.

The punk was slow—the sort of person who would need *SAFE HOUSE* spelled out for him on an annotated map with directions to his destination. He figured it out eventually, though, for as Russell Troy advanced on him, he tried to drag a Glock pistol from his waistband.

Troy stabbed him through the eye.

The big blade jammed through the eye socket, penetrating deeply into the brain. The skinhead's face was a rictus of pain and disbelief. He sat down heavily, not really sitting at all, but falling into a seated position. When he slumped over sideways, the knife went with him.

Troy pulled the empty scabbard from his belt and tossed it aside.

Nobody moved. The few patrons and servers in the truck stop remained frozen in place. Troy reached down, picked up the fallen Glock—it was a .40 caliber, just like the one he had lost—and stuck it behind his belt. The skinhead carried three extra magazines. He took those, too.

The bell above the door rang as he stepped out into the night.

He went to his stolen car, climbed in and started the engine. On a whim, he switched on the radio, found a station playing light rock and put on his seat belt.

As Troy pulled back onto the highway, he rolled down his window and felt the cool air on his face. So many things were so much clearer now.

He wasn't sure what he would face at the safe house.

Likely, Hyde would have many men at his disposal. After the encounter with the young cop, however, Troy was more convinced than ever that his decision, his acceptance of his responsibilities, meant he now enjoyed a special sort of protection.

Wearing that shield, he would walk into the lion's den. He would end Shane Hyde's wretched life, and he could then rejoin his family.

The night would help. The night would cover him as he moved. It would help him travel. The trip wasn't long. There was time enough yet.

There was just enough darkness to see him through.

CHAPTER NINETEEN

Dawn was coming. The stillness just before sunrise was the most vulnerable part of the human sleep cycle, when disruptions carried the most weight and when a motivated force could put a defensive contingent off balance by the greatest amount. The vulnerability was hardwired into the human psyche. That fact, and the knowledge to exploit it, was one of many combat dicta that occupied space within Mack Bolan's brain.

The Farm had transmitted to Bolan updated satellite and thermal imagery of Shane Hyde's last known safe house. It wasn't a "house" at all, really, but an enormous multifamily-size dwelling outside Houston. The structure sat at the end of an artificial canyon formed by an automotive graveyard, where the hulks of stripped cars and trucks, some crushed flat and stacked, were left to bleach and rust in the Texas sun. The fortifications and hazards put in place by Hyde and his people, however, added a much greater level of complexity to breaching the place.

As confirmed by thermal imaging, a system of trenches, almost a maze of interconnected, World War II–style foxholes, snaked through the property. There was no way to tell just how many skinhead guards might be stationed within the maze, or how many could enter it to repel an attack. It was also possible that the

Twelfth Reich forces had more antiaircraft weaponry, which precluded a flyover and insertion from above.

All that was fine with Bolan, who had a very special plan in mind, using one of the largest pieces of ordnance stowed in the belly of the Pave Hawk. Grimaldi, operating from what was, for the chopper, a safe distance, was going to put in some time on the ground.

There were no alternate approaches, by vehicle or on foot, to the safe house. One way in and one way out: that made sense, from a fortress standpoint, and it worked both for and against the soldier. It was good, in that Hyde, once ensconced in his fortress, was unlikely to try to leave it. He would believe his salvation lay in the strong walls and the ranks of muscle arrayed for his protection between him and his enemies.

It was bad, in that Bolan would have to run a gauntlet to get to Hyde.

The terrain and the layout meant that the soldier had no choice but to breach the defenses from the front. He couldn't circumvent them; to do so would be to expose himself to whatever defenses and fields of fire the skinheads had set up for that purpose. The elaborate setup of cover, concealment, barricades and switchbacks used by or erected for the skinheads was his only means of gaining access to the building. He would have to fight his way through those twists and turns, using to his own benefit the very barricades behind which Twelfth Reich's army of gunmen would hide.

From where the chopper waited, Grimaldi would be keeping an eye on the real-time satellite imaging of the site. If Hyde did try to make a run for it, such as in a vehicle, or if he tried to escape by tunnel, the satellite's thermal scopes would ferret him out and alert the Executioner. Again, Bolan didn't think that likely. After his losses, Hyde needed to feel safe. The amount of time and effort he had invested in making this place a fortress meant he wouldn't give it up easily.

"Striker to G-Force," Bolan said quietly.

"G-Force, go."

"I'm entering the auto graveyard," Bolan said

"Good luck, Sarge."

"Out."

He crept forward, staying reasonably low but moving fast. There was a lot of ground to cover.

The first sentry he encountered was asleep.

Luck was a funny thing, and Bolan had to admit this was a lucky break. He slipped up to the sentry, who was sitting against a stack of crushed cars, and buttstroked him in the head with the M4 carbine.

The skinhead collapsed in a heap. He never woke up; he simply traded one unconscious state for another. Bolan fastened the man's wrists and ankles behind his back with cable ties taken from his war bag.

As he was securing the prisoner, another sentry rounded a stack of flattened cars. Bolan snapped up his carbine and punched a round through the man's neck. The skinhead dropped.

The soldier flexed both of his hands in turn. Not too bad so far. He was managing.

He crept to the next line of sight. The maze created by the rows of crushed cars was higher here, obscuring his vision of the terrain ahead.

Gunfire drove him back.

An alarm sounded, a long, low wail as if from an

antique, hand-cranked air-raid siren, which was probably exactly what it was. Somewhere forward of the safe house, flares were popped in the dim morning light, casting slightly more illumination on the scene but really just making noise and smoke.

So much for the element of surprise.

The sun was rising, the gray light giving way to the first yellow rays of true dawn. Bolan reached into his war bag, produced a fragmentation grenade, pulled the pin and let the spoon pop free. Then he chucked the bomb over the wall of crushed cars separating him from the skinheads on the other side.

He did it again.

And again.

He crouched as the first explosions rocked the auto yard and threw showers of dirt, gravel and metal shrapnel through the air. The staggered blasts that came after it brought screams from the men it wounded. The third, on the heels of the first two, set the skinheads to howling. Clods of earth and pieces of metal rained down now in every direction, bouncing and careening off the stacks of wrecked autos.

The momentum was Bolan's for the taking. He rushed around the corner, carbine at his shoulder, and triggered double and triple blasts that took down the wounded skinheads scrambling to recover their weapons. When he vaulted over a low stack of paint cans and overturned oil drums, he found himself facing a long, empty court of packed earth. At the opposite end was a pair of stripped Volkswagen Beetles.

Between them was an M-60 machine gun.

The belt-fed weapon was braced on a bipod and

manned by two skinheads. The open court was one long trap, a killing field through which invaders had to travel to progress farther.

The machine gun began to vomit flame and lead.

Bolan hit the dirt, knowing the rounds would skim by just overtop him, judging by the level of the weapon's muzzle. The skinheads weren't trained shooters and could barely control the gun. They tracked right, trying to keep the bucking M60 on target. He rolled to his right, opposite the line of their fire, shooting as he went, squeezing off 3-round burst after 3-round burst. The little 5.56 mm rounds drew sparks from the Volkswagens and dirt from the ground—then blood from the gunners. The M60 went silent.

He heard racing footfalls and knew that reinforcements were coming to man the gun. Standing and running for all he was worth, Bolan fired on the move, shooting methodically, burning down one, then a second, then a third skinhead, each man falling short of the machine gun.

He reached the makeshift machine-gun nest and took cover behind one of the rusted Beetle hulks. There was shouting from the lines and ranks of derelict cars beyond. The size, the scope of this auto yard, was daunting, and made it the perfect first battlefield for the terrorists hiding behind their fortifications.

Bolan swapped magazines in the M4, checked quickly around the corner, then took cover again. He could hear skinheads moving beyond the next piles of metal. He couldn't, however, leave the M60 behind, to be used against him. The soldier ripped out the ammo belt and partially disassembled the familiar weapon, lifting out the barrel and tossing it as far as he could. The ammunition he pitched in the opposite direction.

As he moved through the narrow passage between the Volkswagens, Bolan saw more cans of paint and several silver cans without labels. On impulse, he bent to check one, sniffing its contents.

Paint thinner.

There were at least a dozen cans. He tucked his M4 under his arm, then took out his Sting knife and, reversing it, punched diamond-shaped holes in the bases of the cans. Snatching up several in each hand, he ran for the barriers, moving in and out, avoiding random shots from the skinheads hiding near his position. When he had fixed each of them, he began pitching cans, which crashed and bounced and splattered, showering the cowering skinheads with the flammable paint thinner and in some cases injuring them as the heavy containers hit home.

Bolan stopped, turned on his heel and knelt in the dirt. He could hear the yowls of skinheads drenched in paint thinner. A few were shooting back, but many more were temporarily out of commission, the chemicals in their eyes, the fumes making them cough.

Bolan reached into his war bag and produced several incendiary grenades.

He knelt at the end of the open court, near several sets of barricades skinheads were hiding behind. Popping the grenades and scattering the spoons, he threw two bombs to his left and two to his right. Then he put his hands over his head, bent as if bowing toward Mecca, and counted off the numbers.

The incendiaries blazed. They ignited the paint thinner, causing sheets of flame to engulf his enemies.

Half a dozen human torches screamed inhumanly from where they stood. The agony was palpable. The fires of Hades had come to these men only too soon, as they would again in death

The Executioner stood, shouldered the M4 once more, and tracked each blazing, walking, burning terrorist, delivering mercy rounds. The sickening smell of charred human flesh filled the air.

Bolan hurried on.

The brutal tactics he was using weren't simple ruthlessness, although one man arrayed against an army as crude as this had to be ruthless to a point. No, Bolan's methods were as much a matter of psychological warfare as they were mechanical tactics. He had relied on similar means many times before. The terrorists were now learning what it meant to be terrified. He was bringing their war to them; he was taking their balance; he was making them believe, deep in the blackened core of their beings, that they weren't safe, that an implacable, invincible foe advanced on them with their deaths in his heart.

It wasn't so far from the truth, really, although Bolan had no illusions of being indestructible.

"Striker to G-Force," he said.

"G-Force," the voice said in his ear.

"Jack, ready the payload."

"I'm on it, Sarge," Grimaldi said. "How are things going down there?"

Bolan froze, dropped to one knee and fired three times, punching all three rounds into the face of a skinhead sniper lying prone on a stack of compressed car cubes. The soldier stepped over and picked up the gunman's weapon, a Remington 30.06 hunting rifle with a fairly powerful scope mounted to it. He popped the magazine, threw it, removed the bolt and tossed that, as well. He left the rifle itself with the dead man.

"Fairly uneventful so far," he said.

"I'd hate to see your idea of busy," Grimaldi commented.

"I'm moving through the last of the barriers to the trenches," Bolan reported. "Keep an eye out. If anyone makes a break for it, don't wait for my signal. You know what to do."

"Roger, Sarge," Grimaldi stated. "Out."

A narrow pathway appeared ahead of Bolan. Beyond it, he could see the corrugated-metal fence of the auto junkyard. He had made it to the other side. Through an arch made of two crushed cars standing on end and capped with a third, he could see the beginning of the trench maze that separated the junkyard from the safe house.

He thought he heard water. That struck him as odd, until he stepped through the arch and saw a small pool dug into the ground. A pit had been lined with a black plastic tarp of some sort. Brackish water filled the pool. Bubbles rose at its center.

Bolan frowned. He took his M4, lowered the barrel and raked the pool with several tribursts. Then he waited. The water, already brown, turned a darker shade. A body floated up to the surface. The man with a shotgun who had been lying in wait beneath the water moved his mouth like a fish.

Bolan leaned closer.

"Che…" the man said.

"What?" Bolan asked.

"Check…mate, ass…hole…." the dying skinhead whispered.

Bolan turned, too late.

There were three of them, carrying handguns and sporting the usual shaved heads, body piercings and bad attitudes. All were dressed in cast-off camouflage fatigues. The man in the center, the biggest of the three, gestured with his gun. The wail of the air-raid siren and the pops of the flares continued behind him, lending the scene a surreal atmosphere.

"On your knees, you son of a bitch," the first one said.

"I honestly," Bolan said, bending to place the M4 gently in the dirt at his feet, "can't tell you three apart. It's like you were all manufactured in the same scumbag factory. Are your serial numbers consecutive?"

"You talk pretty big for a man who's about to die," the third skinhead said. "We caught you. Our Leader will reward us well. We win and you lose."

"About that," Bolan said.

"Shut up!" the first skinhead ordered. He took a pair of handcuffs from his back pocket and threw them in the dirt. "Put those on!"

"Sorry," Bolan said. "Those look 'personal use' to me. I don't think I want to wear anything your girl-friend has had on."

"I said—"

"Or either of these two, for that matter." Bolan jerked his chin at the other skinheads.

"I'm gonna do him in right here," the second man said. He started to raise his handgun.

"There's something you should know, before you do that," Bolan said. His expression darkened.

"What's that?" the first skinhead demanded.

"I'm going to kill your friend first," Bolan said.

He kicked out with his leg. The butt of the M4 was leaning against his toe, where he had deliberately placed it. The carbine flipped up and into the face of the second skinhead, laying it open as the shoulder stock whipped into his eyes. Bolan pivoted and broke the first skinhead's knee with a driving piston kick, then stepped in and smashed his elbow across the third man's face.

"Funny thing about bravado," Bolan said. He bent, picked up the M4 and checked it, making sure the action and barrel hadn't been fouled. "It's easy to talk tough behind the barrel of a gun. A smashed knee, a broken face... These things aren't so easy to sneer at." He stepped back and pointed the M4. "Neither is this."

The skinheads went for their fallen guns. As he reached for his pistol, the one with the smashed knee said, through teeth gritted in pain, "You can go f—"

Bolan shot him, then his friend. The third man put out one hand while reaching behind his back with the other. "Stop! I'm not armed!"

"I'm not a trusting kind of guy," Bolan said. He shot the man through the face.

The hideout pistol, a derringer, fell from the terrorist's nerveless fingers.

Bolan kicked the trio into the oily pool of water, where they floated with the fourth corpse.

He wasn't done taking out the trash.

CHAPTER TWENTY

When Bolan was in position at the mouth of the trench maze, he worked his way into the descending pit and then keyed his transceiver.

"Okay, Jack," Bolan said. "Let's wake the neighbors."

"You got it, Sarge. Pleasure going to war with you."

"Fire," Bolan ordered.

The 60 mm M224 Lightweight Mortar was a smooth-bore, high-angle-of-fire cannon attached to a bipod and mounted to a shock-absorbing assembly. The little man-portable artillery piece had a maximum effective range of more than two miles and a sustained rate of fire of twenty rounds per minute. Grimaldi had a small stack of M888 point-detonating, high-explosive mortar rounds and instructions to spare none of them.

Hell was coming to Twelfth Reich, and with it, Mack Bolan.

The first of the mortar rounds struck short of the house, exploding with a thump that rattled the building and vibrated against Bolan's chest. The next round was only seconds later in coming, and that one hit closer. Grimaldi was walking them in, destroying terrain as he went, targeting the house itself. When a mortar round clipped the sprawling structure and took out the lower corner of its front facade, splinters of siding and window framing came down like snow.

There was nothing for Bolan to do now except make his way through the trench field. He knew that he could expect resistance; that was the purpose of such a structure. The only question was when and how.

He hadn't gone more than twenty feet when he encountered the first trip wire.

Grimaldi's mortar rounds continued to hammer the safe house as Bolan pressed his M4 against his chest, went prone and turned over on his back. He shimmied under the trip wires, mindful of each one, using the barrel of the M4 to adjust them with faint pressure as he wriggled past. It was disorienting to move on his back through the dirt, but he needed to be able to see each wire, to monitor its position as he slid his chest under and past it.

The wires got tighter and lower.

Too late, he realized he had fallen for the trick. He had begun crawling under the wires, only to end up in an awkward position, trapped between those over his chest and lower ones near his neck. Drawing the Sting knife from his waistband, carefully moving his arm to avoid pulling out a trip wire with his elbow, he began very carefully cutting his way through.

The first wire was the hardest. The skinheads didn't strike him as the sophisticated type. He had pegged the wires as connecting to grenades or other pull-free explosive triggers. Cutting such wires shouldn't cause the explosives to detonate, but there was always the possibility that a more sophisticated bomb, triggered by the release of tension, could explode when its trip wire was severed. He reached the end of the section, however, without blowing himself up.

Then the footfalls came.

He had been waiting for them. Funneled into the trench, the soldier made a tempting target. The mortar rounds were slowing now. Grimaldi's supply of shells would be almost gone. That was all right; the attack had jarred the skinheads, softened them up and taken the initiative from them. Anything they did now was reaction to Bolan's attack, which gave the Executioner the psychological advantage.

He got to his knees, shouldering the M4, and pressed himself against the wall of the trench. Then he stopped moving. His breathing became shallow; his muscles relaxed.

He waited.

Any man who hunted game could tell you that the simplest way to achieve success on the hunt was to be still. The smaller, less sophisticated creatures, such as squirrels and other rodents, would quickly forget you existed. The longer you remained unmoving, the more you became just another part of the landscape. Larger, smarter creatures, like deer, wouldn't be fooled if they could see and smell you. But stillness expanded the envelope the hunter could occupy before spooking nearby life.

It was the same when hunting men.

Mack Bolan had hunted men in every major population center of the globe. He had fought in every jungle, faced many predators. He was a master at the hunting of men, a "dangerous game" that was no game at all. His patience was unrivaled; his stillness was almost inhuman.

He waited again.

The skinheads were rabble. Bolan had fought better soldiers, more ferocious warriors, more times than he could count or name. These thugs' patience broke easily, and when they decided to rush down the trench, trusting to their superior numbers, he simply shot the first of them through the chest with the M4.

As the man went down, Bolan stepped over his corpse. There was no way to miss—and no way to be missed. He dropped to his knees, leaned back and let their Kalashnikov fire burn the air over his head as he chopped them down at stomach level.

When the next wave came, they did so over the top of the trenches. Bolan had been anticipating that move, too, so he didn't let it worry him. He shrugged off the first man, lowered his shoulder and bulled through the second. Then he fired a reflexive palm-heel blow into the face of the third, wincing as pain rocketed up his arm.

Old habits…

He almost didn't see the needle-sharp tomahawk that arced toward his face.

He had time to bring up the M4. The tomahawk's spike dug deep into the weapon, gouging into the ejection port and the bolt. The rifle was wrenched from Bolan's grasp. The skinhead threw it far from them both, and then lunged again, swinging his weapon like a clawhammer, trying to bury the point in Bolan's skull.

The soldier let him make his clumsy pass, then slapped the arm down, shoving the blade of the tomahawk up and into the skinhead's groin. The scream the man made was chilling. Bolan smashed an elbow across his face, putting him down for good, and wrenched the tomahawk free.

He drew his Beretta.

Pistol and tomahawk in hand, he stalked the trenches. The sun continued to rise, casting slanting shadows. Rays of light caused the exposed metal of traps concealed within the next stretch to glitter. Bolan stopped.

He reached out with the tomahawk. Smacking the spike against a protruding metal cylinder, he succeeded in tripping the crude cartridge trap.

The Executioner had seen that type of thing before. There were few anti-infantry booby traps he hadn't seen. The Vietnamese had been famous for many, and as he traversed the trench, he saw several examples obviously copied from accounts of that war or from manuals based on those accounts. There were hollow spikes in pits, barely concealed beneath plastic tarps whose thin layers of dirt had been disturbed. There were more trip wires connected to the pins of grenades. He avoided these easily.

There were also toe-popper cartridge traps, both in the floor and mounted on the walls of the trench. These were as simple as a hollow tube to serve as a barrel, with a cartridge nestled over a sharp actuator. Stepping or brushing against them hard enough would cause the actuator to strike the primer of the cartridge, which would then build pressure within the tube and exit as if from a gun.

Several times Bolan was forced to step over man-traps, deep secondary pits dug into the floor of the trench and covered with dirt-soiled plastic. There were so many traps, in fact, that it was a wonder some of

Hyde's men didn't manage to blunder into them. Then Bolan realized that the traps were set in specific sections of the maze, no doubt memorized as no-go zones by the terrorists. The rest of the way was free of such hazards.

He cleared the traps and looked up from his position within the maze. He was close enough now, he judged. It was time to keep up the psy-ops pressure that, he firmly believed, was working to his advantage. It was time Shane Hyde understood exactly what he faced.

The solider tucked his captured tomahawk into his belt, reached into his war bag and removed a compact electric bullhorn. He put it to his lips and keyed, triggering a long blast of sound.

"Shane Hyde," he called, his voice loud through the bullhorn. "Attention, Shane Hyde. Leader of the failed terrorist cell Twelfth Reich. You have one chance to lay down your weapons and surrender!"

He paused, hearing distant shouts, then screams that weren't so distant. The skinheads within the sprawling safe house were massing somewhere near the end of the trench maze, which wasn't far from his position now.

"Shane Hyde," Bolan repeated. He deliberately pitched his voice lower, layering his words with obvious contempt. "Shane Hyde, you gutless coward. Have your bald minions seen enough of your failures for one day?"

He waited again. The shouts were louder now.

"Screw you!" someone cried out.

"Race-traitor!" another roared.

It was working. They were reacting. The moment an enemy's mind could be engaged in dialogue, no matter how trivial the conversation, that enemy would be distracted. The part of the brain that handled such exchanges preoccupied just enough of a man's awareness to slow his reflexes, dull his decisions. It was why street muggers frequently threw questions at their victims.

"How many times do you have to be humiliated before your own men before you react, Hyde?" Bolan shouted into the bullhorn. "Have you no pride? What about the master race? From where I sit, you're looking pretty inferior!"

There was a squeal of feedback. From somewhere in the huge safe house, an amplified voice answered.

"Identify yourself!" it said. "I am Shane Hyde, the Führer of the Twelfth Reich and the man who will mount your severed head on a pike in that trench!"

"The führer?" Bolan called back mockingly. He wondered just how long it would take for Hyde, while bantering this way, to organize a large force and send them in Bolan's direction. The trenches offered the soldier a unique opportunity, a choke point the likes of which he probably wouldn't find so easily within the house. Not of this narrow width.

Most adults were familiar with the story of the outnumbered Spartan warriors who held a mountain pass against a much larger army, displaying great bravery and impressive skills as warriors. When one understood basic military tactics and strategy, the feat was no less admirable, but it was a lot more believable. In a narrow pass or choke point, such as the trenches, having a much larger armed force was meaningless. If only a few men at a time could move through the opening, Bolan could fight them in ones or twos. He wouldn't be forced to take them all at once, as a mob.

The skinheads were slow; that much he had learned, although Hyde himself had repeatedly proved to be smart and cunning.

"You're a sorry bunch of Hitler Youth," Bolan taunted. "Teenagers staying home at night, shaving each other's heads and playing with guns. You'll never be more than a bunch of pretenders. If the Twelfth Reich is remembered at all, it will be remembered for failure. I hear that O'Connor Petroleum's stock is up! Guess my investment paid off!"

He hadn't heard anything of the kind, of course, nor was he a shareholder in OPP or any other company.

"I am the *future,* you Jew-loving tool of the Zionist occupation!" Hyde yelled back. "I demand you identify yourself! Unless you're afraid? Unless you think perhaps we'll come to your house and kill your family, too?"

"Oh, that's right," Bolan said. "That's what you do, isn't it, Hyde? You torture, rape and murder innocent women and children. That's certainly the act of a master race. That's something only the superior human beings among us would do. I bet it takes a lot of courage to put a gun to a woman's head. That's bravery, all right."

"Who are you?" Hyde screamed into his own bullhorn.

"My name is Matt Cooper," Bolan said. "I'm with the Justice Department. I'm here for you, Shane Hyde. I'm here to bring you to justice. You can save yourself a lot of time and a lot of pain if you walk out now and surrender. Of course, that will mean you look like a complete coward in front of your own men. And it means you go straight to prison."

"Silence!" Hyde demanded.

"Weaklings don't last long in prison, Hyde," Bolan said. "But there are ways around that. I'm sure in jail you can find a nice bunk mate who'll protect you. And if not, maybe he can sell you to somebody who'll take you under his wing, so to speak. What do you suppose the going rate is for failed neo-Nazi cult leaders? Two packs of smokes? Three?"

"I'll kill you!" Hyde roared. "I'll cut the flesh from your bones! I'll keep you alive and make you watch while I do it!"

"That's funny," Bolan said. "Because it looks like I'm standing right here, on your own property, Hyde. And the Twelfth Reich is hiding inside its clubhouse, afraid of one man."

What he didn't say, as he goaded Hyde and his men, was that Hyde was right to be scared. Grimaldi's mortar rounds had destroyed much of the front of the building, leaving gaping holes in the facade and punching several craters in the trench maze. There was a blast hole not far from where Bolan stood. He marked its location. If he was forced to retreat, he could use it to make the jump to the next trench, a switchback that would lead him through the maze in reverse.

"You're a coward, you prick!" Hyde called. "A coward!"

"I'm not the one who ran from that train," Bolan said. "Do your fellow skinheads know you were going to abandon most of your attack force? I bet you didn't say anything to them about that. I worked your plan over in my head for a while, Hyde, and I couldn't figure how you thought you were going to evacuate everybody on just a handful of motorcycles. Then I realized you never had any intention of getting them all out. Just the important ones, right? Just the ones who mattered. Do the rank and file know they don't matter, Hyde? Do they know their lives are meaningless to you?"

"Shut up!" Shane Hyde screamed. "Shut up! Lies! All lies!"

Sporadic gunfire cut the morning air. Bolan couldn't determine its location, but realized it was far from where he stood.

Had Hyde's people fixed his position so incompetently that they were shooting at shadows on the far side of the property? It didn't seem likely.

Whatever his men were firing at, Hyde didn't let it distract him from his verbal sparring match with Bolan. The Executioner was growing tired of the exchange. He would have to cut deeper, get to the core of what made Hyde most volatile. He needed to encourage the man to order the type of reckless rush that would work to Bolan's advantage.

"I've read your Army file, Hyde," Bolan called out. "Do your fellow shavetails know why you were really kicked out? I bet you told them it was because you were always fighting with those 'inferior races' you're always talking about."

"Shut up!"

"Seems you kept failing psych evaluations," Bolan said. "And of course this was back when certain tendencies were more frowned upon than they are now. Isn't that right, Hyde? Identity issues? Delusions? Maybe even a tendency to fraternize a little too much?"

"I will drink your blood," Shane Hyde said, his am-

plified voice dead and flat. To the men fighting with him, he said, "Go! Go now!"

They went after Bolan then, running through the trenches, carrying guns and clubs and knives and rifles. It was a small army, what had to be a huge percentage of the force within the safe house. The guns they carried were largely useless, for most of them couldn't shoot for fear of hitting the men in front of them.

It was just as Bolan had planned.

He dropped the bullhorn, drew the tomahawk and raised his Beretta.

Battle was joined.

Bullets pocked the dirt walls of the trench. Bolan crouched, firing judiciously, turning his body to present the narrowest target he could. As the throng of enemies reached him, he used the butt of the Beretta to strike out against them, smashing the 20-round magazine against an eye here, a nose there, a vulnerable cheekbone in between.

He used to deadly effect the spike of the tomahawk. The blade flashed as he buried its short, sharp edge in body after body, then brought it back and around on the reverse strokes. To strike from target to target in the crush of bodies like this required a man to load one side of his body as he unloaded the other, stepping left and right, left and right, into and through and over the opposition. There were screams and streams of blood and cries for mercy. There were vows of terrible revenge that gave way to wails of pain. There were shouts for help.

Men died. They fell away as Bolan fought through them, the center of a vortex of destruction, the eye of a maelstrom of deadly work and deadlier will.

Soon he was stepping over piles of bodies, creating barriers of his foes, as the crush of racist terrorists piled on top of one another. They fell under his blade and his bullets, some rolling away at the last minute, others running, still others charging him out of fear, out of hate, out of determination, or from some combination of all three. He couldn't be dissuaded. He couldn't be discouraged. He didn't know fear, not as they understood it.

The soldier had come to right the wrongs they represented. He had come to put them down. He had come to bring them to justice.

There was nothing they could do to stop him.

The 20-round magazine of the Beretta was empty. He dropped it free of the weapon's butt, drew another from his war bag and slapped it home. His palms were warm, cracking and bloody beneath his bandages, but he no longer felt them.

When Bolan reached the terminus of the trench maze, he stopped, paused and looked back. Smoke rose from the barrel of the Beretta 93R. Blood dripped from the head, from the blade and spike, of the tomahawk in his hand.

His chest heaved. He fought to catch his breath.

An army of wounded and dead men lay in his wake.

Splintered and scarred, the double doors of the safe house lay before him. He reached out, tried the knob and found it wouldn't turn. Rearing back, he planted the sole of his combat boot next to the center slit.

The lock gave. The doors parted.

Mack Bolan stepped inside.

CHAPTER TWENTY-ONE

The enormous safe house had once been a miniature mansion, of sorts. The entrance was a great room, dominated by two huge, curving staircases. There was old furniture here, covered in dust and dry rot, and plenty of trash. The walls were a spray-painted collage of profanity and white-power slogans.

Sandbags had been piled almost haphazardly in the center and corners of the room and at the top of a staircase. The skinheads were gathered behind them, lying in wait, ready to strike whoever entered. Bolan didn't wait, knowing that if he stood framed in the doorway, he made a tempting target. Instead, as he entered the room, he threw himself to the side, landing heavily on his shoulder, feeling the grit and heat as gunfire ripped the air and sprayed him with splinters.

He rolled to the nearest pile of sandbags, vaulted it and collided with the terrorist crouching there. Burying the tomahawk in the skull of the enemy, spike first, he shoved the dead man aside, picked up the Kalashnikov the man had held, and snapped the selector to full-auto. Then he was up, spraying out the recovered weapon, punching holes in the sandbags and the walls of the house, laying down a curtain of hot lead that caught first one, then another of the enemy.

The damage done by Grimaldi's mortar rounds had

left portions of the walls and ceiling in shambles. As Bolan took the right staircase, switching his Beretta to his left hand and drawing his Desert Eagle with his right, more pieces of the ceiling fell. The vibrations of the firefight within the great room were jostling free portions of the structure. The Executioner ignored it, dodging the falling debris, shooting down his foes and continuing on.

Shane Hyde was here somewhere. Bolan was finally within striking distance of the goal for which he had fought so hard.

At the top of the staircase, the soldier was presented with a choice. He could go left or continue right. He blasted the skinheads crouched behind the sandbags, cutting them down like chaff.

In the breathing room that resulted, the pause between spurts of combat during which his foes recoiled, Bolan knelt. His war bag was growing steadily lighter. He emptied it further, removing a grab bag of incendiary, white phosphorous and fragmentation grenades. Yanking the pins free of each in turn, he threw the grenades down the left hallway, watching them bounce and roll as their spoons snapped free and the grenades disappeared along the route he chose not to travel.

Up once again, he was only a few yards down the right hallway when the grenades detonated. They blew one after another, the explosions separated by the mere seconds it had taken to pull each pin. The noise within the safe house set Bolan's ears to ringing. The screams and cries of the wounded or killed were faint in comparison.

Resistance was collapsing.

Skinheads remained on this floor, but now they were running, fleeing before him, shooting behind them in the vain hope of distracting their implacable enemy long enough to make good their escape. Where the men thought they were going, Bolan didn't know, until he pursued a knot of them through a shattered side doorway and into a bedroom that had been ripped open to the outside air by Grimaldi's mortar assault.

They were still cursing, still shooting at Bolan, as they threw themselves out the hole in the building. His pistol held ready, the soldier moved toward the gap, stepping over a filthy mattress covered in debris and smoldering where one corner had caught fire.

The skinheads on the ground below writhed in agony. The building was too high; they had fallen a long way. One man's leg was twisted at an unnatural angle, and surely broken. Another man grabbed at his ankles, screaming in pain. Still another skinhead didn't move at all. The fall had knocked him unconscious or killed him.

Bolan turned toward the interior.

A new series of sandbag barricades awaited. Popping up like Whac-a-Moles, skinheads with Uzi submachine guns began laying down fire, driving Bolan to the floor, causing him to roll into the barrier closest to him. There was a skinhead on the opposite side. Bolan simply reached up and over with the Beretta, triggering several 3-round bursts. His target stopped moving.

The Executioner stood, ducked, then rose again. Skinheads fired, but they were desperate now. They fought not because they wanted to win but because they were afraid to lose. As Bolan drew nearer, their resolve faded, and when they broke to flee, he mowed them down.

Mack Bolan continued on, reloading on the run.

He searched the rooms he came to, concerned that he might find more evidence of the inhumanity Hyde's people had displayed before. He was worried he might encounter murdered slaves, for example, inconvenient lives snuffed out as if the terrorists were throwing light switches. The casual way in which Hyde's men had been prepared to murder the human beings they were holding prisoner—and the fact that they had held slaves at all—had hit home, hard. It was evidence of just how rapidly society would descend into madness were men like Shane Hyde ever to take the power they sought.

Fortunately, there was no evidence of that. Bolan's ears had stopped ringing, and he was now vigilant for the sounds of movement as he stalked through the safe house. Hyde could be anywhere, unless he had already fled the grounds. Some sixth sense told the soldier that Hyde wouldn't leave this place willingly, however. The house was a warren, a lair, a wounded animal's den. Hyde would put his back to the wall and trust to his innate viciousness to carry the day. Fear and instinct would do the rest.

"G-Force to Striker," Grimaldi said in his ear.

"Striker here, go," Bolan replied.

"Sarge, I think I'm going to risk a flyover," Grimaldi said. "You've got them on the run down there. Did you see any evidence of antiaircraft weaponry?"

"None," Bolan reported. "I have to admit an eye in the sky would be helpful. I want to make sure Hyde doesn't sneak away."

"No sign of him?"

"Not yet."

"I'll keep my eyes peeled."

"Don't be afraid to use that automated gun," Bolan said. "Wood's going to be sorry he missed out. If you see any skinhead stragglers, take them down. We're stopping this here and now, Jack."

"You got it, Sarge," Grimaldi said. "G-Force, out."

It was another nail in the coffin of Twelfth Reich. With Bolan burning them out at ground level and Grimaldi covering them from the air, there would be no escape. The two men formed the blades of scissors, coming together to sever the opposition caught between them.

The crackle of fires, igniting by his incendiaries or burning since the mortar assault, began to filter through the fading sounds of gunfire. The safe house was burning, somewhere. The soldier could smell scorched insulation and black smoke.

The hallway ran in a rectangle around the perimeter of the upper floor. Turning a corner, Bolan encountered a plywood barrier braced with two-by-fours. In the center a hollow-core wooden door had been set.

He reached out and wrenched it open.

The trap was an obvious one; his method of springing it had been simply to brazen through it. The skinhead who lunged from the other side carried a curved knife so large it might have been a short samurai sword. Bolan sidestepped, then smashed the butt of the Beretta against the back of the skinhead's neck.

The would-be killer fell to his knees, dead or unconscious.

The Executioner wrenched open another makeshift door. A wrecked bedroom lay beyond.

Shane Hyde waited within.

"Stop!" Hyde ordered. He held a 1911 pistol to the head of a naked woman. She looked scared and she looked angry. Evidently being taken hostage hadn't been part of the program.

Hyde was himself shirtless. Bolan's attack must have caught the terrorist leader slightly indisposed. Fleeing, he had to have returned here, knowing that there was at least one hostage he could still use to his advantage.

Well, too bad for Hyde. There would be no romance where he was going…at least, not of the kind the racist murderer would appreciate.

"Mister, *please*," the woman begged.

"Hyde, I'm from the Justice Department. Lay down your weapon and come with me. There are people who want very much to talk to you."

"I don't think so," Hyde replied.

"Mister," the woman pleaded.

Bolan took a menacing step forward. "She's pretty. Do you ever look at her and think of the families you've destroyed? Wives, daughters? Women just as attractive who'll never be attractive again, if they were alive at all when you were done with them?"

"What are you talking about?" Hyde demanded.

"Russell Troy," Bolan said.

"Russ?" Hyde laughed. "Have you seen him? Is he with you? Russ and I had quite a conversation on the train. It was like old home week."

"You know what you did to him," Bolan said. "You know what you did to his family. For that alone, among all your crimes, I should cut off pieces of you until you beg me to kill you."

The vehemence in Bolan's words brought Shane Hyde up short. He looked into the soldier's eyes and saw the terrible, dark certainty there, the commitment to bringing Shane Hyde and all like him to brutal justice.

"I don't expect you to understand," Hyde said. "Nobody ever has. Not you. Not the voices."

"Why don't you tell me about that?" Bolan asked. Hyde's file had said he was delusional; his psych profile had contained references to possible schizophrenia. If Hyde were hearing voices, that would explain a lot.

"Don't you see that what I'm doing, I'm doing to *help* our race?" Hyde pleaded. "I didn't set out to be a murderer. A great man has to do terrible things. Have you read Machiavelli?"

Bolan said nothing. His finger tightened slightly on the Beretta's trigger.

"'Men ought either to be well treated or crushed,'" Hyde quoted, "because they can avenge themselves of lighter injuries, of more serious ones they cannot...'"

"This," Bolan said, "is the avenge part."

"Who are you but a government pawn?" Hyde demanded. "What difference does it make to you? You're white. Can't you *see?* Don't you ever wonder what kind of future white men, white women, white *children* will have? We're being swamped. We're being overrun. If men like me don't do something, we'll lose. This nation will be lost forever to the legions of alien brown people, bringing their strange ways and their foreign languages to our shores. Or we'll be eaten alive from within by the animal mud people, whose dark skin masks darker souls."

"Darker souls," Bolan repeated. "That's poetic. How dark is the soul of a man who would kill a child, Hyde?"

"I've had to do awful things," he admitted. "Sometimes because the voices told me to. Bob understands. He'll explain it to you."

Bolan didn't know or care who "Bob" might be. He knew a ploy when he heard one. The muscles of Hyde's shoulders tensed. He was getting ready to make a move.

The woman sensed it. She knew, too, that the moment he made a play, the chances she might catch a bullet increased a hundredfold.

"Please, baby," she whispered. "Maybe…maybe he's right. Maybe you should just go with him."

Hyde looked at her. The gun pressed more tightly against her head. "You would ask me to betray our race? Give up our dream?"

"I don't want to die," the woman cried. Tears streamed down her face. "Please, Shane. Please. Don't kill me. Don't make *him* kill me."

"You knew what he was," Bolan told her, "when you climbed into bed with him. I wonder how many people have begged him for their lives. How many men, women and children have begged his skinhead minions for mercy?"

"Russell Troy did," Hyde snarled. He pointed his gun at Bolan, now using the woman as a shield. "I made him watch. I made him see what his betrayal cost."

The roar of the fire at the far end of the building was growing louder. Bolan could smell smoke. The air within this portion of the safe house was beginning to take on a pall, a haze, as smoke started to filter through the building.

Time was running out.

"Enough," Bolan said. "You're coming with me."

"I created Russell Troy!" Hyde screamed. "I gave him the will to live! If he finally learns to love his race, it will be because I made it happen! I will be the leader of the new order!"

"You'll be a piece of meat in a cell, bled for what you can tell the authorities," Bolan said. "And then you'll be nothing."

Hyde yelled incoherently and shoved the woman at Bolan. She came toward him, terror in her eyes, and Bolan, remembering only too well the knife-wielding woman he'd faced before, took no chances. He sidestepped. As she hit the floor and rolled onto the dirty mattress, yelping, Hyde leveled his pistol.

"No!" Bolan shouted.

Hyde fired. The bullet tore into the woman's chest between her breasts, drilling her through the heart. She tried to cry out, but no sound emerged. She stared at the ceiling, suddenly very dead.

"You soulless bastard," Bolan said softly.

Hyde pointed his pistol. The slide was locked back. He had spent the last of his ammunition on the unnecessary murder.

"She reaped what she sowed!" he shrieked. "You stay back!"

"The gun's empty," Bolan said, advancing on him. "And you're out of time."

Hyde suddenly laughed and threw the gun away. "You can't kill me, can you? You could have shot me at any moment and you didn't. All this is because you want me alive!"

"You're going to spill what you know, Hyde," Bolan said. There was no speculation in his voice. It was a statement of fact. "You're going to tell us everything. Every terror group, every person you've financed, every half-baked plan you've put into motion. Anything and everything. Twelfth Reich died today, Hyde. And as far as the world is concerned, so did you."

"I have rights," Hyde said, wild-eyed. "I'm an American citizen. You can't make me testify."

"You're not a citizen," Bolan countered. "You're not even human. You're a torturing, murdering monster. You're going to disappear, Hyde. Where you're going, there are no ACLU lawyers to complain to. No Red Cross care packages. No visits with the outside world. Life as you know it is over. Get down on the floor. Put your hands behind your head and interlace your fingers."

Through the holes in the walls ripped open by the mortar attack, Bolan could hear the rotors of Grimaldi's heavy Pave Hawk in the sky above. The fire was growing still louder. He wasn't sure how long it would take, but soon the big structure would be a roaring inferno. They needed to leave.

"Enough talk," Bolan said. "Do it. Now. Or I'll kneecap you and do it myself."

Hyde sneered. "And if I choose to throw myself out of the building? Take my own life?"

"Then I'll kneecap you sooner rather than later."

"You are a wretched excuse for a white man," Hyde

said. "Tell me something. It was you at the train, wasn't it? Leading the government action to stop me?"

"Something like that," Bolan said.

"And you've fought your way through my army, smashed the ranks of my men. Tell me. Are you alone? Did you walk through my defenses by yourself?"

"Something like that," Bolan said again.

"So much power," Hyde stated. "So much strength. You, a white man, a warrior born. Don't you think you've wasted who you could be? You've turned your power against your own race. You're cutting off your nose to spite your face, all because some mud person has told you to do so!"

Bolan thought he could feel the heat of the approaching blaze. The smoke was starting to make his eyes water. He had the stinging sensation of standing too close to a campfire.

"That's enough," Bolan gritted. "We're leaving."

"Think what you could do if you joined me," Hyde said. "Imagine what we could accomplish. A new world order. A world safe for whites. A world free of the evils of the muds. When the Day of the Rope comes, and our enemies swing from light poles, we'll—"

"If you don't shut him up," said a voice, "then I'm definitely going to."

Bolan turned, leveling his gun.

Russell Troy held an AK on him.

CHAPTER TWENTY-TWO

Hyde broke and ran.

Troy cut loose with his Kalashnikov, spraying the room, forcing Bolan to hit the floor. As Hyde dashed out of the room, a section of the hallway farther on collapsed in a fiery heap. The blaze was consuming half the building now, hungry for more, eager to envelop the whole structure.

The terrorist ran through the barricades and the homemade doorways, making a beeline for the front of the building, the only way out. Troy pursued.

Bolan went after them.

Hyde made for the stairway, followed by Troy, who was firing on the move. The Executioner was forced to throw himself down the opposite stairs, rolling over and over again, feeling the wooden steps smash his arms, his elbows, his ribs, his knees. Troy's shots didn't pursue him, however. The rogue agent was concerned only with Hyde, and continued running on out the door of the safe house.

There was an earsplitting crash. Bolan looked up, seeing the beams burst into orange flame. Sparks poured down. The fire was inside the walls, inside the rafters. Black smoke roiled overhead in thick, billowing clouds.

The ceiling was collapsing.

"Jack! Jack! I have Hyde and Russell Troy on the grounds!" Bolan called into his transmitter. "I need you!"

"Affirmative!" Grimaldi called back.

Bolan cleared the entrance of the safe house just as the center of the great room came crashing down, the flaming beams pushing a tidal wave of heat that almost blew him through the doorway.

"They are in the trench maze," Bolan said. "I need you to spot for me from above."

The Pave Hawk was louder than ever now as the massive chopper hovered just above Bolan's position. Gunfire sounded—the hollow metallic clatter of the Kalashnikov. The bullets weren't intended for the chopper. Bolan didn't think Troy would waste time worrying about Grimaldi.

The man had come all this way, fought past being left for dead more than once, for a very clear reason.

He wanted revenge on Hyde.

How many vigilantes had Bolan encountered in his travels? How many men like Troy had he fought with and against, all of them motivated by the desire to set things right as they saw them? Countless.

Bolan took to the trenches. Beretta in hand, he ran, searching his memory of the maze, knowing that if Troy's pursuit or Hyde's desperation caused the men to blunder into the booby-trapped sections, the entire mission might end with Hyde spitted on the end of one of his own traps.

Gunfire pinned the soldier, and he ducked. Somewhere in the maze, Troy was trying to hold him back, keep him off the trail. Much as Bolan could sympathize with his motives, the rogue agent couldn't be allowed to call the play. Bolan returned fire blindly, knowing he had no shot, hoping to drive Troy off. When he stuck his head out again, there was no answering fire. Troy had moved on. Bolan gave chase.

The Pave Hawk threw up great clouds of dust and dirt as Grimaldi hovered low. Bolan squinted through the grit that tore at his face. He didn't even feel the ache in his hands anymore. He was too keyed up on adrenaline, on the need to bring this mission to a close. He was numb to everything else.

"I've got them, Sarge," Grimaldi reported. "On your nine, on your nine, the dogleg to your left and back."

"Pursuing!" Bolan reported. He ran. As he traversed the section of maze Grimaldi had called out, he realized he hadn't seen this portion of the trenches before. It was at the far west end, to the right of the freely burning safe house. If Hyde had come here trying to escape Troy, had the move been deliberate? Could he have weapons stashed here?

Hell, Bolan thought. Hyde didn't need to have caches of weapons stored on the grounds. There were dead men everywhere, fallen guns and blades free for the taking as soon as he stumbled on one.

The soldier ducked under a pair of two-by-fours that had been set at the mouth of the dogleg. Too late, he realized what those boards might signify. It was a way of delineating a section of trench, which meant more traps.

Hyde and Troy stood staring at each other, just ahead of him.

Something was wrong. Troy's weapon wasn't even

pointed at his nemesis, and he had a curiously elated expression on his face.

Bolan leveled his gun. "Nobody move!" he ordered. "Facedown, on the ground, now! Troy, don't make me kill you!"

The rogue agent tossed his AK farther into the trenches, as hard as he could.

It hit the ground and exploded.

Bolan ducked. When he realized what had happened, he also realized that neither Troy nor Hyde had moved an inch. Hyde was pale and sweating.

Land mines.

Hyde had blundered into a field of land mines planted in the trenches, in what was obviously a killing stretch.

"He's standing on one," Troy explained. "We both heard it click. It hasn't gone off yet."

"You idiot," Bolan said to Hyde. "What did you plant? What is it?"

"B-b-b-bouncing Betty," he stammered.

Bolan cursed under his breath. He had thought as much. The Bouncing Betty was an antipersonnel mine with a particularly brutal twist. Stepping on the device armed it. Stepping off again detonated it. On detonation, the mine expelled a charge that rose to waist height before exploding. The Bouncing Betty didn't just blow off feet or legs. It was designed to kill.

"Listen to me," Bolan told Troy. "Listen very carefully."

"Sure."

"We can't let him die."

Troy looked at Bolan curiously. "Why would you say something like that?"

"My mission all along has been to capture Hyde," Bolan said. "To bring him in. He has valuable intelligence about terrorist operations in the Unites States and on foreign soil. The attacks Twelfth Reich has mounted already are nothing compared to what its allied organizations might do in the future. We need to know what he knows. We can't let him take it to his grave."

"All this time," Troy said with wonder. "You've been fighting to take him alive?"

"Yeah," Bolan replied.

"Who are you with?" Troy asked. "You're not like any government agent I've ever worked with. Are you NSA? CIA?"

"Justice Department," Bolan said. "My name is Matt Cooper. Listen to me, Troy. You have to let me try to disarm that mine. If Hyde dies, everything is for nothing. The information he has—"

"Don't you realize who you're talking to?" the rogue agent said. His voice was oddly flat. He didn't sound angry or outraged. He didn't even sound particularly bothered. It was more that he was disbelieving. That was it; Troy was incredulous.

"I know only too well," Bolan said. "I know what Hyde did to your family. I know why."

"I don't think you do," Troy stated. "Not really. Okay, you've read my files. I can imagine what the Bureau put in the report. I'm curious. I never did read the write-up of my last mission. Does it say that the failure was mine? That I slipped up, gave myself away? I did the one thing an undercover agent is never supposed to do, Cooper. I forgot myself, and in that one moment, everything I did to get to that point, every filthy thing I did to my family and to my own person…it was worthless. That is what it means for all your work to be for nothing. So believe me, Cooper, I know."

"You're a good man," Bolan said. "You're fallible. We all are. I told you, I've read the files, Troy. I know you were a good agent. A dedicated family man—"

"Please don't talk about my family."

"I'm sorry."

"It's not what you're thinking." Troy shook his head. "I'm not angry. I'm not even angry at *him* anymore." He jerked his chin at Hyde, who remained completely still. Sweat poured down the sides of his face.

"He may not have much time," Bolan said. "If he shifts his weight—"

"I feel," Troy said, "like I'm waking up from a dream. They tried to explain it to me in the recovery home, you know. A 'fugue state,' I think they called it. I wasn't really listening."

"I can get you help, if you'll let me."

"I don't need help, Cooper," Troy said. "That's what I'm trying to explain. It's not that I'm well. I know that. I won't ever be."

The Pave Hawk was hovering high above. Grimaldi, listening in to Bolan's transceiver, knew what was happening. He had taken the chopper up to prevent the rotor wash from blowing over Hyde. The terrorist leader looked as if he was ready to urinate himself from fear.

"You're in shock," Bolan said. "You've suffered great trauma."

Troy laughed. "You're joking, right? Of course I've suffered trauma. Listen to me, Cooper. I'm okay. Really."

"Then help me," the Executioner told him.

"What do you want me to do?"

"I need to try to disarm the mine," Bolan said. "It's got to be now. The slightest movement on his part could trigger it. The explosion might take you out, too, close as you are. Move away. Let me take care of it."

"No, Cooper," Troy said. "I can't let you do that."

"Why not? Revenge isn't—"

"No," Troy interrupted. "Not revenge. Cooper, we're standing in a minefield. If you come closer, you might trigger one, too. Then you die and Hyde dies. My own life doesn't matter."

"It does. It does to me."

"You know, I think you mean that," Troy said. He looked up at the sky, at the chopper. The sound of the rotors beat in time to Bolan's pounding heart. "You're not who you say you are," Troy said. "The Justice Department doesn't field helicopter-borne commandos. I've seen you do what you do. And I've heard…things."

"Troy, we don't have time for this."

"Cooper, I have all the time I'm ever going to need. I want you to do something for me. I want you to hear me out."

Bolan paused. "All right. I'm listening."

"Do you know what you value, Cooper? Do you know what's really important in your life? I thought I did. I became my job. I defined myself by how well I did it. Nothing was ever good enough for me. I had to keep trying. Keep doing more. Keep taking on more. You could call it ambition, I guess."

"You're not to blame for—"

"Please," Troy said, interrupting again. "You said

you would listen. I've had so very long to think about my family. To think about how much I loved them. And how I failed them. I never did what mattered when I had them. I passed them over. But I'm not ready to crucify myself for the failure that led to their deaths and will lead to mine. It isn't my place to do that, not now. I *am* human. I failed because I'm human. My crime, Cooper, is that I didn't learn how to live when my family was alive. That time wasted, that world, that life that I'll never get back. That is loss, Cooper. That is tragedy. That is my sin."

"I can help you," Bolan said.

Troy shook his head. "I know. You're worried I'm about to put a bullet in him or something." He lifted his soiled black BDU blouse. There was a Glock pistol tucked in his waistband. "And I could. But I'm not going to."

"Can I ask why not?"

"Have you ever been insane?" Troy asked. "I was. For a long time. It blurs together, after a while. The fugue state thing, I guess you would call it. And then I was manic. I made the decision to kill myself, Cooper, and I thought that was going to make everything right again."

"It won't."

"No," Troy said. "It won't. Killing myself won't bring them back. It won't reunite me with them. I used to think, well, I used to be a religious man. Now I'm not sure what I believe. I haven't been since losing myself to the undercover world. To the world of sex and drugs and wildness."

"It lures you in." Bolan was no stranger to that world.

He had spent many years behind battle masks, pretending to be criminals, gaining the confidence of enemies so he could destroy them from within.

"Yes," Troy said. "It's funny, Cooper. When I shook it off, when I realized I had simply shifted my illness, my insanity, from one focus point to another, well, it all melted away."

"Troy," Bolan said. "I have to defuse that mine."

"No, I can't let you do that, Cooper. It's too risky. You're a good man. You don't deserve to die for this... this creature."

"I need him," Bolan said. "The country needs what he knows."

"Yes, yes." Troy shook his head impatiently. "I get that, Cooper. I do. Do you know what I decided, before I followed him here? I decided I wanted to live."

"You can," Bolan said.

"But I can't. That's where you're wrong. Have you ever heard that old story, the moral dilemma about the criminally insane?"

"I don't think so," the soldier replied.

"It's said that there are people who murder who aren't responsible for their crimes," Troy said, "because they're crazy. They don't know what they're doing. Now imagine that it was possible to cure those people. That they could be restored to sanity, and with that restoration, they would no longer be murderers."

"All right," Bolan said.

"Well, wouldn't that be the most monstrous thing you could do to such a person?" Troy said. "Give him back his mind, and with it the knowledge of the terrible things he's done?"

Bolan had nothing to say to that.

"I'm a murderer," Troy said. He rubbed absently at the stubs of his missing fingers. "I've killed in cold blood. And I remember everything. Everything I did while I was a member on the fringes of Twelfth Reich. Everything he did to my family, and to me, to pay me back for trying to betray him."

Hyde looked nervously from Troy to Bolan and back again. He could obviously sense that Troy was finally getting it out of his system, had finally said what he needed to say—and now something was going to happen.

"I can see your footsteps in the dirt," Bolan said, "leading to where you're now standing. I can follow your steps until I get within reach of Hyde. Then I can try to dig out the mine and deactivate it. The mission can still be salvaged."

"All right," Troy said. "You've been more than kind to me. You could simply have shot me and done what you need to do. I'm grateful you didn't." He raised his shirt slowly. "I'm going to take out my gun and throw it away. Please don't kill me."

"Go ahead."

Troy drew the Glock, careful not to point it at Hyde. He ejected the magazine, shucked the round in the chamber and tossed the gun into the dirt nearby. Bolan flinched, half expecting it to touch off another mine. It didn't.

"Come ahead, Cooper."

Bolan holstered his Beretta and moved in, stepping where the ex-agent had stepped. Troy's feet were slightly smaller than his, which increased the risk, but there was nothing to be done about that.

He reached the two men without incident. Hyde had, in fact, soiled himself. Bolan didn't comment on that.

"Striker to G-Force," he said.

"I've got you, Sarge," Grimaldi said in his ear. "You're…you're not doing what I think you're doing, are you?"

"You know I am," Bolan said.

"Be careful, Sarge," Grimaldi stated. "For what it's worth, I agree with you. Hyde doesn't deserve to live. Don't give up your life for that piece of trash."

"Nobody's given up their life for anyone," Bolan said. "Not just yet."

He drew the Sting knife from his waistband. Knives used by bomb disposal and deactivation technicians were typically nonmagnetic, to avoid detonating certain types of explosives. He looked up at Hyde. "Does this mine have any advanced electromagnetic signature technology?"

"What?" Hyde said. "Uh, no. No. They're Soviet surplus. Old technology."

"Well, that's something, at least," Bolan said. He began digging in the dirt with the blade of his knife, defining the edges of the mine.

"Jack," he said.

"Who is Jack?" Hyde asked.

"Shut up, Hyde," Bolan replied.

"Yeah, Sarge," Grimaldi said.

"If something goes wrong, tell Barb…"

"Yeah, Sarge," Grimaldi said. "I will."

"Who are you—" Hyde began.

"If you don't shut up," Bolan said, "I'll punch you in the balls and watch you explode."

Hyde said nothing more. Troy simply watched as Bolan probed the mine, gently scraping away dirt until he had uncovered most of the device. Hyde's foot had squarely depressed the firing stud. Fortunately, his weight was centered on the trigger.

"I'm going to dig under the mine now," Bolan stated.

"But if it shifts…" Hyde muttered.

"If it shifts," Bolan told him, "it will go off, and they'll never be able to tell which of us was which. Go back to shutting up."

Carefully, oh so carefully, he dug a narrow trench beneath the mine. He removed his combat light from his pocket and shone it into the hole, holding the light in his mouth as he worked.

"There's the pin," he said. A fuse beneath the mine held the key to the device's destructive payload. Removing that pin would allow him to disassemble the mine from beneath…if he was careful.

He probed the pin with the blade of his knife. First, he would need to unscrew it. Using the Sting as a screwdriver, he eased the blade in.

The pin wouldn't move.

"Uh-oh," Bolan said.

"What?" Hyde demanded. "What is it? What's happening?"

"Jack," Bolan said, "I have a problem."

"Is Jack like my friend Bob?" Hyde asked nervously.

"Would you shut the *hell* up?" Bolan said.

"G-Force," Grimaldi responded. "Go, Sarge."

"Problem," Bolan said. "The mine is rusted shut. If I exert enough force to break it open, it'll shift."

"You've got to abort, Striker," Grimaldi said. "Let him die. You did your best."

"Yeah," Bolan said, shaking his head. "Yeah." He looked to Troy. "There's nothing I can do."

"Walk out the way you came in," Troy told him. "I could follow."

"Don't you leave me!" Hyde screamed. "Don't you leave! I could step off this mine and kill us both!"

"Then do it," Bolan ordered.

Hyde didn't move.

"Didn't think so." He stepped out, again following Troy's prints. When he was clear of the mined area, he gestured for the ex-agent to follow.

"Come on," Bolan said.

"No, Cooper." Troy smiled. "I think I finally understand what I can do. It won't make up for the wrong I've done, but, if it helps now, it's the right thing."

"What?" Bolan said. "Troy, don't—"

"All I wanted was justice for my family," he said. "You can understand that, right?"

"Yeah," Bolan said. "I can understand that."

"Thank you, Agent Cooper. And goodbye."

He jumped.

CHAPTER TWENTY-THREE

Troy tackled Hyde, knocking him clear of the mined section of the trench. The Bouncing Betty detonated, its deadly payload shooting into the air as if in slow motion, whirling lethally. Bolan couldn't be sure, but he thought he saw Troy reach for the spherical charge, as if he meant to grab and squeeze the Betty like a rubber ball.

The explosion killed Troy, splattering Hyde with the rogue agent's blood.

Hyde ran.

He knocked Bolan aside and fled as if Satan himself were on his heels. The soldier was momentarily stunned by the concussion and shocked by Troy's sacrifice. Hyde bulled past Bolan and continued through the trenches before he could recover and go after him.

The two men played cat and mouse as Hyde took them through cutouts and switchbacks, seemingly struggling to remember the layout of his own defensive maze. Whether he was trying to confuse and elude Bolan, or really having trouble getting away didn't matter. The soldier knew that if he let Hyde get to the junkyard and then off the property, everything he had done over the last twenty-four hours, every sacrifice that had been made—including Russell Troy's last, valiant act of redemption—would be for nothing.

"Jack, eyes in the sky!" Bolan ordered. "Track Hyde!"

"On him," Grimaldi replied. "He's trying to double back to the house."

"I don't want him going there," Bolan said. "If he gets burned alive going for some secret tunnel or something, that's all she wrote."

"I'll herd him for you," Grimaldi said. He fired up his chopper's electric Gatling gun and began shooting across Hyde's path, driving the skinhead leader back toward the other end of the trench field.

"Running like a rabbit, Sarge," Grimaldi said. "Like his tail's on fire."

"Thanks, Jack," Bolan said. "Stand by. We've got to corral him. I can't risk losing him completely, not now that we're so close."

"Will do. Sarge, did Troy..."

"He did."

"Man," Grimaldi said.

"Yeah."

The soldier chased the terrorist. They had nearly cleared the trenches when Bolan caught up to his prey. Hyde had reached the edge of the junkyard when he tripped and fell into the bloody pool of corpses. Thrashing in the murky, bloody water, Hyde screamed. He came up with a shotgun. Water poured from the double barrels of the weapon.

Bolan stopped short as Hyde pointed the gun.

"You *can't* kill me!" he screamed with glee. "That fool, Troy, gave his life to stop me from dying. You need me alive! And that, race-traitor, is why *you're* going to die."

"I'm really sick of being called that," Bolan stated.

Hyde pulled the twin triggers of the sawed-off shotgun.

Nothing happened.

"Too long in the water," Bolan said. He lashed out with a kick that snapped Hyde's head back, dropping him back into the pool.

Reaching down, the soldier grabbed Hyde's collar and dragged the man out of the pool. "I had a lousy day yesterday," he said. "It started with burning my hands, and only got worse from there. Today hasn't been much better, but it has the advantage of me seeing you where you belong—on your knees in the dirt." He kicked Hyde in the gut, doubling the terrorist over.

Shane Hyde wasn't out of tricks.

The switchblade appeared as if by magic, coming up and almost flaying Bolan's face. The soldier ducked and drew his Sting again, holstering his useless pistol. He couldn't risk killing Hyde.

"You're coming with me," Bolan said. "Alive and talking."

Hyde lunged and slashed, driving forward. The soldier understood the tactic. It wasn't the desperation ploy it appeared. Hyde would lure him in with wild, exaggerated strikes, then drive that knife between Bolan's ribs or into his neck the moment he let down his guard or underestimated his enemy.

"I'm sorry, Dad," Hyde said. "The voices say you've got to go now. I got you the whiskey you like."

Hyde had stopped slashing. He stood now, breathing heavily, looking around as if he didn't recognize his own fortifications. "Dad?" he said. "You understand, right? You know I'm not angry. It isn't your fault. But you've got to go. Mom and I need you to leave."

He's gone completely insane, Bolan thought. If he ever was stable, which he probably wasn't.

Hyde's face changed again. "Come on! Come kill me, then! But you can't, can you, Cooper?" The terrorist laughed maniacally. "I can kill you, and all you can do is try to stop me! How's that for a metaphor for the modern war on terror, government man! You have to succeed every time. I only have to connect once."

Bolan tripped him.

He lashed out with his leg and swept Hyde's feet out from under him, dropping him to the dirt. Then Bolan tackled the terrorist, scrambling for position, straddling him. Astride Hyde's chest, he began punching the terrorist leader in the face. His blows were weakened by the painful feedback in his palms, but they were effective nonetheless. Hyde's eyes were soon swollen, his lips puffy and bleeding, his nose crushed. He had dropped his switchblade.

"Dad, stop hitting Mom. She's a drunk. She doesn't know what she's saying."

Bolan was beating a lunatic. He eased up. Hyde had no idea what he was—

Shane Hyde had planted his feet. Now he arched his back and rolled Bolan off him in the moment when the soldier's balance was lost as he pulled back from his attack. The terrorist was laughing when he planted a solid combination across Bolan's jaw. Pushing to his knees, then his feet, Hyde landed a vicious kick to the soldier's ribs.

Bolan dropped to his side and hunched slightly.

Bending his knee, he rotated in place, keeping his kicking leg between himself and Hyde. When Hyde tried to come in, the soldier hammered him in the shin, hard. The brutal piston-kick raised a bloody welt under Hyde's pant leg. He hobbled, but maintained his attack, kicking and circling as Bolan tried to keep him from coming in to achieve a mount of his own.

"Fell for it, didn't you?" Hyde taunted. "I've been using that 'I hear voices' shtick for years. I mean, sure, I used to hear them. Sometimes I still do. But I haven't exactly been worried about it. And I don't lie awake at night wondering why Mommy didn't hug me, or reliving my father's death."

Bolan wasted no breath on conversation. He slashed out again with another kick.

"Daddy drinks—" Hyde laughed "—because you cry!" He dived in. The impact caused Bolan to drop his knife in the dirt.

Hyde managed to pin the soldier beneath him and start throwing punches, which Bolan blocked by covering his head. Hyde, flailing in the dirt, came up with Bolan's knife. He pressed the blade against his adversary's throat.

Bolan froze.

"I want to tell you a story," Hyde said. "About the little boy who grew up to be the leader of a very powerful organization. They called him a terrorist, but he knew that he was really a freedom fighter. Was fighting for his race. He was fighting for the freedom to raise his kids in a world free of its lesser races, animals who polluted everything with their stink, with their culture of criminality."

"If you're going to talk," Bolan said, "I wish you would kill me already. I don't want to be tortured."

Hyde's eyes widened.

Bolan smashed him in the side of the head with his balled fist.

The blow brought stars to the soldier's eyes, as well as, he assumed, to Hyde's. It was enough to extricate himself from his adversary's mount, and the two scrambled to their feet. The Sting was lost again. Bolan saw it in the dirt and kicked it away. He couldn't stab Hyde, anyway, not in any part of his body that really mattered.

"Last chance to surrender," he said.

"You don't seriously think that's going to happen, do you?" the neo-Nazi asked. "You don't seem stupid to me."

"I'm an incurable optimist."

Hyde turned and ran.

Bolan gave chase. Hyde was running through the stacks of crushed cars in the junkyard maze. Above, Grimaldi hovered with the Pave Hawk, and served as a spotter.

"On your ten," the pilot reported. "He's moving left…. No, he's cut right. On your eleven now. About twenty yards, behind that stack of old cars. Okay, you're dead-on. Get him, Sarge."

They played out the scenario several times. Hyde was working his way closer and closer to the entrance of the junkyard. From there, he could take a gravel access road back to the closest paved road, and then to a highway. He was trying to escape.

Bolan didn't intend to let him.

At the last instance, Hyde cut right when he should

have gone left, by rights, to leave the junkyard. Near a stack of crushed cars, he pulled at a dirt-covered tarp revealing a four-wheeler. Leaping on, he reached for the controls, but had trouble starting it. By the time the engine roared to life, Bolan, directed by Grimaldi, was almost on top of him.

The four-wheeler took off as Hyde gunned it. Bolan made a flying leap and the two were suddenly grappling on the back of the all-terrain vehicle. Hyde punched him; the soldier punched Hyde. Bolan had to remind himself to hold back, not to risk doing permanent injury to his adversary. Breaking an arm would be one thing, but causing the terrorist leader brain damage, at this point, would be terribly self-defeating.

The four-wheeler careened this way and that along the gravel road. Above them, the Pave Hawk churned gravel and road dust into a nebula that surrounded and obscured them. Bolan, tiring of the game, reached out and grabbed both of Hyde's ears from behind, wrenching his head down and over.

It was like steering a car. Hyde shrieked and turned the control yoke. The four-wheeler turned, too sharply, throwing both men to the ground. The vehicle itself rolled over several times before coming to rest with the engine still running. It died a moment after that.

Hyde picked himself up and began running again. Bolan stood, sprinted and tackled him, dragging him down. He drove an elbow into his chest, which caused the terrorist to choke and cough.

Bolan pressed his knee against Hyde's stomach, pinning him. "Not so easy to breathe like that, is it?" he said.

Hyde turned red, then purple. Bolan let up the pressure, but when Hyde started to struggle gain, the soldier drove his knee back into the terrorist's gut. He repeated the process several times before Hyde, his eyes bloody, finally shook his head and put up his hand.

"No...no more..." he begged. "I'll cooperate."

Bolan was breathing heavily. He climbed off Hyde and grabbed the man by the shirt. Then he dragged him to his feet. Removing a plastic zip tie from his war bag, the soldier secured Hyde's hands behind his back.

"All right, Jack," he said. "Come get us."

Grimaldi brought the chopper in for a landing. Bolan took Hyde by the arm and led him into the fuselage. Hyde kept squirming, shifting his hands back and forth.

"These cuffs are too tight," he complained.

"Live with it," Bolan said.

As the helicopter bore them skyward, Bolan looked out from the open fuselage, surveying the carnage below. A great cloud of black smoke, doubtless visible for miles, rose over the burning safe house, which was completely engulfed. From the air, the damage done by Grimaldi's mortar attack was visible, too. The Executioner had truly brought a war to the doorstep of Twelfth Reich. If there were any skinheads left alive down there, they weren't moving where Bolan or Grimaldi could see them.

"Call it in, Jack," Bolan said. "We have Shane Hyde, alive."

"Roger, Sarge," Grimaldi said. He looked back. "Did a number on 'em, didn't we?"

"Yeah. You didn't leave the mortar behind for the neighborhood kids to play with, I hope."

"Of course not." Grimaldi chuckled. "It's stowed in the cargo pod in the belly with the rest of the special toys." He looked back again. "Sarge! He's loose!"

Hyde had snapped his zip ties. The razor blade, apparently hidden in his sleeve, was still in his hand. He slashed at Bolan with it, but the soldier smashed one fist and one palm in a cross-scissors motion into the terrorist's wrist. The little blade was sent flying.

"Maybe," Hyde yelled over the rotor wash, "I'll just throw myself out of this chopper! Dying can't be any worse than being a prisoner for the rest of my life! And after you worked so hard to keep me alive, too!" He made as if to take a leap for it. "What a terrible shame for poor, noble Russell Troy, dead for no reason! I'll let you in on a little secret, Cooper. I raped his wife before I killed her. I made him watch the first time, sure. Video-taped it for him. But when the camera wasn't rolling, before I turned it back on and snuffed her, I made her a deal. I told her if she really cooperated, if she made me feel good, if she gave herself to me willingly, I'd spare her husband and her child."

"Shut up, Hyde," Bolan said. His voice was sharp as honed steel.

"Oh, she was such a little fireball," Hyde said. "When the stakes were clear to her, she couldn't get enough! Oh, it was so sweet. Maybe the best I've ever had. She was screaming and bucking and holding on to me like I was the best she'd ever had, and let me tell you, I was. There was nothing she wouldn't do, not by the time I got done with her. And of course, the kid, well, I had to—"

Bolan chopped him in the throat.

Hyde hit the deck, choking and wheezing. The edge-of-hand blow had been just enough to hurt him, but not enough to crush his windpipe.

"Jack," Bolan said, "get the medical kit. We're going to need to treat him for shock so he doesn't die."

Grimaldi looked back. "Sarge, are you sure? I don't think—"

"I'm positive, Jack," Bolan said. He raised his leg and snapped Hyde's ankle with a single stomping kick.

Hyde howled in agony.

Bolan reached out, grabbed the man's left wrist and slammed it into the deck of the chopper. Bones snapped.

Hyde writhed there, pale and sweating. The soldier took the medical kit from Grimaldi's hand as the pilot handed it back.

"Call it in, Jack," Mack Bolan said again. "Tell the Farm we have Shane Hyde. Alive."

EPILOGUE

Alexandria, Virginia

Mack Bolan brought the rented Dodge Challenger to a halt in one of the condominium's designated spaces. The morning was bright, crisp and clear. Rolling the window down, he inhaled deeply. It was going to be a beautiful day.

His secure satellite phone buzzed. He snapped it open and put it to his ear.

"Striker," Hal Brognola said. "Where are you?"

"Not far away. Running a little errand."

"I've just finished reading your debrief at the Farm," Brognola said. "I have to admit, you had me a little worried there."

"You know me, Hal. Or you should."

"Yes," Brognola agreed. "I should. And I do."

"You saw my request?" Bolan asked.

"I did. And I can make those arrangements."

"Good," Bolan said. "I want Russell Troy's record sealed. He deserves to be buried with honors. He's a hero. If not for him, Hyde would be dead. Whatever he did wrong, whatever else he tried, Russell Troy gave his life doing the right thing."

"I'll explain it to the Man," Brognola said. "I don't think it will be too hard a sell. We're already gleaning useful intelligence in the interrogation of Shane Hyde, which is what the President wanted in the first place. That goes a long way."

"How is Hyde, anyway?" Bolan asked.

"The doctors say he'll live." Brognola's voice turned sour. "Which is not to say he'll ever play the piano, or even feed himself again, necessarily."

Bolan had nothing to say to that.

"There's something else," Brognola said. "Hyde gave up a cache of documents in a storage area, materials Twelfth Reich were archiving. There were videotapes, recordings of everything from television shows to, well, Hyde's torture sessions."

"I'm not surprised."

"We believe, in going through the evidence, we'll be able to make several more arrests. Your operation racked up quite a body count, Striker, and a lot of members of Twelfth Reich are dead. Using what we now have, we'll be able to round up the others relatively easily. And we have ironclad evidence of their guilt, of their association with Hyde's terrorist group."

"Good," Bolan said. "What about the European terror ops and the Reich's other domestic targets?"

"Without Hyde to ramrod things on this end, the domestic issues are effectively ended," Brognola said. "We have teams of blacksuits conducting raids this morning to collect any stragglers and verify from Hyde's notes and records that nothing he was thinking of doing in future is being executed by any of his followers."

"If you need help," Bolan said, "I'll be free shortly."

"We should have it under control," Brognola replied. He paused. Bolan could sense his hesitation.

"What is it, Hal?"

"Striker, I've watched the video of what was done to Troy's family."

"I'm sorry," Bolan said.

"I wish I could un-see it," Brognola admitted. "But Hyde's injuries…"

"Are you going to tell me I was excessive?" Bolan said without inflection.

"No," Brognola stated. "I was going to say I admire your restraint."

Bolan digested that. "Troy went astray. He took the wrong path. He chose revenge over justice, when what he wanted—what he needed—was the second of the two. But he came back at the end. Nobody understands that choice better than I do."

"No, of course not," Brognola said. "Now, looking through your report, I do have some questions."

"Shoot."

"I see that you've recommended the FBI's Michael Wood for commendation."

"Service above and beyond the call, Hal," Bolan said. "And posthumously, an Agent Greene."

"Yes, I have it here," Brognola said. "I'll see to it."

"Thanks," Bolan said.

"How are your hands?"

"Healing well," Bolan said. "They itch a bit now. Peeling skin and so on. The Farm's medical team said it was like I sunburned my palms."

Brognola clucked his tongue admonishingly. "I've read the report. They said it was a bit more serious than that. Frankly, you're lucky to have suffered no permanent ill effects. If you were anyone else I'd have ordered you out of the field after incurring an injury like that."

"I wouldn't have gone."

"But I'd have ordered," Brognola said.

Bolan laughed. "Understood. Anything else?"

"A few things, yes. Among them, I have here on my desk a rather damning report. From the boss of a Harmon Margrave of Homeland Security."

"Really?"

"Yes," Brognola said. "Striker, Margrave's laid it on pretty thick. Accuses you of everything from a 'psychopathic disregard for authority' to 'violent tendencies' and 'poor impulse control.' Says you suffer from a 'pathological disregard for the hierarchy of command,' that you're a danger to yourself and others…. Well, it goes on. He's also appended a medical bill."

"Medical bill?"

"I'll spare you the exact language," Brognola said. "It essentially says you broke his face."

"You want me to turn in my decoder ring?" Bolan asked.

"Given what was included in your debrief concerning Margrave," Brognola said, "I really don't believe that's going to be necessary. Actually, I was thinking a transfer might be in order for Harmon Margrave. Somewhere his particular talents can best be put to use in the service of the United States government."

"Did you have something in mind?"

"Alaska," Brognola said. "Definitely Alaska. Northern Alaska, in fact."

"I can't disagree," Bolan replied.

"Speaking of DHS, we've uncovered some breaches

using the Farm's back-trace program, now that we know what to look for," Brognola said. "Sensitive information about your assignment was passed from one Peter Copley, a paper pusher at DHS, to Troy. Copley's facing a pretty dark hole, unfortunately for him. He rolled over almost immediately when he was detained for questioning."

"That's not the only housecleaning needed," Bolan said. "Barb gave me the particulars on Wong, the FBI employee fingered by one of Troy's rogue agents. That's where I am now."

"Benjamin 'Buster' Wong, yes," Brognola said. "I have the file here. It was a given that Troy had sympathizers within the Bureau or a connected agency, of course. He knew everything the Bureau and DHS knew about Hyde's organization, and it was from those sources that we built our mission plans. That's how Troy was able to keep up with us, and with them. The Department of Homeland Security knew about your involvement per your Justice cover, but only the FBI had the priority target list from which Troy culled the safe house locations in Alamogordo, not to mention the details of the train hijacking."

"Maybe Wong and Copley can room together in Club Fed," Bolan said.

"Be careful, Striker," Brognola said. "Our liaison within the Bureau tells me they've notified Wong that he's the subject of an internal investigation. The cat is out of the bag. If you come knocking on his door, he may realize he's caught, and try to put a bullet in you."

"I always assume that's a possibility when I meet new people," Bolan said, only half joking. "Whose bright idea was it to tip off Wong that we were onto him? That's not exactly standard procedure."

"It's either bureaucratic foolishness," Brognola said, "or someone sympathetic within the FBI trying to give Wong advance warning so he could skip town."

Bolan glanced out his window at the driveway of Wong's condominium. "His car is still here. Unless he walked, it doesn't look like he's left Alexandria just yet."

"I'll check into the matter as far as is possible," Brognola promised. "But I don't think it's likely we'll find anyone else to put our hands on, not just yet. Some level of interdepartmental corruption is always going to exist."

"I know," Bolan said. "But I don't have to like it. Striker out." He snapped the phone shut.

Making sure no one noticed him, the soldier circled around to the back of the condominium. Wong's unit was on the second floor. Bolan took the stairs and, positioning himself next to the door, rapped on it.

No one stirred within. He knocked again. When there was no response, he checked the area and, deciding his lock pick would take more time than he wished to invest, he prepared to fire off a kick near the doorknob. Before he could do so, however, a thought occurred to him. He stopped, planted his foot and tried the knob.

The door swung inward.

Bolan stepped into the living room, which was empty. In the kitchen he found empty bottles of vodka on the counter and an ashtray overflowing with cigarette butts on the table. The smell of stale smoke hung heavily throughout the condominium suite.

He found Buster Wong in the bathroom.

Wong had used an extension cord. He had tied it to the showerhead, wrapping the other end around his throat, and had let his body weight do the rest. Bolan checked for a note, but there was none.

Wong had died badly. There had been no opportunity for a clean neck break here. The disgraced FBI agent had instead slowly strangled as the cord dug deeply into the flesh of his neck.

Bolan left the bathroom. He made his way back out through the living room, running one last visual check to make sure everything was in order. There were no signs of foul play. Buster Wong had been unable to handle the consequences of his actions and had ended his own life.

The soldier left the dead man's home, quietly closing the door behind him. He had come here to make sure justice was done.

Justice, for a change, had gotten there before him.

* * * * *

TAKE 'EM FREE
2 action-packed novels plus a mystery bonus

NO RISK
NO OBLIGATION TO BUY

The Executioner® Don Pendleton's
FINAL JUDGMENT

A war-crimes trial becomes a deadly hostage situation.

When neo-Nazis seize a U.S. courthouse and demand the release of their leader, Mack Bolan is called in to go under the radar and eliminate the gunmen. But before he can finish the job the jailed WWII Nazi leader escapes...with hostages. This time there will be no escape for the leader, as the Executioner is ready to deliver his own form of justice.

Available in July wherever books are sold.